A FAST HORSE NEVER BRINGS GOOD NEWS

Five Stories

CARY FAGAN

Book*hug Press
Toronto 2025

FIRST EDITION

Library and Archives Canada Cataloguing in Publication

Title: A fast horse never brings good news / Cary Fagan.
Names: Fagan, Cary, author
Identifiers: Canadiana (print) 20250205971 | Canadiana (ebook) 2025020598X
ISBN 9781771669511 (softcover)
ISBN 9781771669528 (EPUB)
Subjects: LCGFT: Short stories.
Classification: LCC PS8561.A375 F37 2025 | DDC C813/.54—dc23

The production of this book was made possible through the generous assistance of the Canada Council for the Arts and the Ontario Arts Council. Book*hug Press also acknowledges the support of the Government of Canada through the Canada Book Fund and the Government of Ontario through the Ontario Book Publishing Tax Credit and the Ontario Book Fund.

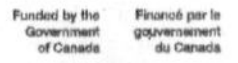

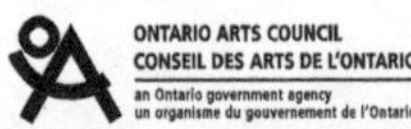

Book*hug Press acknowledges that the land on which we operate is the traditional territory of many nations, including the Mississaugas of the Credit, the Anishnabeg, the Chippewa, the Haudenosaunee, and the Wendat peoples. We recognize the enduring presence of many diverse First Nations, Inuit, and Métis peoples, and are grateful for the opportunity to meet and work on this territory.

Praise for *A Fast Horse Never Brings Good News*

"Using the sparest of prose, Fagan reveals a world both mysterious and amusingly off-kilter. A wonderful collection."
—Robert Hough, author of *Anarchists in Love: A Novel*

"This book is sharp, funny, and quietly profound, crafted with the elegance of a master. Each story feels both timeless and modern, threaded with post-ironic tenderness. This is storytelling at its best: clever, mesmerizing, and a genuine pleasure to read."
—Sarah Selecky, author of *Story Is a State of Mind: Writing and the Art of Creative Curiosity*

"Cary Fagan is one of our most clear-eyed, charming, humane writers. In this collection, he dramatizes so many various lives with confidence, concision, and empathy. This book is for all of us who crave stories about interconnectedness, illuminating our attachments to each other and the more-than-human world."
—Deborah Willis, author of *Girlfriend on Mars*

Praise for *The Animals*

Silver Winner of the 2022 Foreword INDIES Award for Humor

"Fagan's novella distills enchantments from the ordinary while treating the forces that corrupt ordinary life (including religions, governments, and the bored rich) with sardonic incision. Each scene proffers a surprise, strung together to form a sometimes baffling, always delightful whole."
—*Foreword Reviews*

"Fagan's short and addictive novel...is a puzzling and lively parable."
—*Literary Review of Canada*

"*The Animals* is a peculiar and weirdly compelling fable, a version of *Where the Wild Things Are*, but for adults of the kind who find the world as strange as the films of Wes Anderson."
—Antanas Sileika, author of *Some Unfinished Business*

"Funny, provocative, magical, and warmly engaging."
—*Vancouver Sun*

"Adopting a wolf, weasel, or wolverine sounds like an extremely bad idea, but in Cary Fagan's novel *The Animals*, it adds to the overall zaniness of the topsy-turvy world he creates."
—*Winnipeg Free Press*

for Rebecca

Contents

The Big Story . . . 9

Indivisible Property . . . 21

Higher and Higher . . . 55

Muswell Hill . . . 93

The Musicianers . . . 147

THE BIG STORY

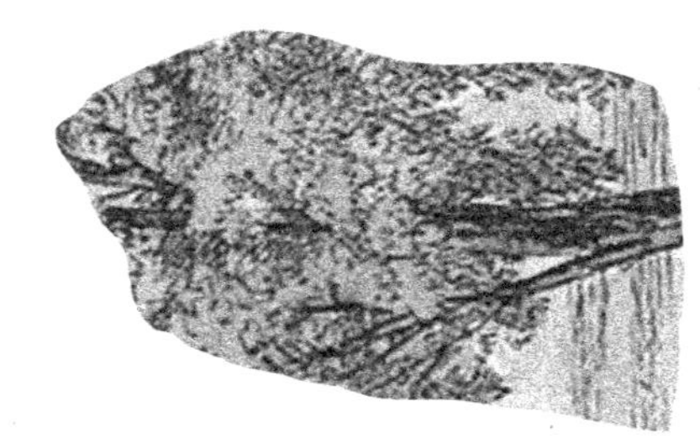

THE IDEA OF DINNER WITH STRANGERS IN A RESTAURANT with a dress code—who could possibly find that appealing? But I was in town for work and my boss asked me to present myself, representing our office, as it were. I put on a dress, something conservative but nice, and got there ten minutes after the hour to find that the five of us had been put into a private room, which I considered even worse. Airless and without the distraction of other people coming and going, waiters opening bottles, couples having arguments, it felt to me like a kind of incarceration. I was the second-last to arrive—good timing, I thought—and we all sat down at the oval table with the white cloth and the properly laid-out silver and glasses and the wine-coloured carpet under our feet and the hunting prints on the walls. Immediately wine was poured, and it turned out that the menu had been pre-chosen, so at least I didn't have to listen to the others hemming and hawing over their choices.

We exchanged names. Eileen, Burak, Simone, Orin, and me. Eileen and Burak were a couple and Eileen and Simone knew each other from some yoga retreat. That left only Orin and myself as complete strangers, but I didn't respond to his sympathetic glance. Not looking for any allies, thank you very much. I just wanted to get through the evening and have myself a long hotel-room bath.

The appetizer arrived, a sprinkling of roasted vegetables on a bed of wild rice. As we started to eat, Eileen made a reference to somebody's big story. To my surprise they all started talking, and although I'd planned to keep quiet, I couldn't help opening my mouth. "Sorry but I'm not following. What do you mean by a big story?"

"I'm sure you know," Simone said, smiling with encouragement. "That idea everyone's been posting about."

"I don't think so."

The others exchanged glances, which rather annoyed me. Burak said, "It's this theory that's going around."

"Not a theory," Eileen said. "It's the truth. It's real."

Others nodded. I was starting to feel like the backward kid in class who just couldn't get long division. "Okay, I'll bite. What is it?"

Only now did Orin admit that he, too, had never heard of the big story. What a coward! And so they explained, Eileen starting, Burak jumping in, Simone adding detail. None of them knew the origin, but it was really quite simple. Every person, so the theory went, had a story from childhood that explained them in the deepest, most essential way. Of course people had childhood anecdotes, but this was different, the big story that explained why a person grew into the adult they had become.

"I don't mean to disrespect anyone's belief," I said, "but doesn't that seem a little simplistic to you all?"

"I suppose it makes sense to you or it doesn't." Simone sounded a little defensive.

"It's easy to be cynical," said Burak.

"I'm not trying to be and I'm sorry if I sound that way. Maybe you could tell me more. I mean, what's your own big story, then?"

It was as if I'd shoved open a window and let ice-cold air into the room. This was not going the way my boss had wanted. I would have to find a way to change the subject and, with luck, the mood.

But then Simone said, "I'll tell you mine."

"You don't have to," Orin said. "I mean, I've never heard of this before, but it seems to me that a person might want to keep such a thing to themselves."

"It won't be the first time I've told it," Simone went on. "It's good for me, I think. Isn't that also the point, that knowing your big story and telling it gives you a greater self-knowledge? I was very young. In the night I woke from a nightmare. My room was dark—I wasn't allowed any sort of light, you see—and I called out for my mother. But she didn't answer. Even though I was scared, I got out of bed. I can remember very precisely the cold floor on the soles of my feet. I went out of my room and tiptoed down the apartment hall to my parents' bedroom door. The rule was to knock, but I thought they would be sleeping so I opened it up slowly and peeked in. No mother or father. The bed still made. I went to the sitting room and the kitchen and even the toilet, but I didn't find them. And that is when I knew that the monster from my dreams had eaten them up. I was overcome with terror but I managed to crawl under the dining room table. I wept as quietly as I could since I knew the monster had extremely good hearing. My sobs grew less controllable and louder, and I thought I might start screaming, when the apartment door opened. In came my parents, holding on to one another. Tipsy, laughing. In that instant I understood that they had left me all alone to go to the bar next door. I managed to slip back to my room undetected. But after that, I hated my parents and now as an adult I live on a different continent and rarely call. It's the reason I mistrust people and fear being abandoned. My partner, Constance—it's a good name, no?—she has to give me constant reassurance, and even then I am convinced she will leave me one day."

Everyone looked grave. By now the main course—baked cod with roasted potatoes—had been served. I was hungry but didn't want to be first and so I waited for Simone to finally pick up her fork. She said, "Is it just me or does this fish seem dry?"

"And too salty," said Eileen. "But I can't resist a free dinner. Do you want to hear my story?"

"Your *big* story?" said Simone.

"Yes, my big story. I was older, almost eleven, and went on holiday with my family. To the ocean, which I'd never seen before. I fell in love the moment I saw it, and with the beach, too. I'd only been on stone beaches and lakes. My mom couldn't get me out of the water. I'd play in the shallows, swim out a short way, let the waves bring me back in. I remember one late afternoon when I was pretending to be a porpoise, diving down, touching the sandy bottom, rising up again. I'd gone out just far enough so that I could keep my head above water if I was on my toes. But then the tide started to come in—gradually, so that I didn't realize it until a big wave rolled up and swamped me. I went down, swallowed water, and came up sputtering. I tried to stand, but my feet flailed without touching bottom. I felt a rising panic and slipped under again. This time I managed to hold my breath until I could fight my way to the surface. It was hard to see because of the waves and the water in my eyes, but I could tell that I had drifted farther from the shore. Another big wave came, I held my breath, I went under and came up. I was growing tired. I was no longer certain which way was land. I was sure—I'm still sure—I was going to drown. My head went under again. And then two arms appeared around me. They took me around the waist and hauled me up so I could breathe. Of course I knew instantly that it was my big brother. I started coughing. He swam toward the shore while holding on to me. It couldn't have been easy, because I was fighting him the whole way. And then finally when he tried to let go of me, I clung to him. But we were back in the shallows, and when I did let go I fell on all fours. I just stayed there shaking and trying to breathe."

"So your brother was a hero," Orin said.

"He was only fourteen. I was too upset to thank him or even talk about it, and to this day we never have. But here's the thing. It didn't make me afraid of the water or anything else. It had the opposite effect. Since then I've carried this unshakable belief that no matter what I do, no matter what risk I take, I'm always going to be all right."

We were silent. Finally Simone said, "I like your story better than mine." Everybody laughed.

We had all finished our cod except for Eileen, who had been talking, and she began to eat ravenously. It was while they were clearing away the main dishes and bringing us small bowls of salad that Burak began telling us about his big story. "I was nine years old and my entire identity was wrapped up in playing the violin. I'd started on the Suzuki method when I was six, which wasn't even that young. My parents had both been amateur musicians, playing in a municipal orchestra. In fact, that's how they met. So they were thrilled to find that I had a natural talent and I loved playing. I never had to be told to practise. If anything, they had to make me stop and go play outside. But the one thing I didn't like doing was performing for an audience. Whenever my parents had a party, they would ask me and I always made up some excuse, like I had a stomach ache or one of my violin strings had broken. I had performed once at the music school concert, but I was seven and it was with a bunch of other kids. I'd avoided doing it again, but when I turned nine my teacher phoned my parents to make sure I was going to be in the concert that year. She said I was the best student she'd had in a long time and had assigned me a solo to learn, the first movement of Mozart's *Violin Concerto No. 3 in G Major,* with her accompaniment on the piano. I loved practising it but I still didn't want to perform."

"But why?" asked Simone. "When it was your joy."

"At the time I couldn't understand my feelings. It seems so obvious to me now. My teacher. She was a failed and disappointed concert violinist and was living vicariously through me. I couldn't see how manipulative she was, cold one day and affectionate the next, making me so hyper-aware of her moods that I would try to anticipate what she wanted. What a thrill I felt when she touched my arm or gave me a compliment. Those lessons always left me feeling sick. That's the only way I can describe it. But even though I wanted to make her happy, I thought performing was just too much for me. So on the day of the concert I refused even to get into the little suit my mother had bought for me. My parents couldn't understand it. They saw how I lived to play; why wouldn't I want to share my talent? But they let me decide. Finally I resigned myself and got dressed, slumping into the back of the car. The school had rented an auditorium and it was pretty full. I sat with my parents, and when my turn came, I went up onto the stage and tuned my violin and my teacher nodded at me and I started to play. How well I performed I can't say—I have no memory of it. But I can recall everything immediately afterwards, the standing ovation, my teacher beaming. And as I stood there I knew I would never, ever touch the violin again. And I've kept to my vow."

Somebody put down a spoon. A chair creaked.

"Of course I know this story," Eileen said. "But I don't understand why you can't start again, even now. Just for your own pleasure."

"No, it's too late. And there's no positive end to my big story. I was robbed of something I can't ever get back. And it has left me with a melancholy that never completely goes away."

Simone said, "I'm so sorry that happened to you." But her sympathy was cut short by the arrival of one waiter to take away the salad bowls and another with dessert. Crème brûlée with a dollop of house-made whipped cream and a sprinkling of raspberries on the side.

"What about you, Orin," Burak said. "I know you're hearing about this for the first time, but most people know immediately what their big story is."

Orin looked up, his spoon posed in the air. He looked as scared as a kid who'd been caught shoplifting a dirty magazine. "I...well, to be honest, I don't think I have one."

"Come on," said Eileen.

"Really. I've been thinking about it while you've all been talking. In fact, I've been racking my brain. There was this one time when a clown scared me at a birthday party. And another when I was ten and somehow managed to break my arm in an elevator. But I wouldn't call them life-changing. I don't really ever think about them. Or much about my childhood, really. It wasn't bad or anything. It was pretty ordinary. I don't think I have a big story."

"If you don't want to tell us, you can just say so." Simone sounded miffed.

"No, I would tell you if it was that."

"Hey," said Burak. "Not everyone is naturally self-reflective."

There was another change in the air, either from disapproval of Burak's comment or a loss of interest in Orin. Everyone ate their dessert in silence except for Eileen, who took only one bite of hers. Orin himself looked pretty uncomfortable. I saw him glance surreptitiously at his watch.

The waiter came in with coffee. "Do you have decaf?" Eileen asked.

"Perhaps it's not fair to ask someone without warning," Simone said, nodding at me. "We can just change the subject."

"Unless *you* actually know your big story," Burak said.

"Right," Eileen nodded. "We might as well give you the option."

Now they were all looking at me. Even disgraced Orin. I glanced at the door, tempted to make a run for it. I could feel myself chewing my lip, the way I did when I got anxious.

Picking up my coffee, I downed half of it in a gulp. "Maybe I have one."

"We'd love you to share," Eileen said.

"All right. I was seven—no, eight. I'd already had my birthday. It was late spring, I remember. Been raining for a week and then finally the sun came out. I had these yellow boots that I loved, and I put them on to go into the backyard. I used to walk around saying hello to everything. 'Hello, fence. Hello, grass. Hello, rock. Hello, tree.'"

"Cute," said Eileen.

"'Hello,' the tree said back to me. Huh? I looked up and saw this woman up in our tree. Crouching on a branch. There was a man, too. And a boy and a girl. And a baby in the woman's arms. And an old man with a white beard and also a little dog."

"Are you serious?" asked Simone.

"I am. The woman started nursing the baby. She said it was a very nice tree and would it be all right if they stayed in it for a while? So I ran inside. I told my dad there was a family in the tree. Could they stay awhile? He didn't see why not, as long as it was okay with my mother. She was in the living room. I asked her the same thing. My mom didn't see why not, as long as it was okay with my father. I ran out again and told them they could stay. I spent the whole afternoon playing with the boy and girl. The boy and I played catch—he tossed the ball down from the tree and I threw it back up, which wasn't so easy. The girl made each of us a crown of leaves and twigs. I wore it on my head for hours."

Burak said, "I've never heard anything like this."

"Maybe I won't tell the rest."

"No, go on. Please."

"All right. So the next morning I put on my jacket and ran out to the backyard. The man and the woman were cooking breakfast in the tree on this little portable stove. The boy was playing guitar, trying to figure out some chord. The girl was stringing beads onto a necklace. The old man was doing calisthenics."

Orin said, "You forgot about the baby and the dog."

"I don't remember what they were doing. The woman asked me if I'd like some pancakes, only she didn't call them pancakes but something else. They were warm and delicious. It's not as if I didn't know this was weird. Why would a family hang out in a tree? But I didn't feel right about asking them.

"In the middle of the night when I got up to pee, I looked out the window and saw them all sleeping. Summer came. I went out every day. I've no idea how they relieved themselves. One morning I went into the kitchen and said to my parents, 'You haven't met the family in the tree. Do you want to come to the backyard with me?' They said of course. So we all went out. 'Oh my,' my mother said, and put her hand up to her mouth. The tree had blossomed. It was full of these tiny white flowers, so many that even I could hardly see the family. 'Amazing,' my father said. 'That tree hasn't blossomed in years.'"

"Your parents didn't see them?"

"Not as far as I could tell. The summer grew warm. I watched the old man teach the girl how to waltz. The boy got kind of moody and didn't always want to play. I tried to cheer him up by playing the one song I knew on my plastic recorder. It grew cooler, and one day the girl said, 'Catch!' and threw me something. An apple. Not large but crisp and sweet. The boy and girl picked more apples and tossed them down to me. I caught them in my shirt and took them inside.

"'Why, that tree hasn't had apples since we moved here,' my father said.

"'I'm going to make an apple pie,' my mother said.

"It grew colder. I had to put a sweater on under my jacket. The family put on sweaters, too. Leaves started to fall. Sometimes it rained. They started to look miserable. And then early one morning it began to snow. I jumped out of bed, got dressed in my winter boots and coat, and went out. The family was climbing down from the tree. First the woman. Then the man. Then the boy carrying the baby and the old man holding the girl's hand. Last came the dog, jumping into the man's arms.

"'Goodbye,' called the woman. 'Goodbye,' said the boy and girl. The dog ran up to me, and when I leaned down, it licked my face. I followed them to the front of the house and watched them go down the sidewalk until they turned the corner and I couldn't see them anymore."

The waiter came in and asked if anyone wanted a liqueur. Orin asked for a Drambuie.

Eileen said, "But what do you think now? I mean, were they homeless people? Refugees? Did you possibly dream it?"

"I can only tell you that I remember it perfectly."

"And what does it say to you?" asked Simone.

"Right," Burek nodded. "Did it change your life in some way?"

I shrugged but said nothing. There was a long pause, and then they gave up waiting and began to push back their chairs. We filed out of that stuffy room, through the half-empty restaurant, and onto the street. It was dark except for the circles cast by the street lights and a few neon shop signs. The others decided to walk back to the hotel together. I said I wanted some air and quickly went in the other direction. I walked several blocks, buttoning up my jacket against the chill. A small park appeared and I followed the path that crossed it. I stopped at a tree that had mostly lost its leaves. What kind it was I didn't know, but it had the right sort of branches for climbing, strong and set apart. But I was too old to climb and just put my hand on the trunk. Well, of course, I thought. Doesn't every story change something? And then I started walking again.

INDIVISIBLE PROPERTY

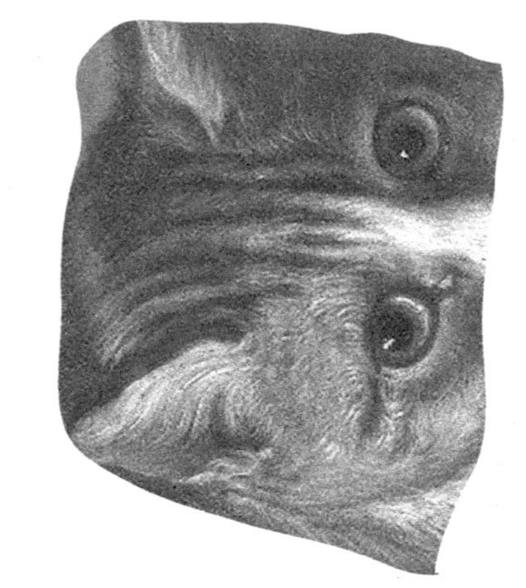

BEFORE THE ANIMALS BEGAN TO TALK CAME THE BREAKUP.

It was 10 a.m., an unlikely time for the ending of a relationship. But Ryan and Jessica had been up all night. Perhaps Ryan had slept a little; it was pretty hard to keep him awake, no matter what the catastrophe. Several years earlier he'd fallen asleep in a hospital chair in the middle of the afternoon and so had missed the moment of his father's passing from this world.

They were dressed now, pale-faced and bleary, sitting at the 1950s Formica table they had bought together in a retro furniture store. There was a Bodum coffee press on the table, not pushed down yet but giving out its heavy aroma, and a couple of mismatched cups they had found in a free box, one from Disneyland and the other from CWS Chartered Accountants. Also in the room were Moochie, the six-year-old basset hound who was snuffling under the table, and Crook, the eight-year-old tabby, hunched on top of the cookbook case. Neither had been fed.

"I wish—I wish just for once," Ryan said, and stopped. It wasn't clear that he knew what in fact he wished for.

"We both know it's not about one crummy night." Jessica yawned. She stood up and for no reason picked up the candlestick that stood by the toaster.

"I know it isn't. And I'm not blaming anyone. You're not going to throw that candlestick at me, are you?"

"Very funny. And I *am* blaming someone. I'm blaming both of us, Big time. Big fucking time. We ruined what we had."

Ryan didn't answer right away. In a sullen voice he said, "Not everything."

"But what good does it do if we're miserable? The world is going to shit, and instead of comforting one another we manage to find our own ways to make life worse. If you ask me, it's pretty fucking selfish."

"Maybe bringing the world into it just complicates things."

She made that sound he hated, blowing air out of pursed lips. The dog wiggled out from between two chair legs and gave out his glorious howl.

Jessica put down the candlestick. "We haven't even fed them."

"And what *about* Moochie and Crook?" Ryan said. "What are we going to do about them?"

The night before, they had gone with friends to see a play at the Tarragon, based on the life of Anna Akhmatova. Ryan and Jessica almost never went to the theatre; the last thing they had seen was that musical about Mormons, which he had found funny and she offensive. They were more into movies, although he preferred the old black-and-whites while Jessica leaned toward science fiction and weird foreign films. But their friends were crazy about plays and what they reverently called the "small theatre scene." Getting ready to go, Jessica and Ryan had admitted to one another feeling a bit intimidated at the prospect of having to discuss the show afterwards over drinks. That had been a nice moment—Jessica laughing as she put her hand on Ryan's arm, even if it had caused him to cut himself shaving.

Unlike their friends, neither Jessica nor Ryan had known before who Osip Mandelstam, another historical character in the play, was, but they had googled him, each on their laptop. When the play was over and they were leaving the theatre, Nadia and Samesh said they always waited until they had drinks in their hands before talking about it. They walked down to Bloor Street and went to Paupers, which turned out to be crowded on all three floors, so they had to squeeze together at the end of a bar. Overhead a television showed the Leafs–Bruins game and Ryan had to keep pulling his eyes from the screen.

"So what did you think?" Samesh asked.

For Ryan this was a difficult moment. He'd neither understood nor particularly liked the play. But if he said that, their friends—and possibly Jessica—would consider him a cretin. Also, the cast had been diverse, and they might think he was criticizing colour-blind casting.

He said, "I thought it was great. Talk about a lot of ideas to think about!"

"Wasn't it?" Nadia agreed. "The way it pivoted between realism and those meta-fictional moments of pure theatricality? I haven't seen so much creativity onstage for a long time. What did you think, Jess?"

Jessica didn't answer. There was a long awkward silence as their friends saw what Ryan already knew, that Jessica was glaring at him, her thin eyebrows arrowed down and her mouth grim.

"Why can't you ever just tell people the truth?"

"I'm not sure what's going on," Samesh said.

"Me?" Ryan's voice broke. "You're the one who wanted to pretend we were eager to come."

"So Ryan didn't actually like the play?" Samesh asked.

"I don't think this is about the play," Nadia answered.

At which point Jessica began to cry.

"Oh, that's a bit unfair," Ryan said.

Nadia took Jessica to the washroom, leaving the men at the table.

"What the fuck?" Samesh said. "Is somebody cheating? Are you screwing a student?"

"I teach middle school," Ryan said.

"Then what is it?"

"I can't even put it into words for myself. Differences in character, maybe. Mutual selfishness? We're just worn down from arguing all the time, God knows about what. We don't seem to even try to make each other happy anymore."

The women returned. "That washroom is disgusting," Nadia said. "Maybe we should all go home."

"I'm having another drink," said Jessica. She was wearing a pair of sunglasses Ryan didn't recognize; they must have belonged to Nadia. And they must have been too dark to wear indoors, especially in a bar, because a moment later she knocked over the remains of Ryan's beer, soaking his lap.

They had arrived home to find Moochie and Crook in the vestibule of the apartment. Usually they'd have been asleep, the dog in his bed on the kitchen floor, the cat on the end of the double bed or sofa. Officially the dog belonged to Ryan and the cat to Jessica, each having brought the animal with them, and they sometimes joked that Moochie's resigned personality closely resembled Ryan's just as Crook's touchy restlessness did Jessica's. Now Ryan took Moochie for a short walk. It was almost midnight when they got into bed.

In retrospect, it was easy to see the mistake in trying to have sex, considering the mood they were in. But in the past (if not recently), sex had been the best solution for a fight, renewing the intimacy they both wanted. On this night they were in too deep a hole and their touching felt forced, their kisses almost reluctant, and while Ryan just managed to finish, Jessica didn't even try. They turned their backs on one another and pretended to sleep.

So here they were at the kitchen table, the animals fed and Moochie lying on Ryan's feet while Crook walked across the table, swishing her tail. A door had closed on it five years ago, leaving the tip crooked. She pushed her face into Jessica's.

"Ugh, fur in my mouth. Anyway, that's why I think we should separate for a while."

"You mean break up."

"Do I? I don't know."

"Is there any point in us holding out some false hope? It'll just make things harder."

"You're right. It seems ironic that we finally agree on something."

"Shit."

"Please don't cry, Ryan. I hate when you cry. You look horrible. You're no happier than I am. You would just never say it first. You're too nice."

She reached her hand across the table and laid it palm up for him. It was their first genuine gesture in weeks. He laid his own hand on hers.

"Neither of us can afford this apartment on our own," Ryan said.

"I thought of that, too. We'll have to give it up. I really liked this place."

"I guess it's lucky that the lease is about up."

"What about the animals?" she said.

He sighed. "In legal terms, I believe they are what is called 'indivisible property.' We can't cut them in half and share them, so I guess we take the one that came with us. Maybe we can have visiting rights."

"It'll just make it harder if we keep seeing each other. For me, anyway."

"That's just as true for me. Sorry, Crook. So long, pal." He scratched the cat behind the ears. "It was nice knowing you."

Jessica reached down and stroked Moochie's back so that the dog moaned. "That goes for you, too," she said.

It's one thing to say you are breaking up and another thing to do it. Jessica had previously lived with a guy for a year while Ryan had only gone back and forth between a girlfriend's place and his own, but these three years together had been in another category for both of them. Everybody said they'd be fighting tooth and nail about who owned this vinyl album or that band T-shirt, but for the most part they made the decisions amicably.

"It feels like there's someone dead in the next room," Ryan said.

"Right. And we're making the funeral arrangements."

And they smiled at one another.

Jessica found herself a one-bedroom on the fourth floor of a small building with no elevator, parquet floors, and windows that only slid one-third open. Ryan alarmed her (given how easily he caught cold) by taking a basement apartment in a house. But the basement had been dug out for higher ceilings, had a modern kitchen and a washer-dryer, and the family said he could use the backyard. Neither of them actually went to see the other's place, although they texted photos. They also managed to avoid saying an official goodbye, busy as they were loading up (Jessica with hired movers and a van, Ryan with a couple of old high school friends) and corralling their respective animals.

The last time Ryan saw Crook, she was mewling in her carrying case. Jessica had taken some private time in the empty apartment with Moochie.

Jessica's text: *Hope you're really happy there!*

Ryan's reply: *You too!*

And that was that.

The first thing Jessica did was buy a lot of plants. She put an old repainted table by the living room window and covered it in Virginia creepers and orchids and nasturtiums. She hung the series of photographs she'd taken in Japan. The futon sofa, two small armchairs, the Formica table (generously given up by Ryan), the bed and side table and dresser and rugs and standing lamp all found their place.

The first weekend, a cold late October, she kept to herself, reading *Wives and Daughters* while curled in the armchair, putting together a thousand-piece jigsaw puzzle of Van Gogh's *Wheatfield with Crows*, listening to other people's lists on Spotify, making banana bread. She got to know the local Korean grocery and the still-independent drugstore on the corner. She found a nice café and a used book and record store. She saw a record Ryan might like, a reissue of the Nitty Gritty Dirt Band, and got halfway to the cash before putting it back.

She did more for herself in this one weekend than she had in months. And she had time left over for a couple of cries, one while drinking a third glass of Malbec. She missed the sound of Ryan's voice, his little solicitations, but she also felt some small buried part of her making its presence known.

Crook was another matter. She vocalized all the way to the new building, and when Jessica let her out, she made a beeline under the bed and didn't come out. In the morning, Jessica discovered that instead of using the litter box, she had shat in the bathtub. Only the next day did the cat emerge in daylight, refusing to let Jessica touch her, prowling through the apartment while uttering guttural complaints.

Of course cats dislike changes to their environment. They are ridiculously fussy creatures, like an old person who hasn't altered a thing for decades. Jessica was sympathetic to Crook's distress, even if the third time she used the bathtub seemed a touch aggressive. No doubt she missed Ryan, who used to give her treats several times a day despite Jessica saying she didn't want to end up with one of those obese cats.

She did, however, get annoyed when Crook jumped onto the table and knocked three plants to the floor, spilling earth and dislodging roots. "Oh, you stupid thing," she said, going for the dustpan.

The cat stared at her as she swept, watching her put back the earth and tamp it down. And then, in a vibrating whine, the cat said, "No, *you're* the stupid thing."

"What?"

Jessica thought she must have been daydreaming. She pressed

a palm to her chest. "You didn't just... No, of course you didn't."

The cat stepped to the edge of the table and landed, not delicately, on the floor. "I don't care a rodent's tail for your plants," she said. "They can piss off, and so can you."

Whiskers twitching, she walked to the bedroom and retreated once more underneath the bed.

Ryan had not gone into the relationship with a lot of furniture. After his friends finished the pizzas he'd ordered and the two six-packs he'd picked up from the beer store, he was left alone in a basement apartment that looked barely inhabited. He duct-taped together four pizza boxes into a cube for a table and used it for ten days before making the trip to Ikea and furnishing the place in one fell swoop. He couldn't decide if the minimalist furniture reflected, or did not reflect, his taste.

He quickly discovered that he did not enjoy living alone. Of course there had been times he wouldn't have minded having a couple of days to himself, and then there were the excruciating arguments when it was actually painful to be together. Well, here he was with only Moochie's snoring for company. He felt as if he'd woken up in some dystopian movie, the last non-zombie on earth. And then the family who lived upstairs came back from holiday. He heard children's feet pounding overhead like a herd of antelope. He heard shrieks of laughter and screams of defiance and bursts of tears and the *zip-bing* of video games. Somebody was learning to play the piano. One evening he could make out the voice of Robin Williams in *Mrs. Doubtfire.*

Occasionally he would encounter one or another family member as he used the private side entrance or sat on a folding chair in the toy-strewn backyard. The youngest child was afraid of Moochie, which to Ryan seemed hard to believe, given the animal's short legs and dopey face, but the oldest one would lift up his ears and cry, "Look, it's Dumbo!"

Ryan grew used to the footfalls overhead and the muffled

voices, signs that there was human life on the planet after all. Occasionally Mrs. D. would knock on his door with a slice of birthday cake or a plate of steaming lasagna. Every so often he helped the oldest child with his math homework.

How Moochie took to the new life was hard to tell at first because he spent so much time sleeping. The family's return made him more alert, if only because those supersensitive ears kept picking up the noises above. Once he looked up at the ceiling and began to bay mournfully, putting a dead stop to whatever was going on up there.

Moochie was a generally unfussy animal who made few demands. "The two of you could form a band," Jessica had once said. "The Phlegmatics." It was the kind of funny remark she used to make when she was annoyed at Ryan for no discernible reason, really just for his Ryan-ness. But though Moochie was easygoing by nature, Ryan could see that something was off. He was more listless, melancholy even, and when Ryan came home from work, he didn't scoot over with tail wagging but merely raised those Eugene Levy eyebrows.

One Sunday morning Ryan decided to take the dog to the wooded park on the other side of town. He drove with Moochie lounging on the back seat, and when they got to the park Ryan kept the leash on since hounds have a tendency to follow an interesting scent to the ends of the earth. He walked slowly so that Moochie could stick his nose into the mouldering leaves. But today his heart didn't seem in it.

"What's wrong, Mooch? You always love a good stink."

The dog stopped and half-turned his head. "You," he said. "You are what's wrong. You'd be a disappointment to any canine, I'm sure. But to me in particular." He started walking again, pulling on the leash.

"Disappointing how?" Ryan said. And then, "Wait...what?"

Jessica did not attempt to speak with the cat again. Instead, she went out as much as she could, keeping away from the apartment. She took her breakfast at the café down the block, went to work, headed to the gym to tire herself out even more. Every night that week she met one friend or another for a drink, dinner, or a movie. Obviously, her friends thought she was having a hard time adjusting to the single life. *Don't worry, it gets better,* they all said, and each time she lowered her eyes, trying to look doubtful so she wouldn't blurt out the truth: she had hallucinated a talking cat.

On Saturday morning, her head aching from too many shots, she blurred into consciousness with the feeling that something was pressing down on her chest. Crook. Green eyes staring into hers.

"Jesus!" she screamed, and flung the cat onto the floor.

"Oof! Are you trying to kill me?"

That same weedy voice. That could only come from, yes, a cat. Jessica sat up.

The cat laced its claws into the quilt and half-climbed, half-leapt back up. "Do you see the sun is up? I'm hungry."

"I am freaking out right now," Jessica said. "I just *sound* calm."

"You don't sound all that calm to me. Of course I'm sensitive to that sort of thing. More as a survival instinct."

"So you actually talk."

The cat tilted her head as if to say, *Obviously.*

"Have you always been able to talk?"

"Now, that's an interesting question, Jess. Let me think. I don't believe so, but on the other hand I've never tried before."

"Can other cats talk?"

"I've no idea. It's not something that has ever come up. But it seems unlikely that I'm the only one. On the other hand, I've always felt rather special."

"All cats think they're special."

"True that."

"This is incredible. So what do you think about all day?"

"The usual things. Where should I sleep? Is it worth bothering to go to the kitchen or should I just drink out of the toilet?"

"Ugh, really?"

The cat gave her another look. Apparently the animal had a natural understanding of irony. "So are you going to get up and feed me or do I have to grow a pair of hands?"

"You have a weird sense of humour," she said, pushing off the covers. "And I don't think you're as cute now that you talk."

"Cuteness is overrated."

"I feel like I'm in a Disney movie. One of the lousy ones from the sixties."

The cat began to groom her whiskers. "Sometimes I have no idea what you are talking about."

Jessica felt shy undressing, so she changed under a towel, beach-style. Turning around again, she saw Crook lying in a patch of sunlight on the oval rug under the window. She hesitated, then kneeled down to stroke her.

"Oh, yeah. That's nice. Do my head, do my head. Harder. You're not going to break me."

"Hey, you still purr."

"Why wouldn't I? I'm a cat."

As Jessica got the bag of food from the pantry, she heard that Crook liked salmon best but preferred some variety once in a while. Also, that she wanted a new scratching post to replace the one that got thrown out during the move. "Unless you want me to use the sofa leg."

"I'll get one today."

"Good. And please open the window. It smells like my own farts in here."

"This is incredible," Ryan said. "Why didn't you tell me you could talk?"

"Uh, because you never asked? Sorry, I couldn't resist." Moochie was lying on the floor. He began licking his left paw.

"All this time I've been talking away to you. That's what people do, they talk to their dogs. Weren't you ever tempted to answer?"

"Honestly, I can't recall. I have a kind of selective memory. Like that time you gave me the bone from your T-bone steak. Now, that I remember perfectly!"

"It was only two weeks ago."

"See?"

"Anyway, Mooch old boy, you can talk to me now."

"Can I say something? Not meaning to criticize, I realize you think it's an endearment, but that 'old boy'—"

"You don't like it?"

"I'm five, Ryan. I'm in my prime."

"Six, actually."

"Really? No wonder my joints ache when it rains."

"Fine. So listen, I was thinking of taking you with me to Richie's. It's poker night. I'm going to love seeing how they react. Like you can say, 'I believe it's my deal' or 'I thought you had four aces' or something like that. It'll be a scream."

The dog shook himself, splaying out his ears for a moment. "Hey, I'm sorry, Ryan, but I'm pretty sure I can only talk to you."

"Really? Why?"

"It's weird, I know. But that's how it feels. I can just tell."

Ryan scratched his head. That was pretty disappointing. He remembered a cartoon he'd seen as a kid, about a guy finding a frog that could dance while singing "Hello, My Baby." But when the guy put the frog onstage before a big audience, all it did was ribbit. Ruined the guy's life.

"Okay. So you want to go for a walk?"

"I'm game. And bring a bag. I have to you-know-what."

"Sure. We'll go to the park. You haven't chased a squirrel for a while."

"I'd like that. You think maybe I'll catch him?"

"Going by your track record, I'd have to say not a chance."

"But it could happen. The squirrel might not be looking, or might trip on a stick. Or run head-first into a tree..."

"If you say so."

"I'm feeling lucky today."

"Here, let me clip on the leash."

"I don't mean to be a dick, but I do find that leash a tad humiliating. What am I, a poodle?"

"You'll have to promise never to run off."

"Of course. Unless I pick up a fresh scent. Or see one of those squirrels across the road—"

"You're wearing the leash."

"Ever get the feeling you're in an unequal relationship?"

"Yes, actually. I work so that I can buy your food. I pick up your poop. I take you for walks when I don't feel like it..."

"Okay, okay. Maybe I should thank you more often."

"Or even just once. Anyway, I chose to live with you, Mooch. You're a good companion."

"Aw, I'm blushing. At least I think so. Now can we have that walk? Because I really have to go."

She had phoned in sick and now, still in her pyjamas, her fuzzy socks keeping her feet warm, she was making banana bread in the kitchen, mashing the bananas into a bowl while the oven warmed up.

"I know what's going on," said the cat. She had somehow got herself on top of the dish cupboard, but because there were only a few inches between it and the ceiling, she was flattened down, her paws hanging over the edge.

"Is that comfortable?" Jessica asked.

"Doesn't it look comfortable? You should try it. Plus I can see everything going on. Nothing can swoop down and grab me from above."

"That's a concern, is it? Raptors in the apartment."

"If there's one thing I'm sure about, it's that you should listen to your instincts."

Jessica laughed a little maniacally as she used the spatula to push the batter into the loaf pan. "It seems to me that you're sure of a lot of things. By the way, what did you mean?"

"What did I mean when?" The cat yawned, showing her impressive incisors.

"When you said before that you know what's going on."

"Oh, that. Never mind."

"Come on, Crook."

She put the pan in the oven. Behind her a loud thump made her start. The cat was back on the floor. She began sauntering out of the kitchen.

"Hey, are you walking out on me?"

Crook stopped and turned to groom her raised shoulder. "I know you've got cleaning up to do."

"Wow, are you being avoidant."

The cat turned to face her. She looked at Jessica with her unblinking green eyes. "Fine. What's going on is Ryan."

"Ryan? What are you talking about?"

"What's going on is that you've got a broken heart. Is that clear enough for you?"

"But I'm perfectly happy on my own. I mean, sure, it's still new, but I think it's going well. It's getting used to you—the new you—that I'm having trouble with."

"Keep telling yourself that, sweetheart."

The cat padded out of the room.

"I feel like your dog is staring at me."

"Moochie? Oh, don't mind him. He's a little eccentric."

"I don't think he likes me."

"Not true, Helen. Moochie likes everybody."

"Can't you hear that? He's growling."

"It's his deviated septum. Come back here."

Ryan was sitting with Helen on the sofa. They had gone for drinks and then a walk, during which they had stopped to kiss. Now here on the sofa she was doing the buttons of her blouse back up.

"It's late. I promised my sister I would meet her at the gym tomorrow morning."

"Do you really have to go?" He followed her to the stairs. The dog came after them, still making noises.

"I had a good time," she said, pulling on her low boots.

"I'll walk you home. Or get you an Uber. Whatever you want."

"No, really, I'm fine. Call me, okay?"

"Definitely."

The kiss lingered and then she was gone. Moochie was waiting as he turned around. Ryan looked at him. "Exactly what was that little show about?"

The dog waddled back to the sofa. He girded himself before the jump up. "I think I'm getting fat. Maybe you should put me on a diet. Just kidding."

"You really were growling at her."

"I couldn't help it. I tried not to."

"I know you, Mooch. That was very deliberate."

"Mind scratching my belly?"

"Forget it."

"Come on, be a sport."

Ryan shook his head but came over. "Fine."

"That's it. A bit lower."

"So what's the problem with Helen?"

"For one thing, she looks like a badger."

"That's the stupidest thing I've ever heard."

"For another, she doesn't like dogs."

"She didn't do anything to you."

"Exactly. She pretended to be interested in me but she couldn't have cared less. 'Isn't he sweet!' You could hear the insincerity just dripping."

"Not everybody has to love dogs."

"Everybody who comes around here does. And speaking of dating, don't you think it's too soon? Jessica left like five minutes ago. Or maybe five months, I'm not good with time passing. But I don't think it was very long."

Ryan let himself fall back on the sofa. "Maybe it is a bit early. Helen's a friend of Richie's girlfriend. He convinced me that going out is the best way to move on. I have to start sometime."

"I hear you, buddy, I do." The dog lay his head on Ryan's lap.

"If I'm not careful, I'll just end up with you." He played with the dog's ears.

"Hardy har har. By the way, if you really want to hear my opinion, Helen is no Jessica."

"Why do you say that?"

"Because the Jessmeister was the best. You'll never meet someone as good as her."

"Please don't say that. It's not helpful. I actually feel like I'm starting to get over her. In fact I've been feeling much better. And I like Helen."

"You like her boobies, you mean."

"Jesus, are you two years old?"

"Okay, how about this. Sometimes a person needs a break from having any relationship. It's better to be on your own for a while. You know, howl at the moon, run with your pack."

Ryan shrugged.

"I bet she thinks it was a mistake."

"Helen?"

"Jessica. Breaking up."

"I doubt it. Once she makes up her mind, she generally sticks to it."

"This time might be different."

"I'm not calling Jessica. I'm going to call Helen tomorrow. And now I'm going to bed." He got up, pulling his T-shirt over his head.

"I'm telling you, Ryan. Don't settle for no-name kibble when you can have fresh liver."

"Ugh. Stop talking, Mooch."

* * *

She was watching *Dodsworth* again. The part where Mr. and Mrs. Dodsworth agree to live apart.

"See?" Jessica said. "Walter Houston will be a lot better off without her. He's going to find happiness with Mary Astor."

She had her laptop propped on her knees in bed, a bowl of popcorn beside her. The cat was stretched out on the other side.

"Let me get this straight," Crook said. "You're comparing yourself to a woman who's cheating on her husband with a gigolo?"

"How do you even know those words? My point is that people need to feel pain before they can heal."

"I believe it was Ryan who introduced you to this film."

"So?"

"He also introduced you to Hitchcock. Preston Sturges. Howard Hawks..."

"You've made your point, Crook. And I introduced him to a lot of things. Like restaurants that serve more than shawarma. Roller skating. Louis Malle. Adrienne Rich."

"But did he really like those Adrienne Rich poems or was he just trying to please you because he's such a nice guy?"

"I'm *trying* to watch this movie. I love the part with Mary Astor on the terrace."

"Sometimes Ryan cries during films. He's an unusually sensitive man. He could be watching this same film right now in his lonely apartment. And there would be tears running down his cheeks."

Jessica slammed shut the laptop. "I'm going to sleep," she said, pushing the cat off the bed.

"Well, thanks a lot, Moochie."

"What did I do?"

Ryan stood naked in his living room. With the basement windows so high, there was little chance of being seen from outside.

The dog looked up at him, head tilted to one side. "Have you lost weight? I'm starting to worry about you."

"You chased her out, Mooch."

"Who?"

"Helen, that's who."

"I can't keep her name in my head. There's just nothing memorable about her."

"I finally got her to come back and you pushed your way into the bedroom. You bared your teeth!"

"I was *smiling*."

"You looked like a vampire. How vulnerable do you think a naked woman might feel?"

"I don't know. You don't see me wearing clothes."

Ryan fell into a chair. "I don't get it. You used to be such a swell dog. A real companion. And now that you can talk, I don't see it as any improvement. It feels like you're sabotaging my life."

"Wow." The dog shook his ears. "I can't believe you just said that. We're very sensitive about humans, Ryan. We're like emotional Geiger counters. And my needle has been waving in the red like crazy. You're unhappy. You're depressed. You're giving up."

"I'm not."

"You didn't really even want to put your thingy into Helen."

"I did so."

"You're just licking a wound that isn't healing, my friend. Let me spell it out for you. Helen. Is. Not. Jessica."

"I'm not looking for Jessica 2.0, you know. I'm not even really looking, except to have some fun. Helen is a nice person, she's interesting, and she even seems to like me."

"You know what I hear, Ryan? Blah, blah, blah, blah, blah."

Ryan kicked the sofa leg, making the dog start. "You're fucking impossible. I've heard about good dogs that go bad as they get older. Maybe that's what's happening. Maybe I should dump you at the pound."

"I'd be upset if I thought you meant it."

"You know what? I ought to talk to Jessica. She's the only other person who might know how to deal with you."

"I think that's a great idea. Where's your phone?"

"She used to tell me that I spoiled you way too much. Now I see that she was right. Ugh, you're slobbering all over it. Put my phone down."

Moochie dropped it at Ryan's feet. "If I could press the buttons, I would."

"It's one in the morning. I'm not going to wake her up."

"Just a little bit of advice here, don't tell her that I can talk."

"Why is that?"

"Because she'll think you're nuts, that's why."

"She's so lucky that she got the cat," Ryan said. He turned, went into the bedroom, and shut the door.

"And by the way," Moochie said from the other side. "Do you know if it's possible to get *un*-neutered?"

They chose a café where neither had been—"neutral territory," as Jessica joked in a text. It turned out to be more of a tea room, with mauve walls and shelves of bric-a-brac and old stuffed furniture. Jessica arrived first so that she was already at a table with a cup in front of her and phone in hand. He went to the counter to order, then sat across from her, careful not to pull his chair too close.

"Hi."

"Hi."

Awkward smiles. He said, "I was a little surprised to get your text. I was actually thinking of messaging you myself."

"Some time has passed, right?" she said. "I figured it would be all right. But I hope you didn't feel obligated. I wasn't trying to make some big thing. The opposite, really."

"For sure, I get that. Hang on, my cappuccino's ready."

He went to the counter to fetch it. "Oh damn"—a small spill on his jeans. "Clumsy as always," he shrugged, taking a sip.

"You just think of yourself that way," she said. "It's not true."

"Anyway, so how are you?"

"Great," she said. "Well, fine. You know. It's an adjustment. You?"

"Definitely the same. Trying a few new things. I'm going to the gym."

"Great. I've joined a woman's bowling league."

"That's wild."

"I know. And I'm not bad, either. Plus there's the drinking after."

"The real draw. And I finally started writing my novel. I don't care if it never gets published."

"You've been talking about that since the day I met you. I'm taking pottery classes. I've made a lopsided bowl and a cup that won't stand up."

He laughed. "That sounds like a lot of fun. I don't know why we didn't do these things before."

"Really."

She sipped her coffee, he sipped his. The silence lasted long enough to make them both uncomfortable.

Finally he said, "So how's Crook?"

"What?" She almost choked on her tea.

"You know, that mangy cat who lives with you."

"She's fine. You know cats, always land on their feet. Heavily in her case. She's pretty demanding, though."

"I guess she always was, for a cat, anyway."

"And Moochie?"

"He's a little strange, to be honest."

"Strange how?"

"How can I describe it? He vocalizes more."

"Hounds are like that."

"Sometimes I think he's trying to tell me something."

"I know what you mean. With Crook I feel like I'm living with a nagging roommate. Sometimes I think..."

"...I'm going crazy." They said it at the same time. And looked at each other.

"Are we being too loud?" she said.

"There's nobody else in here. You know, Jess, I'm starting to think that I don't know the first thing about life."

She smiled at him, but her mind seemed to have drifted elsewhere.

"Hey, Ryanovsky, there's a call for you." It was Eddie, who sat in the cubicle across the barrier from him.

"Thanks, I got it." He picked up the receiver. "Ryan speaking."

"It's Helen."

"Oh, hi! I forgot that I gave you my work number. You want to meet for a drink later? I know we're seeing Springsteen on the weekend, but why wait, eh?"

"You have to stop, Ryan."

"Stop?"

"Calling. Leaving those messages."

"I'm not sure—"

"Those disgusting slurp sounds. And then the heavy breathing. Three nights in a row. Do you think it's funny? Or sexy? Because it's just plain creepy."

"Helen, I don't know what you're talking about. Is somebody making sick phone calls to you? Did you ask the police to trace the number?"

"They're coming from your cell, Ryan. You haven't even bothered to hide the number. Three in the morning. Four in the morning. I can't take it anymore. I *will* call the police—"

"But that's crazy. I'd never do that. There must be some glitch."

"Glitch in your brain, maybe. Don't call me anymore. Don't show up at my place or my work. If you do I'll get a restraining order."

"But the Springsteen tickets—"

The line went dead.

* * *

Jessica downed another shot. "I might take someone home with me tonight."

"As long as it's none of those guys in hockey shirts," Sandra said.

"I do look hot in this dress, don't I? Or does it say 'desperate and trying too hard'?"

"Okay," Melanie said. "I'm all for guilt-free bonking. But something must have happened to you at work today."

"Nothing happened at work." Jessica leaned against the edge of the bar. "Unless you mean losing the Knit Love account."

"Those cute shops? What happened?"

"I told the owner her promotion sucked. I mean, not like that. I was diplomatic about it."

"Apparently not," said Sandra.

"Knitting cafés are stupid, anyway," Jessica said. "And I was tired. I was just so tired."

"You still having insomnia?" Melanie asked.

"I'm having catsomnia."

"What is your little pussy cat doing to you?"

"Biting my feet. Jumping on my head. Yattering in my ears."

"I heard that Siamese cats are always 'talking.' Do you think she's part Siamese?" Sandra asked.

"I think she's part Freddy Krueger." Jessica pointed to one of the hockey-shirt guys. "That one. I'm going to ask him if he'll take me to his place. Then I won't have to go home. But first I'm going to make sure he has no pets."

Ryan stared at the machines, or more accurately at the muscled and glistening men and women using them. Lifting legs, thrusting arms, grunting and panting. He regretted having turned down the free training session, even though he disliked taking instruction. Now he tried to look purposeful as he walked over to the free weights. The twenty-fives didn't look too big, so he picked one up in each hand. Jesus, were they mislabelled? He put them down and picked up the tens.

As he raised them over his head, a memory of high school came to him. He'd spent several gym classes trying to climb the rope that hung from the ceiling. Once he got about a third of the way up and then slipped down, giving himself a thigh-burn. The teacher took pity on Ryan and offered him a skipping rope.

It was hard not to feel self-conscious. There was simply no way he was ever going to look like the rest of them, so what was the point of trying? He put the weights back and headed for the showers. He wasn't thrilled at the idea of standing among a bunch of wet and naked men, so he just put his clothes back on and left.

It was seven blocks to his basement apartment, down one of the tree-lined streets. The fridge was all but empty so he stopped at the overpriced corner market and filled a bag with groceries. Walking on, he remembered that the dog had been pestering him for some canned food, the idea of which had apparently been haunting the animal's dreams. He went into the variety and bought a can of beef-flavoured and another of chicken. When he got to the house, he could see the top of Moochie's ears in the basement window. The dog must have been standing on the back of the sofa. Now Ryan could see a rump and wagging tail.

"Very mature," he said, coming in.

The dog half-jumped, half-slid off the sofa. "Did you get some, did you? Did you get some canned food?"

Ryan pulled a can out of his backpack. Without a word he went into the kitchen and took a plate from the cupboard. He pulled off the lid and used a large spoon to scoop the gelatinous mass onto the plate. He put it down on the floor. "Eat your heart out."

The dog waddled quickly over as Ryan went into the living room and dropped onto the sofa. He sat there doing nothing until the dog came back in, running his tongue over his lips.

"It wasn't as good as I thought it was going to be," the dog said, and belched. "But it was still good."

"I didn't think you'd ever move back here," Jessica said. She cut a small piece of blackened catfish and brought it to her mouth. The restaurant was a piece of imaginary New Orleans—hanging beads, naive paintings, trad jazz on the speakers.

"I never intended to stay forever," Andrew said. "L.A. was a great place to get experience and to make some money. It allowed me to come back and buy some property. My house is a ten-minute walk from here."

She almost did a spit take with her Chardonnay. "You own a house? In *this* city? I don't know anybody our age who does."

Andrew Delgado was an ex, the one she had lived with before Ryan. Why had she ended it? The reasons seemed vague to her now. He was tanned with slightly receding hair cut close to his scalp, a sculpted chest visible through the stretch shirt. A honking big Rolex on his wrist.

"Weren't you living with somebody?" he said. "I thought I heard that."

"I was for a while. Well, three years."

"I'd call that a while. What happened?"

"I guess it just ran its course."

"Hmm. Like us?"

She paused. What message did she want to send? She decided to hedge her bets. "We were pretty young." She looked up at him and smiled.

He didn't smile and then he did. "If you want to see my house, we could walk over." He refilled her glass. She didn't answer and was no doubt confusing him. But when the meal was over they began to stroll, looking in store windows. Every so often his shoulder or hand would brush against hers. She tacitly agreed to turn down his street. Detached houses and big trees. A Volvo was parked in his drive. Not the biggest house on the block but more than comfortable.

"It's really nice. I'm envious."

"Do you want the royal tour?"

"Maybe next time. I have to work tomorrow."

"So there'll be a next time? I'm glad. At least I can drive you home."

"It's too much trouble," she said, but again acquiesced. He let her off in front of her building after a quick kiss. A slight trepidation made her hesitate before unlocking the apartment door, but she was relieved to find no pillows had been shredded, no surprises left on the living room rug.

"Crook?"

No answer. She looked behind the sofa, in the kitchen, and finally found the cat inside the bedroom closet, sitting on Jessica's clothes and preening herself. "Why didn't you answer me?"

The cat licked her side one last time, then turned to stare at Jessica before starting on a paw. Could it be over? Could the cat have gone back to being a regular—

"I feel very betrayed."

Nope, still talking. "Why is that?" Jessica asked with a sigh.

"Because Andrew never liked me. Once he even kicked me."

"He was pretending. You'd ripped the sleeve of his leather jacket."

"Oh, right. That was quite fun."

"Strange, you never damaged anything belonging to Ryan."

"Ryan used to give me tummy rubs. He was good for you, too."

"As if you should be the judge."

"Face the truth, kiddo. You miss him. You're sorry you broke up. Your life is a sad little pantomime."

"I still don't get how you know some things and not others. Now go sleep somewhere else," she said. "You're getting hair all over my clothes."

"Gladly." The cat walked out of the bedroom, tail raised high.

"Do I really need the leash?" Moochie grumped.

"Shhh, I can't talk to you when we're outside." Ryan tried not to move his lips too much.

"There's nobody around. Give me a break, would you?"

"All right, I'll take off the leash. But if you decide to run after the scent of some skunk, I'm not going to come after you."

"A skunk! As if I was born yesterday."

Ryan unclasped the leash from the collar. "Go find something disgusting to roll in."

"You're really developing a chip on your shoulder," said the dog, who then began to roll in some dank leaves. They were just inside the east entrance to High Park, where Ryan and Jessica used to come with Moochie all the time. It was full-on autumn now, the crimson leaves brittle underfoot. He saw a chestnut on the ground and picked it up, but it was already puckered from drying out so he found a better one and touched the smooth mahogany sheen. As a kid he had treasured chestnuts and would carry one in his jacket pocket for months, until one day it wouldn't be there. And now he remembered telling that story to Jessica and how in their first year together they had brought home a couple of handfuls to keep in a bowl.

Up ahead was the bench where they'd often sat with cappuccinos from a nearby café. There was a woman sitting there now in a red coat and with hair cut short, a style he'd always liked on women but could never convince Jessica to try. She was looking into the middle distance, apparently unaware of the leaf that had landed on her shoulder. It took him another moment to realize that the woman was Jessica.

He'd never seen her in anything other than black or grey. That and the short hair were, he supposed, meant to be markers of inner change.

"Mooch," he whispered.

"I'm busy here."

"Jessica's over there."

"What? Where? You know I'm near-sighted."

"On the bench."

The dog scrambled out of the leaves and was making for her as fast as his short legs could go. Ryan followed slowly, hands in his jacket pockets. He thought that Jessica looked thin and sad and beautiful. She saw the dog running toward her, but it took another beat for her to recognize Moochie. Her face broke into a smile.

"Mooch, what are you doing here?"

The dog gave a howl and a moment later had his snout in her lap while she leaned over and kissed him all over his head. Ryan couldn't hear what she was saying until he got up closer, but then he stopped a few feet away and waited for her to look up.

"He's getting fat," she said. "What are you feeding him? Hey, sweet boy, did you miss me?"

Evidently he did, judging by the way his butt was waggling. Ryan waited to see whether the dog would say anything. He could understand not talking to other humans, but to Jessica?

"Jesus, he's so excited he's tinkling. I think he got the cuff of my pants."

The dog made whimpering sounds.

"It's funny that we've met, this is the first time I've been here on my own."

"It's still a habit with Moochie and me. Would it be okay if I sat down?"

"Sure."

He left a space between them. "Too bad you can't walk Crook here."

"I've tried walking with her, but she wouldn't agree to a leash."

"Agree?"

"Well, you know. She practically scratched my eyes out. Actually, I was going to call you."

"Yes?"

"I think"—she paused, as if considering her next words—"this break was a good thing for us. Painful, of course. I mean, it's so easy to start taking things for granted."

"And get in a rut."

"Exactly. Not really seeing each other except as someone we think we've already figured out." She turned on the bench to look at him. "I don't think it's our fault. It's what usually happens."

"But it doesn't have to." He looked back at her. "It could be different."

"Could *we* be different, do you think?"

He held back his answer for a moment. "Yes, I think so. I know so."

"I know it, too."

They kept looking at one another, as if not knowing what to do next. The obvious thing was to kiss, but neither was prepared for that. And so Jessica patted his hand and he took hers. Really that was all they needed to do.

A fresh start demanded a fresh place. Each favoured their latest neighbourhood, but in the end they found somewhere in between, a one-bedroom with dining room, living room, and den in a midtown fourplex.

They planned to move in on the same day, but a last-minute work problem came up for Ryan, so Jessica moved in first. Really it was easier than competing for the doorway and gave Jessica a night alone in the new place. She could hear the television in the apartment above, but it went off early and the rest of the evening was quiet. She opened a bottle of wine, kicked off her flats, and stretched out on the sofa below the bay window.

"I wish you would stop pacing," she said. "It's driving me a little crazy."

The cat stopped in the middle of the room. "Do you really have such weak territorial instincts? I need to make the place my own."

"I think you're just nervous because Ryan is coming tomorrow. Admit it. You think he's nicer than me."

"Talk about projection." The cat resumed her pacing.

* * *

His friend had sold his truck, so Ryan rented a U-Haul. After it was loaded, he decided to leave the dog in the empty apartment and come back when everything was in. "Otherwise you'll get under our feet like last time. It'll be bad enough with the cat freaking out over the commotion."

"I don't want to stay in this tomb alone. What if I promise to keep out of the way?"

"I can't remember the last time you kept a promise."

"That's harsh."

When he arrived with his friends, Jessica was at work. They weren't done until two, when he went back for the dog, who was waiting at the door. "You took your sweet time." They drove to the new place and Ryan parked by the curb.

"Here it is," he said. "Home sweet home. Now, I know you've gotten used to being king of the castle but I want you to be nice to Crook."

He expected some snide remark, but the dog remained silent, merely staring out the car window at the building. He let the animal out, not bothering with the leash, and together they went up the walkway to the front door, which was still propped open. Then up a half-stair to the apartment. He opened the door.

The dog looked in warily.

"Come on, Mooch. Everything's going to be fine."

Jessica was back, unpacking a box of books. The cat was standing on the seat of an armchair, its tail twitching.

Mooch crept in, keeping low. The cat stayed where she was.

"Is that the best place for the bookcase?" Ryan said.

"It is, in my opinion."

"All right, but maybe we can shift the sofa."

"Then it won't get the light."

Crook jumped down from the chair. Moochie approached, then stopped a foot or so away. The two stared at one another.

"You want to hang some pictures?" Jessica asked.

Being together again felt less different than either of them had expected. What exactly had changed? In the morning, Jessica took a shower while Ryan got the coffee on. He read the news on his iPad, she listened to a podcast with earbuds. They took turns shopping for dinner. They started watching the new Darren Star series on Netflix.

While she was dressing he called to Moochie. "Time for walkies! Let's go, I have to get to work."

Outside, Ryan said, "Aren't you going to tell me how you think the word *walkies* is infantilizing?" But Moochie just tilted his head and trotted on. They walked to the nearby parkette, where the animal did his business. Ryan bagged it and tossed it in the trash can. "So what do you think of the new place?"

Nothing.

When they got back, Jessica was already gone. He looked to see if she had left him one of her little notes, but there was nothing on the table. While Moochie thumped his tail, Ryan got a treat from the cupboard. "Okay, you two. Get along."

The cat looked at him from the armchair and then began cleaning herself. The dog went into the kitchen, nails tapping, and lapped from his water bowl. Ryan was beginning to feel as if he had dreamt the whole thing.

They decided to eat at home on Saturday night. Candles were lit. A bottle of Côte du Rhône was opened. Ryan's "famous" penne arrabbiata was served.

"Well, this is something I missed, anyway," Jessica said.

"What do you mean by 'anyway'?"

"I don't mean anything. By the way, where are the animals?"

"Sleeping, I guess. I'd like to have their life."

"Tell me about it. But they always used to sit by the table, hoping we'd give them a scrap or drop something."

"That's true. I don't think they've done that since we've been together again." He speared some of the penne. "I haven't told you this, but when I was on my own I spent a lot of time talking to Mooch."

"I did the same thing with Crook."

"Sure. But it was as if..." He hesitated.

She poured the wine. "As if he talked back to you?"

"Yes."

"I know. Because Crook really did talk to me. I swear."

"When you say 'talk,' you mean, like, words?"

"Don't think I'm insane."

"I don't, because I had the same experience."

They stared at one another. "What are we saying exactly?"

"I'll tell you what else. I see now that Moochie was doing a number on me. He applied a lot of pressure. I guess he really missed you."

"Crook did the same. She told me that I'd never be happy without you. That I'd be lonely and miserable. I guess she missed you, too."

"And were you?" Ryan asked. "Lonely and miserable, I mean."

She took a sip of wine. "Not really. I was growing into it. What about you?"

"I did miss you," he said. "But there were good things about being on my own, too. Sometimes I would wake up on the weekend and feel almost transcendentally happy. I hope that isn't—"

"No, I completely understand. I felt the same way sometimes."

"Wow."

They continued to eat. "One thing I don't get," she said. "You say that Mooch must have missed me. But other than our reunion, he hasn't paid me much attention. Half the time he doesn't come when I call."

"I didn't even get a greeting from Crook."

They ate.

"So where are they exactly?" Ryan asked.

"Maybe we should find out."

They both stood up. She put her finger to her lips. Carefully they lifted their chairs away and tiptoed through the dining room to the hall.

Ryan pointed: the bedroom.

The door was closed. They crept forward and stopped. Ryan raised an eyebrow. Gingerly, Jessica turned the knob and pushed it open.

They were on the bed, sleeping. The cat on her side, head on Jessica's pillow. Behind her lay the dog with his head on Ryan's pillow. He was up against her. Spooning.

"Mooch?" said Ryan.

"Crook?"

The cat yawned but didn't wake.

The dog opened one eye, then slowly lifted his head. "Shut the door, would you?"

Jessica gaped. She and Ryan turned to stare at one another.

Ryan pulled the door closed.

HIGHER AND HIGHER

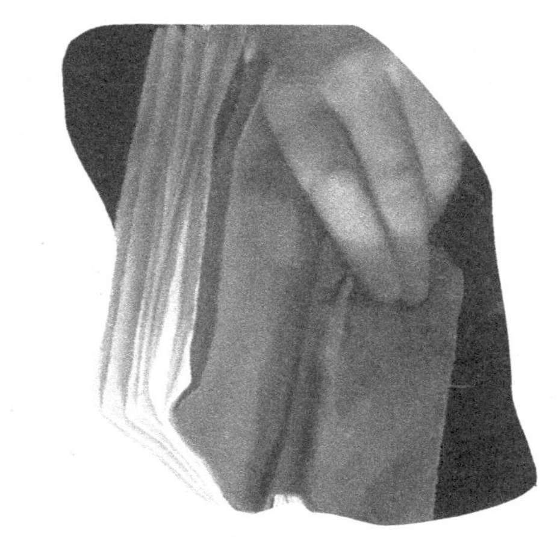

HER NAME IS ELIZABETH JAQUELINE PARTNOY-KATZ. SHE IS fifteen but short for her age, in knee-torn jeans, vintage baseball jacket, Converse sneakers, Herschel backpack, and she is jumping Greenwich Avenue potholes on her Death's Head skateboard. Billie Eilish is playing on her Bluetooth earbuds even though a lot of Lizzie's friends have turned against her.

She heads the wrong way down West 10th, stops, kickflips her board. In front of her is the blue wooden front of Three Lives & Co. bookshop. The rows of books in the pretty windows. Some tourist couple from Fucktown, Ohio, are oohing over how deliciously quaint it is. People can be so pathetically sentimental about books, she thinks. They get all excited by some *Times* review or go on about how their book club loved it.

Someone ought to throw a brick through that pretty window.

But not Lizzie. Because she needs a book to write a book report for Essler, the prick. It isn't the whole class that needs to but just her, because she said that reading dead authors was a waste of time. This after he assigned this week Leo Tolstoy and his fucking little book *The Forged Coupon*. Private school is so pretentious. Essler had to explain what a coupon even was. Dead authors don't know shit about the fires in Australia or the latest school shooting or whatever. But instead of arguing the point with her, Essler just said that if she felt that way she could find a book by a living author and write a paper on that. For tomorrow.

Her phone pings. She looks at the message and decides not to answer because she hates group chat. Besides, she's on a mission. To go into the pretty little bookstore and find a book and then—fuck you, Essler—steal it.

From her backpack she takes a baseball cap and puts it on, bending down the brim. It doesn't hurt to make herself less identifiable. A woman comes through the red door, gift-wrapped book in hand, and Lizzie slips inside. She pauses to take in the wooden shelves against brick walls, the lamps and tin ceiling and old tables. Tinkly classical music. Four people are browsing, which gives her some cover, especially since both employees are behind the cash—a woman with a grey bun and enormous glasses and a young, skinny guy with a red beard. The skinny guy is unpacking a box and talking about some "amazing" poetry reading, as if that's possible. The counter is high and there are book stands on it, so it's hard for them to see anybody who isn't right in front of them. This is going to be easier than Lizzie expected.

Now to find the right book. The important thing is that it has to be short like the Tolstoy. But also easy to read, not like that *Heart of Darkness* she made the mistake of choosing last year. Sure enough there's a table of cute little paperbacks beneath a sign that says *Small Books, Big Stories*. She doesn't recognize any of the names. She picks up a book with a flame on the cover and two flying birds. *The Animals*, it's called. Looks inside to make sure the type isn't minuscule. Nope, she can get through this easily.

The two employees are kidding around. "Stop it, Daniel, you're incorrigible," laughs the bun lady, batting her eyelashes at the young guy. Cross-generation flirting is gross. In one casual move Lizzie picks up the book and slips it into her jacket pocket. There's a corner sticking up that she covers with her hand. Now she turns to the door.

And sees a man staring at her. In a pinstripe suit and stupid bow tie. He raises an eyebrow slowly, as if to say, *You're going to put that back, aren't you?* She gives him a fakey smile and puts an elbow in his ribs as she goes by. A moment later she's dropping her board onto the sidewalk and pushing up Waverly. Heart pounding, she skims past pedestrians, hops two curbs, skips between cars, and makes it to wide Eighth Avenue. Breathe, she tells herself. She weaves across four lanes of traffic to reach the bike path, and then it's clear sailing.

Lizzie is surprised by how scared she was. Her heart's still going like a hummingbird's. She looks for somewhere to stop, spots a bubble tea shop, grabs her board, and goes inside. It's all pink walls and polka-dot tables that are unoccupied except for three Asian girls in school uniforms slurping on fat straws. Lizzie gets a tall milk tea and takes a table by the window. She pulls the book out of her pocket, bends back the cover, and creases it with her hand to stay open.

She sips and reads. Reads and sips. Gets up to use the washroom, comes back to read some more. There's this main character who might be the hero but he seems too pathetic and reminds her of her uncle Tony, who still talks about his high school girlfriend and spends his time baking bread. Except the guy in the book makes these miniature wooden models and he's gaga over this woman who's six feet tall and then people start taking wild animals into their houses for some government program that seems kind of random.

The man behind the counter is starting to glare at her, so she buys another drink and tries to read fast, skimming here and there until she slows down for the last pages. Talk about an unsatisfying ending, you don't even know if he ends up with the tall woman or not. What the fuck is Lizzie going to write? Is this supposed to be serious or funny? Did this actually happen somewhere? It seems doubtful, but the world is so crazy that you never know. Whatever, as long as she writes five hundred words. She pulls out her MacBook Air, the top covered in stickers. She two-finger types the name of the book and the rest of the bibliographical crap. She ponders a moment and then—

I feel sorry for the animals.

Weird thing about essays, she hates having to write them but once she gets started she can get really into it. Like now. By the time the guy behind the counter comes to take her empty cups away, she's at the exhilarating finish.

She stuffs the laptop back in her pack and carries her board into the honking cacophony of the street. Funny thing about the book, how it reminded her of that time when she was maybe seven years old and started bugging her folks for a dog. Any kind of dog, big or little, young or old, half-blind or missing a leg. She begged and pleaded but her parents wouldn't give in.

She's sure she would be a different person if they'd let her have a dog. Basically, they ruined her life.

Elizabeth Jaqueline Partnoy-Katz puts in her earbuds and hits her Spotify mix called "Heavy Traffic" as she begins to move uptown. What did her parents say at breakfast, that they wouldn't be home until ten? She should order in for herself and her little brother.

She shifts around a clutch of hesitating tourists, but there are more of them as she moves into midtown. A black limo gets too close and she gives it the finger but then notices that the person in back is powering down the tinted window and waving. They come to a red light and she sees that it's River Albertson. He's two years older than her, and she can't remember how she knows him, maybe through Janine or from some party. He tosses his hair and motions for her to get closer.

"Nice wheels," he says. "Want a ride up to 68th?"

"Guess so."

"Cool. Get in."

She grabs her board as he pushes open the door.

The driver has a little goatee and smiles at her in the mirror. "So where we going, River?"

"Home. Can you put up the thing?"

"Sure, boss."

The darkened privacy glass rises to separate front from back.

The limo starts to move.

"So what exactly does your dad do?" she asks.

"Some Wall Street bullshit. You want a Coke?"

"No thanks."

He's tapping his phone. "One sec."

"Okay," she says, yanking off her backpack. She leans back into the leather seat, closing her eyes. "I could live in here forever." The movement of the car is soothing. She's been so tense lately—her parents, school, her reject friends, everything. She really could stay here and never move.

And then she feels a hand on her thigh.

Her eyes spring open. He's stroking her skin through a tear in the jeans. "What the fuck?" she says.

"Your name's Lizzie, right? I'm into you. Is there anything wrong with that?" He slides closer and slides his hand up to her right tit.

She shoves him. "Fuck off."

"You accepted the ride, right? I see no problem here. Hey, let me take a picture of us. You can Instagram it, your friends will be impressed."

"Okay, I'll get out now."

"I can't hear you." He gives her a smile and reaches down to unzip his jeans, takes out his pale, semi-erect cock. "Just do this one thing for me."

The first object that Lizzie grasps inside her backpack is the book. She wacks him across the cheek.

"Ow! Are you crazy?"

This time she catches his ear.

"Jesus Christ!"

"Let me out of this car. Now." She starts banging the book repeatedly on the dark glass. "Hey! Pull over!"

As the glass slides down, River Albertson is trying to stuff himself back into his jeans.

"Can I help you?" the driver says.

"Stop the car. Like right now."

He pulls against the curb as passing cars honk.

"You're a bitch. Get out."

"Gladly, jerk-off."

She climbs out of the limo, throws down her board. Somehow River's got the book in his hand. He lowers the window. "Want this?" he says. "Then go fetch it." Reaching out, he tosses it backwards over the roof of the car and into the traffic.

"Don't need it anymore, prick." Her skateboard takes her away.

"This traffic," says Dino Santori. The phone is in its holder on the dashboard of his truck. "Worse every ear. Like it's some deliberate plan, you know? Remember the governor shutting down the bridge because he was in a bad mood or something?"

"Dino, sweetheart, you're getting off track. I absolutely need you to be home on time. *Jewell* needs you to be home."

"You think I don't want to be?"

"But can you actually get to the store on time? Because they just got it back in stock, and if we don't have her present she's going to have a meltdown."

"Remember the days when all she wanted was a new Barbie?"

"Please, you'll make me cry. Just get to the Apple Store."

"That friend of hers got the new one so now Jewell has to have it. Is she going to get her navel pierced, too?"

"Over my dead body. Be on time, Dino."

"Fucking governor of New Jersey."

"So vote Democrat."

"Oh, you're a scream. Why don't I just— *shit!*"

"Dino? You okay? You weren't in an accident, were you? My God—"

"Something just flew in through my window. Is it a bird?"

"Don't touch it, it could be diseased!"

"No, it's...it's a book. What the—"

"Good, because if you're not on time—"

"Traffic's moving. I gotta go."

"Okay, love you."

"Love you, too."

Dino Santori shifts into second and the ten-wheeler groans forward. He planned to take Hudson but now there's a bunch of city workers setting up a blue barricade in front of a geyser that's flooding the street. He pulls around, laying on the horn to hurry a gaggle of jaywalkers, and makes it to Broadway. Miracle of miracles, the cars are moving and he rumbles down to Ann, turns once and again to reach Gold. Now he's peering through the side window, squinting at the numbers painted over the loading docks. And there it is, Silverschmidt International Trading Company. He backs into the dock, turning the wheel with practised ease. There in his left mirror is a guy on the dock waving for him to stop. Dino kills the engine.

He swings open the cab door and jumps down, feeling that pain in his right knee again. He tries not to limp as he approaches the guy. "You with Silverschmidt? I got a pickup."

"I don't know anything about it. I'm waiting for a courier."

"Anyone else who knows?"

"Sorry, I've got strict instructions to get— oh, here he is now."

A bike courier glides past Dino, one of those dreadlocked white guys who's stoned all the time. He pulls an envelope from his bike, gets the guy on the dock to sign for it, and pulls out again.

"Can you at least ask—"

But the guy has gone through the door marked *Employees Only*.

Dino looks down and sees that he's standing in a puddle of oil. "Isn't that just swell."

A buzzer sounds but nobody appears. He looks at his watch, trying to calculate how long it will take him to get to the Apple Store and onto the turnpike. He could call the office, but Harry's going to give him a hard time—

"You from Double-R Trucking?" somebody says. It's a young fellow in a blue suit and tan shoes.

"Yup, that's me. Where's the load?"

"We've had a bit of a delay."

"You serious?"

"The IT guys were supposed to pack up the old desktops, but all they did was disconnect them."

"How long do you think they'll be?"

The young fellow raises his shoulders.

Dino says, "Okay, but I'm leaving in sixty minutes, whether my trailer's empty or full."

He climbs back into the cab. His son, who's doing an MBA in Philadelphia, already sounds like that guy. Dino finds a pack of Juicy Fruit in the cupholder and folds a piece into his mouth. With nothing better to do, he picks up the book that landed on the passenger's seat. The back cover is bent and he tries to flatten it, then begins to read.

Twenty minutes go by. Forty. A truck pulls up in the next dock. The driver calls over to him.

"Are you Larry Ruft?"

"Larry Rust?"

"No, Larry *Ruft*."

"Not me."

"Sorry, I thought we met at a stop in Rhode Island."

Dino goes back to reading. The story makes him think of his Aunt Maria. She had an exotic bird as a pet, some really big parrot. Wouldn't shut up. And it was a jealous bastard, attacking anyone who got close to her. When Maria died, she lay on the sofa with the TV on for two days. But the bird knew. Pulled out half its feathers in grief. Then the undertakers couldn't get near the body until the Humane Society came and netted the damn thing.

He finds half a can of Pringles on the floor and crunches them down as he reads.

A knock on the cab window. It's the fellow in the blue suit.

"They're bringing the stuff down now. It should take about forty-five minutes to load."

"Jesus. I can't take that long."

"I talked to your boss. He said you need to wait."

"You phoned my boss? Who the fuck are you to talk to my boss?"

Blue suit holds up his hands. "Hey, just trying to help."

"I bet. Well, I got to piss. Can I come in and use the can?"

"Sorry, no. There's a Starbucks just to the right at the end of the block."

"Unbelievable. When I get back, that load better be on my truck and belted down."

Blue suit tries to look nonchalant as he turns away. Dino gets down from the cab, using the step this time, then goes back up to grab the book. He walks to the end of the loading dock, turns, passes a shoe repair kiosk, a tie shop, and spots the Starbucks. It's one of those narrow ones with just a few tables and a line of stools along the window. This late in the day it's quiet inside, and he goes up to the counter.

"What can I get you?"

"What the hell, give me a Frappuccino. And the code for the little boys' room."

The washroom is at the back and not all that clean. He unzips his fly. It used to be that he could piss like a horse, but now with the enlarged prostate he just stands there and dribbles. When he comes out again, his drink is waiting for him, the whipped cream already melting into the coffee. He takes it to the window and hikes himself up onto a stool. He starts to read.

Uses a stir stick to get the whipped cream along the rim.

Reads.

Looks out the window at a couple of women walking by.

Reads.

Back when he was a young driver on the road for days at a time, he used to pull over at night to sleep in the bed behind the driver's seat. He kept a *Penthouse* back there to help relieve the itch, which he needed to do nightly. Once in a while he'd meet a waitress in a diner and get lucky. Well, twice anyway. He was more than glad to get married and end all that.

His phone chimes. Lucille's name. What's the point in picking up and telling her he's going to be late? He's got a few more pages to go and he concentrates on finishing the book. Somehow he feels that character could have been him, that it's only because of Lucille putting up with him that he's had a real life. He closes the cover, leaves it on the counter, and as he walks out of Starbucks he calls her back.

Laila Cameron is picking up sugar packets that somebody knocked all over the floor. Her shift is over in ten minutes but she likes to leave the place tidy, not to impress the manager but because her mother trained her so well that she just can't leave anything out of place.

Which is not the same thing as saying she's rule-bound. For example, on some days Laila will speak to Starbucks customers in an Irish, Italian, or even Swedish accent just for practice. Of course there was that time a woman started speaking back to her in rapid Italian and Laila had broken out laughing.

Her real first name is Margot, but she used her middle name on joining Actor's Equity because there was already a Margot Cameron. She still has that first membership card in a little frame by her bedside. Now she takes off her apron and hangs it in the back. She grabs her fun-fur jacket and her bag and sees a burly man leave something on the window counter as he goes out the door. It's a book. She grabs it and follows him out.

"Excuse me, sir, you forgot this!"

The man is on his cell, but he turns back and gives her a smile. "That's okay, honey, I left it for someone else. Just be careful. It's a flying book!"

He keeps going. *Don't "honey" me,* she thinks, and is about throw the book into the lost-and-found box when she decides she doesn't want to go back in and sticks it inside her bag. She walks toward the subway and gets caught up in the flow of office workers pouring out of the surrounding buildings. She swipes her MetroCard twice before it works. Down the stairs to the platform, where she keeps back because of her fear that someone will shove her onto the tracks. How she can be an actor when she's afraid of so many things is beyond explanation, just as the need to act is beyond explanation. Not wanting to feel the other bodies around her, she pulls the book out and starts to read. Lately her reading has been Jesmyn Ward and Colson Whitehead and Brandon Taylor, wanting to read voices she might recognize, and here she is reading somebody who is definitely white. The train that pulls in is already three-quarters full, but she manages to get on and wedges herself in the middle of the car with one hand on a strap and the book in the other.

The train lurches forward and then comes to a halt. An older woman's wig has shifted to one side and Laila would like to reach out and fix it but of course she can't. She goes back to reading.

She hates the 42nd Street Station, which is damp and deep and dismal, so she waits to get off at 50th, then walks over to Seventh Avenue and back down. On the way she picks up some sushi maki and a mango drink and arrives at the Minskoff Theatre, where she is understudying not only the ensemble but also the parts of Sarafina and Nala. In the last five months of steady employment she has taken ensemble roles seventeen times and Sarafina three times but never the larger part of Nala. Mostly she has cooled her heels.

Today there are about two dozen hopefuls lined up at the box office, waiting for last-minute releases. Laila waves at Marsha and Nick in the booth and then backtracks over to the stage door in the alley and rings the buzzer.

Big Ben opens the door, wiping his bearded mouth on his sleeve because he's got a souvlaki in his other hand. "Hey, Laila, did you hear?"

"Hear what?"

"Theresa's got a sore throat."

"No way! I mean, that's terrible. I better check in with Gwen."

"That's what I'm saying, girl."

"Thanks, Benny," she says, squeezing his arm as she goes by. It can't be, Laila thinks, it can't be true that she'll finally get a chance to play Nala. Her heart is already racing. She says hi to everyone she passes, but her mind is flying above the theatre. She goes past the dressing rooms, takes a short staircase, and sees Gwen leaning out her doorway and crooking a finger at her. Gwen is an unusual theatre type in that she has never been known to smile. Laila dutifully follows as Gwen, pushing back her headset, retreats into her office.

"So you hear about Theresa?"

"Is she okay? I know there's a nasty cold going around. It isn't Covid, I hope."

"She's tested negative twice so it looks like just a cold. Theresa says she's okay for today but you better be ready for tomorrow. I'm working on scheduling a morning rehearsal with Jackson and Annalee. It wouldn't hurt to watch some scenes from the wings tonight."

"Definitely."

"Just remember to keep out of the way. There are some fast exits."

"Of course." Does Gwen think Laila is an amateur? She is already turning to her computer screen, so Laila leaves the office. Would it be terrible for her to pray that Theresa gets a bad cold just for a few days? She heads back to the dressing rooms and sees Theresa coming toward her in costume but without her lioness headpiece. In her hand is a steaming mug.

"Terry! Are you feeling any better?"

"Not really. This tea with honey is helping my throat a bit, anyway. But I might collapse after the show. Listen, if it comes to that, I know you'll do fine."

"That's so nice of you to say. But I hope you'll be okay."

"Thanks, cutie."

Theresa goes past her, and Laila heads for the dressing room she shares with two other girls. Fifteen minutes to curtain and Cecile and Jacky are leaning into the mirrors to finish their makeup. Cecile gets up and Laila looks her over, straightening a hem, pulling a sleeve. Jacky has a makeup smear on her neck that Laila blends in with her finger.

"Maybe tomorrow you'll be getting ready, too," Jacky says.

"Oh, I can't talk about it!"

The two disappear. Other people are moving past the open doorway and then it gets quiet. This is the moment that Laila always feels a little sinking of her heart. She takes out her sushi and pulls the tab on the mango drink. She finds the book, then turns the speaker on low and hears the murmur of the audience. The adult Nala doesn't appear before intermission, so she can zone out for a long while. She takes up the ratty armchair in the corner, sushi in her lap, and as she starts to read, the speaker crackles with Rafiki's first long note.

No one disturbs her for a good stretch. Then comes a knock on the door frame. She looks up to see Levon, twenty-one and beautiful and smiling. "You need anything?"

"No, I'm good, thanks. Hey, Levon. You write plays, right?"

"Trying to."

"Had anything put on?"

"At Yale. But I'm sending a script around. Why?"

"It's just this book I'm reading. What would you think of a play about a town where people bring wild animals to live in their houses? I mean, like wolves and bears and shit."

"Do the animals talk?"

"No, they're just animals. Never mind, it's probably a bad idea. So what's your script about?"

"It's about the Obama kids when they're old, like in their

eighties, and looking back to when Dad was president."

"That's awesome crazy."

"Here, have a bottle of water. Got to hydrate."

Levon moves on as "Hakuna Matata" plays over the speaker. Then comes the roar of the audience, and two minutes later Cecile and Jacky are hustling back into the dressing room, laughing about something. Jacky says there was a little problem with one of the giraffes getting off the stage. They take turns in the toilet and Cecile eats half a granola bar while Jacky swigs water and calls home to check in on her two-year-old daughter. Then the five-minute call comes over the speaker and they're gone again.

Laila waits for the opening number to be almost done and then walks through the corridors to the wings on stage right. She keeps away from the tech guys and backs off for exits, then watches "The Madness of King Scar," where Nala plays it comically, and Scar's sexual advances. Now comes Nala's song, the power ballad "Shadowland." Laila watches the female chorus singing and then Theresa's silken voice slide into the lyrics. Just the right inflection and slight vibrato as the rhythm picks up and her voice rises and holds the big notes. Laila has to remind herself that she's got the chops for it and that when she watches Theresa, doubts always creep in. The chorus takes over and then Nala sings in Zulu with that amazing nasal edge and power. Laila knows her voice just isn't as big as Theresa's.

Back in the dressing room, she turns off the speaker and curls up in the chair with the book. Don't think about tomorrow, she tells herself. She reads and reads, but how much she takes in is another matter, at least until the scene with the really old, cantankerous father, who is about to climb a mountain with his nurse. It reminds her of her own grandfather, the most stubborn man on earth. But also the only one in the family who said that if she wanted to sing on Broadway, then that's what she should do. Made her mother mad as anything. If only her grandfather hadn't died, if only he could be in the audience, if only she got to play the role—

She's on the last pages when she can hear the cast coming back from curtain call. Cecile and Jacky hardly notice her, and she just sits there and finishes the book. Then she grabs her stuff, says goodbye over her shoulder, heads down the corridor, and sees Theresa leaning against the wall, looking exhausted.

"I think I have a fever," Theresa says, and one of the dressers takes her inside the dressing room and closes the door.

Laila keeps going. She puts the book down by the house phone, where people leave copies of *Variety* and stuff. She's out the door ahead of the cast and has to pass by the line of fans waiting with their programs and phones. Maybe tomorrow they'll want her autograph, too.

The Minskoff Theatre is dark but for the bare ghost light onstage. All the seats in the vast orchestra and two balconies are empty except for seat BB1. Ali Singh Ahani chafes in his polyester uniform, purchased used from a former employee of Broadway Protection Services. On the seat next to him rests his cap and the wide leather belt that is so weighed down (baton, pepper spray, flashlight, two-way radio) that it gives him a backache.

Ali needs one more year to be re-certified as an anesthesiologist. He studies and attends his hospital internship during the day and watches over the Minskoff five nights a week. So far the only intruders have been a couple of teenage girls who hid in a washroom after the show and cried when he called their parents. But he is not looking for excitement; he's too tired. The dull passing of the hours suits him as he listens to the music of Umm Kulthum and Mohammed Abdel Wahab, old-school singers who remind him of his parents' generation.

Now he is cracking sunflower seeds into a paper cup and reading a book he found by the telephone. His reading comprehension is high—he started learning English as a child—and he prefers the long, immersive novels of Charles Dickens and Anthony Trollope or John Irving and A. S. Byatt. So he turns the pages of this squib of a book, which has clearly been read more than once, as the back cover is bent and there is a small orange stain on the front and the pages smell slightly of fish. Perhaps, he thinks, this is more important than the story itself, that he join the anonymous chain of fellow readers. Although he does find himself strangely relating to the character in the book. And that incident with the prostitute reminds him of the woman in Cairo he once visited, prompted by his brother, who kept making fun of his virginity. She had been very motherly and afterwards he had been apologetic and thankful, discovering only later that she had removed all the money from his wallet. Which of course he had deserved.

It is time for him to make his rounds, so he gets up and puts on his belt and cap. Climbing onto the stage with a grunt, he slips into the wing and then walks all the corridors and rattles the doors. He takes a drink of water and returns to seat BB1 for the last stretch of the book. Sure enough, the character finds the woman at the very end. There is something appealing about her; although he is only five foot five, Ali too finds tall women attractive. But he knows from bitter experience that all women prefer men who are six feet or more. For this reason, if no other, he is rooting for the character and chooses not to find the ending at all ambiguous.

This is his last thought before falling asleep. He has failed to set the alarm on his phone and wakes only when someone taps on the sole of his shoe. He startles awake but is relieved to find Donald standing there in his own uniform, baton in hand. "Time for you to go home, Laurel."

"Yes, yes." Ali rouses himself. Donald calls them Laurel and Hardy because of their contrasting size, Donald being both big and fat. Ali gets up and considers offering Donald the book, but his fellow guard is not a reader. Instead, he's already chuckling over a video on his phone of a person trying to jump over a car and into a child's pool. So Ali heads for the exit. It is 6:40 a.m., the morning light clear, the air almost fresh. He walks along 45th Street, pulling up his trousers every few steps, and heads down Fifth Avenue. Soon he can see the public library's handsome lions. Another in the army of security guards that resentfully guard the city is unlocking the gate to Bryant Park, and Ali makes a sudden decision to be the first person in the park that day. It is so wonderfully lush and yet orderly, the walkways lined with plane trees, the little green tables and folding chairs. He strolls toward the opposite gate, pausing to lay the book down on a table. With his finger he invisibly inscribes his name on the cover in Arabic script. There isn't time for him to go to his apartment, he'll head straight to the hospital for his morning shift.

Four thousand one hundred and twenty-six people will enter Bryant Park over the next five hours. One hundred and seventeen notice the book lying on the table; thirty-four pause to read the title and eleven pick it up, look at the back cover, and put it down again.

At two o'clock in the afternoon there is a sprinkle of rain. Drops patter on the book and a few roll past the fore-edge, dampening the pages. The cloud drifts off toward the East River and the sun shines again.

Mark and Geraldine Reef of Hamilton, Ontario, are standing by the bronze figure of Gertrude Stein and having an argument. They have come from inside the library, where they went up the stairs to see the Reading Room. Arguments have been common lately and the holiday has not improved things. Two of their adult children have become fed up enough to suggest they have a trial separation. The third suggested this trip. And now they are arguing about the September 11 Memorial & Museum.

"Obviously it was a tragedy," Mark says. "You keep deliberately misunderstanding me. I just don't want to pay some ridiculous ticket price to stare at a bunch of twisted metal and listen to American propaganda."

Geraldine says, "Lower your voice. People are going to be insulted. There might even be someone here who knows a person who died. How do you know what the museum is like before you even go?"

"Believe me, I know. If the country accepted even a little responsibility—"

"As soon as you say, 'Believe me,' I know not to believe you. In fact, I'm not even going to listen to you anymore." Who *is* this man she lives with? She recognizes his outline—the crooked nose, the rounded stomach, but not the look in his eyes. He obviously hates her.

"Well, I'm going to the museum. You don't have to come. I'll be done by four thirty. You can meet me down there or not. It's your choice."

She begins to walk away. He wants to run after her but he doesn't. He watches her go down the path in her gold jacket and black pedal pushers, a middle-aged woman with wide hips and dyed blond hair. Somehow his wife. Somehow the person with whom he has spent the formative decades of his life. Adding up to what, he doesn't know.

Mark turns and begins to walk in the other direction. Having no idea what to do with himself, he sits in a metal chair. Nearby sparrows are hopping about in the grass, competing for muffin crumbs thrown by a little girl in braids. He doesn't understand what has been happening to the two of them lately. He knows he's angry and that he's being a jerk to Geraldine. The only thing he can think of is that he's turning forty-nine, the year his own father died. But that seems melodramatic. His father died on a building site, not from some genetically inheritable disease. But people say Mark looks more like his father all the time. He doesn't want to look like him or be anything like him, but maybe he doesn't have a choice.

"Mister, I think you dropped your book." The girl with the muffin has taken up the chair next to his. She's holding a book out to him.

"Sorry, are you talking to me?"

"Here," she says, and puts it in his hand. Then she gets up and runs onto the path and into the crowd. He looks at the book, the pages slightly warped. He's not much of a reader other than the newspaper and Stephen King novels. But with no reason to be sitting there, he can't think of anything better to do than open the book.

As he reads, people move past in a constant, slow-moving stream. Shadows from surrounding buildings creep over the green rectangle. Unlike Stephen King, where you need to know what will happen next, this book is more like a series of moments that might or might not add up to something. More like life maybe, but doesn't a person read a novel to get away from life? He stays there reading and doesn't get up, not once, until he has finished the last page. Only then does he realize how badly he needs to take a piss. So he goes around to the front steps of the library, waits in line for the security check, and as he goes through realizes that he still has the book in his hand. He climbs the marble stairs and goes all the way to the other side of the building to find the men's room, where he waits in line again. The urinal is so big, he thinks, that you could bury a man in one.

On Fifth Avenue the buses are lined up along the curb, making it impossible to see any cabs going by. He has to walk south two blocks before he can start to wave like a drowning man, but the cabs roll by. He's thinking one will never stop and then a cab pulls up so suddenly he leaps backwards for fear of being flattened.

"The 9/11 memorial, please."

The driver pulls out again. There is a scratched Plexiglas divider separating them and a small TV screen showing advertisements for restaurants and Broadway shows. The driver takes the FDR Drive along the East River, the traffic moving all right until they pull off, getting stuck under the ramp to the Brooklyn Bridge. Then they crawl with excruciating slowness while he taps the book on his knee. They emerge into the light, lurch forward, stop, lurch again. Without thinking, he slips the book behind his head, onto the ledge under the back window.

"This is about as close as I can get," the driver says. "Another block and there's a barrier. Just follow the crowd, you'll get to the museum."

Mark hands over some bills and then he's walking. There is a mass of people right up to the wooden barricades funnelling them toward the museum. Cops everywhere. He sees two enormous, square basins of black marble into which water pours from the sides as if into an abyss. He is surprised by the severity of them.

And there is Geraldine, standing near the second basin, quietly crying. Now she is looking for a tissue in her purse. She blows her nose. He thinks she might look up but she doesn't so he walks toward her. Her mascara has run. He comes up to her and at last she sees him.

"It's so..." She doesn't go on.

He puts his arms around her. If only he hadn't hesitated.

Julia Ramirez would never take a cab for her own convenience. But during the last half-hour of her shift she got a text from Roman. Roman used to be her brother Donato's boyfriend and she knows he still loves Don, even if Roman can't take it anymore. And who can blame him, Julia herself has given up so many times.

She waits for the passenger to get out of the cab and then slips in before somebody else can take it. "Brooklyn, please," she says. "New York Community Hospital. Take the tunnel."

As the taxi starts backing up she realizes she's still wearing her headset and transmitter. She's supposed to return them to the office on finishing her last tour, but she was too anxious to remember. She shoves them into her bag while the taxi turns and shoots forward into a sudden hole in the traffic. Julia closes her eyes. She feels exhausted, but whether it's from eight hours on her feet or worrying about her brother, she hardly knows. He was such a beautiful boy, as a teenager she used to think how unfair it was that he got the looks. Their neighbours used to say he would grow up to become a movie star, and everyone wanted to fix him up with their daughters. And to see him now like a scarecrow, and all those scars on his arms—

Her phone chimes. She sees a text from Bill and writes back, *Sue's picking up the kids there's a lasagna in the freezer don't wait for me.* From the tunnel it's pretty much a straight shot down Ocean Parkway. She closes her eyes again and is instantly asleep, waking when the driver slams on the brakes. Actually what wakes her is some object knocking the back of her head. She reaches behind her and finds a book. Some passenger must have left it in the cab.

They're idling in front of the hospital doors. She pays and gets out. The doors slide open and she is immediately greeted by a smiling elderly woman in a blue smock. "May I direct you somewhere?"

"My brother was admitted. I was told he's on the sixth floor."

"Well, dear, you can check at the desk or just take the elevators straight up."

Julia thanks her as she moves on, controlling an urge to run. What if he finally did it, finally killed himself like she accused him of trying to do all these years? How could there be a world without him out there? She gets into the elevator, followed by an orderly pushing a bed. The woman in the bed appears to be asleep. The orderly takes her out on the fourth floor and two doctors get in, talking about a baby shower or engagement party or something. Julia gets out. She walks past the deserted nurses' station and begins to check the names by the doors. At 612 she finds *D. Ramirez / H. Shimotakahara* and looks in. There's nobody in the bed by the door, but behind the half-pulled curtain on the window side she can see feet under a blanket. She steps into the room and peeks around the curtain to see an extremely old Asian man in the bed. He has only a few hairs on his mottled scalp and his skin looks translucent. His mouth is slightly open, his eyes closed. Beside him a woman is sitting in a chair. She's wearing office attire—a blouse and skirt and heels—and is staring at Julia.

"Excuse me?" the woman says.

"I'm looking for my brother, Donato. He's supposed to be in the next bed. Did something happen to him?"

"They released him."

"Already?

"A good thing, with the noise he was making. He was very disruptive."

"I'm sorry."

Julia ought to leave, but something in her lets go and she's suddenly exhausted. Now she'll have to take the subway from Brooklyn across Manhattan to Queens. It'll take her at least an hour and a half. What she really wants to do is lie down on the empty bed.

The woman says, "Can you do me a favour?"

"What favour?"

"I don't want to leave my father by himself. But I have this work thing to do. My fault for not retiring when they offered. It won't take long. Can you just sit beside him for a bit?"

"What's wrong with your father?"

"He's just old. He's ninety-three. Heart failure."

"Is he going to get better?"

"No, he's not."

"I don't know, I really should—"

"Please. Otherwise I'll have to leave him by himself."

"But you are coming back soon, right?"

"He's my father."

"Okay. I can stay for a while."

"Thank you, thank you." She grabs her purse from under the chair and leans forward and speaks Japanese into her father's ear. Then she gets up and, coming around, briefly touches Julia's shoulder.

"Oh, and it would be great if you talked to him."

"Talked?"

"I don't know if he hears or not, but it couldn't hurt. He doesn't speak English well, but just the sound of a voice is good."

The woman hurries out the door. What has just happened? What is she doing with somebody else's father? Julia looks at the doorway a moment and then sighs and sits down in the still-warm chair. The man is much closer to her now, propped up on a couple of pillows, thin blanket pulled almost to his chin. His cheekbones are painfully prominent, his eyes deep in their sockets. None of the surrounding monitors are turned on; there's no IV in his arm.

"Hi," she says.

"I'm Julia," she says.

The man's narrow chest rises a little with each breath.

"Your daughter will be back soon. I'm sorry you don't feel well." What else can she say? If only there was a newspaper to read aloud. She opens her bag and is surprised to find the book that banged her in the cab. She must have unconsciously stuffed it in, fortunately as it turns out. She picks up the ratty thing and looks at the cover.

"I used to read to my girls every night," she says. "They loved it. But now they read themselves and I'm the one who misses it. This book is called *The Animals.* I don't know anything about it, but how bad can it be, right?"

She looks at the man; his eyelashes flutter. Is he communicating with her? She starts to read, not with emphasis or drama like she did with her kids, but in a quiet, even voice. And right at the beginning there's something a little embarrassing, for the man is making a miniature figure of a naked woman and gets aroused by his own creation. Which is pretty ridiculous when you think about it. But it's too hard to skip, so the old man gets to hear it all.

A faint sound from his lips, like the air being released from a balloon.

"Does that mean you like it or you don't, Mr.... Ah, hold on a sec." She goes outside, checks the name plate, and comes back. "Mr. Shimotakahara. That's a nice name, like poetry. Anyway, I'll keep reading."

She does. She reads and reads. Her fatigue has settled into something manageable, and it's actually more pleasant to be sitting here in the dim light than fighting for a seat on the train. When she looks at him, his breath seems a bit shallower. He doesn't look agitated but there is strain in his face, a bare hint of struggle. She reads on. Surely it's a strange occupation to be a writer, an adult who makes up stories. There's something juvenile about it, even if some writers make loads of money. She suspects this writer isn't one of them. Donato used to make up crazy stories for the kids and they'd be riveted. She always wondered how he was able to do that. They loved their uncle, still love him, which makes her only angrier at him for throwing their affection away.

She reads.

She should really be getting home. But she reads on, even though her voice is growing hoarse. It's usually sore at the end of the day from giving so many tours, she always gargles with salt water before bed. And here she is, reading on.

The light has dimmed in the window. At least she's getting to the end. There's the main character, waving from the window of the burning school, the woman he loves looking up at him, arms open as he jumps. And then the chapter ends and there's an epilogue that takes place a year later. That's a bit of a cheat, isn't it?

"Whew," she says, closing the book. "That was a little marathon. What do you think, Mr. Shimotakahara? Any good?"

Looking at him, she sees his colour has changed. He was pale before but now he looks positively grey. His skin is like parchment, his cheekbones almost silvery. He isn't breathing and his mouth has twisted into a slight grimace.

She becomes very still and listens. But there is nothing. Julia stands up. She agreed to sit with the woman's father, not to be with him when he died. Her eyes are wet for a man she didn't know and she wipes them with her sleeve as she goes to the doorway to look for somebody. But there's only an orderly disappearing through a door. She'll have to go to the nurses' station and tell them. As she starts to walk she sees the elevator at the other end open and the man's daughter get out. She doesn't notice Julia because she's tipping up a takeout coffee as she walks. Julia wants to duck in somewhere and hide, but there are only other patients' rooms and now the daughter sees her. They walk toward each other and the woman smiles and nods her head. Julia tries to smile in return as they pass each other. She walks faster and faster as if people are going to come running after her and she doesn't wait for the elevator but throws open the stairway door and hurries down the steps.

For Mike Jastrow it's a good day when nobody dies. Today one man croaked on his shift and another had to be transferred to intensive care. On the other hand, Lola Esposito texted to say she would meet him at the open mic. In his mind, the good news definitely outweighs the bad.

He puts on a new mask and gloves and goes in to disinfect the room of the deceased. Strips the bed and brings in a new mattress, removes what can be sterilized, disinfects everything else. The book left on the chair he drops into the pocket of his scrubs. By the time he's finished, a new patient is parked in the hall, waiting. He nods to the other orderly and dumps his protective wear in the hall bin and whistles his way to the elevator. Down in the bowels he changes into a lumberjack shirt, jeans, and cowboy boots. He used to like wearing an obscure band T-shirt when he performed, but then his last girlfriend told him he was too fat. Said she was trying to be nice.

Since his guitar doesn't fit in the locker, he always has to leave it in the maintenance office, even though Joe is a dick who calls him Mike Jagger or sometimes just Open Mike, ha ha. Mike knocks on the door and goes in. Joe has his feet up on the desk and he's watching something on his computer screen with earbuds in.

"Well, well," Joe says. "If it isn't the Jewish Bob Dylan."

"Bob Dylan *is* Jewish."

"I was going to sell your guitar on Kijiji but I never got around to it."

"That's hilarious, Joe." The case is lying against the wall, and Mike picks it up. "Anyway, thanks for holding on to it." *And go fuck yourself.* Joe is already sticking his earbuds back in.

The darkness outside is always dismaying after nine hours indoors. He calls an Uber and, when it pulls up, gets in the back seat. Fortunately the guy isn't one of those drivers who plies you with sparkling water and wants to know your life story. They take the expressway, pass Prospect Park, and work their way through Cobble Hill to the bar. He pulls the guitar case out after him and heads inside. A woman onstage is reciting a poem to the sound of waves coming from her iPhone. He puts his name on the clipboard, too late to get an early spot. It's not a bad crowd since most performers drag in a few friends, which is the only reason the bar holds an open mic. Mike hasn't asked anyone since that last girlfriend, but tonight Lola is coming, which makes him doubly nervous. It isn't so much his wanting to impress her as not wanting to look like an idiot. They met online two weeks ago and met for a coffee, where they seemed to hit it off. She's maybe a year or two younger than he is, not gorgeous or anything but with a nice face. He liked her clear voice and the way she laughed and how she didn't go on about how great her life was. He actually wanted to hear her talk more than himself for a change. So now it's his turn to show the true guy underneath. There's nothing more vulnerable than singing your own song. And if she doesn't like what she hears, better to know now. But please, he thinks, like what you see.

The poet takes her bow and the MC gets up to introduce an elderly couple who sing Carter Family songs while the woman plays an autoharp. Lola didn't say when she would show up, so he goes to the bar and gets a Michelob, then sits at a back table and takes the book out of his jacket pocket, where he'd transferred it from his scrubs. Of course he's not supposed to take anything from patients' rooms, but he didn't think anybody would want a beat-up book that now smelled like the hospital room of a dying patient. He starts to read but he's always been impatient with print, so he uses the speed-reading technique he learned in high school, running his finger down the centre of the page and following it with his eyes. He turns the pages quickly, although he's a little confused about what the guy in the book does (home renovation?) and why his neighbour keeps a guard dog.

A hipster type is playing a Stella guitar and singing "Dust My Broom" like he's an old Black dude. Mike turns the page and reads on. The guy in the book likes this girl who is either a stripper or a dance instructor. Now another guitar player—too many damn guitars—is doing an imitation of Johnny Cash. Too many damn clones!

So where is Lola? The photograph he'd put up on the dating app was eight years old, yet when Lola met him she hadn't seemed to notice. But maybe it did matter and she's decided not to come. Now the MC is calling him up to the mic. He hates going after the guy with the musical saw. Also, he'd like to wait in case Lola finally comes. Not to mention he's got thirty pages left in the book. But he puts it down on the table and heads for the stage with his guitar. He has some trouble hefting himself up onto the stool and then he strums a chord to check the sound.

"Hi, everyone," he says, leaning into the mic. "I was going to sing only upbeat songs tonight, but fuck it—excuse my French—I'll just do what I feel. This first one comes from my work in a hospital. It's called 'The Dead Never Look Happy.'"

He sings three songs in all, feeling off his game. Probably

because he keeps hoping that Lola will walk in and knowing that she won't. So that's that. He doesn't even say thank you but just gets off the stool and heads to his table. He puts the guitar back in the case. Might as well finish that second beer and read the end of his book. Only the book isn't on the table. Or under it, either. It looks like somebody has swiped it. If that isn't the icing on the fucking cake. But as he's about to go, some words for a new song pop into his head. *We are all animals trying to survive, we are all animals trying to stay alive.* He's not sure there's any difference between surviving and staying alive but he pulls out his little notebook from an inside jacket pocket and writes down the lyric. So he'll get something out of the night at least.

Nodding to the bartender, who ignores him, he heads for the door. He goes through and sees a woman approaching. It takes him a second to recognize Lola.

"Mike," she says, coming up to him. "I'm really sorry but I got tied up with my drama-queen sister on the phone. I didn't have your cell to let you know. Did I miss your set?"

"That's okay." He's enormously glad to see her. "Do you want to go for a walk? It's pretty nice out."

"Sure," she says. And they begin walking slowly, Mike carrying the guitar case. "I hope your sister is okay."

"I'm having a holiday from her starting now," she says, taking his arm.

The bell jingles. The door is opened by Talman, first name unknown. Talman is a book scout whom just about everybody in the business suspects of stealing from one store to sell to another. The Strand has him on the banned list, but George Galanis, whose bookshop looks out onto 12th Street, feels sorry for a man so clearly ridden with physical tics and psychological ailments. Life can't be easy for the guy.

"Hey hey hey hey there, George," Talman says without looking at him. He flicks his hair three times. Talman wears a long overcoat and scarf. He carries a filthy tote bag.

"Got some books. Some good books."

"Did you steal them?"

"No, I swear swear swear." He taps his chin several times with the palm of his hand. "I got most of them from my mom's neighbour on Coney Island. And I found one in a bar."

"Okay, let me take a look. Right off the bat I have to say no to these memoirs of British politicians, thank you. And sorry, I've already got eight copies of *The Handmaid's Tale*. I can take these novels, I guess. What's this little one? Never heard of it and it's in poor condition. Why are you bringing me stuff like this?"

"I read it, George, I read it to the end. Afterwards I went to sleep and had this dream. I'm a bear. A bear in the woods. And I meet this girl."

"I don't need to hear, thanks. All right, I'll take it for the dollar rack outside. Here's ten bucks. Now go away, Talman."

One dollar he can spare. After all, he's got some time to kill. Theodore Glass pulls the heavy cape around his bulk, hardly even looks at the book he pulls off the rack, and goes inside to pay. Then he walks down to Astor Place, for he likes the metal chairs and little tables that anyone can use. The book's cover is half torn off; he should have offered fifty cents. His watch fob tells him he has just over an hour before the next tour, so he adjusts the cape around his shoulders and begins to read.

He cannot read about a place, even a fictional village, without imagining the possibilities for a guided tour. This one has a number of strong attributes—the old buildings, the miniature scenes in the shop windows, the famous author who still lives there. He might also show sites from the book itself—the protagonist's front door, the rustic café where he meets the schoolteacher (a good place for a washroom break), the place by the river where the body is found. Perhaps everyone could ride the same sort of adult tricycle used in the story, he leading them with flag held high. A metafictional tour, taking place in an imaginary village, visiting sites from the fiction itself!

He reaches a split in the binding where the pages will start to come loose if he isn't careful. The time having passed so pleasantly, he puts the book inside his cape and walks straight to Washington Square Park. Three people are lingering by the designated meeting spot, a bench near the man who plays a grand piano on wheels. They have already paid through the website, a couple in their fifties and a young woman from China. He flares his cape and approaches.

"Welcome, good people! Welcome to the History of Washington Square Park Tour. You must be Bert and Harriet from Minnesota. And you are Ming Wong from the garden city of Suzhou. We are a small but select group today. Let us step away from the glorious racket of that piano while I introduce myself. Theodore Glass, PhD, former lecturer in history at Columbia University, former textbook editor, former bread baker, former dog walker, current poet and *flâneur*. A New Yorker through and through. Today we are going to immerse ourselves in the dramatic history of this infamous square. A history that captures the sweep of this entire city. Let us begin."

They follow like ducklings. His stentorian voice needs no amplification as he describes how a marsh near the Sapohanikan Indian settlement became a potter's field. They halt beneath a three-hundred-year-old elm, site of eighteenth-century public hangings. Naturally he discourses at length on the triumphal arch designed by Stanford White, later shot and killed by the jealous husband of his mistress during a theatrical performance of the song "I Could Love a Million Girls." He moves from Edgar Allan Poe to Oscar Wilde to Djuna Barnes to James Baldwin, all nearby inhabitants. He sweeps toward the 1960s, when Jane Jacobs stood before a crowd and denounced Robert Moses' plan to carve a highway through the square. Over here cops once shut down hootenannies of banjo twangers and fiddle scratchers. Over there women raised their fists in outrage at the election of Donald Trump.

He shakes everyone's hand, giving them an opportunity to tip. Before Ming Wong can leave, he asks whether she might like to go dancing tonight, and when she declines he bows graciously and makes his way past the dog park and the chess players. Hungry as always after his exertions, he buys a hot dog, loading it with sauerkraut and pickles, and sits on a bench by the Japanese jazz trio playing "Scrapple from the Apple." From his cape he extracts the book and opens it to his place. Reading on, he is mildly surprised by the sudden appearance of a gun. He is not surprised that the poor fellow does not get laid. A streak of mustard lands on the page; he rubs it in with a finger.

Theodore Glass takes himself home, which means walking up to 14th Street and a couple of blocks east. He lives in a studio apartment above a discount electronics store, which used to be a discount luggage store, which used to be a La-Z-Boy recliner outlet. Perhaps one day a tour guide will stand before it and speak of *his* mark on the city. Fat chance. He knows he will become a mere stain, to be washed away by rain and snow and succeeding stains. The thought does not ruffle him. In the apartment he has one joint left in the Altoids tin on his dresser. He has an episode of *The Crown* to watch. He has the memory of Miss Ming Wong's fine oval face.

On the sidewalk outside the metal door is a box of objects abandoned by the tenant who moved out on the weekend. A cracked Frisbee. A plastic ukulele with a broken string. Theodore gently lays the book down, unlocks the door, and girds himself for the effort of climbing the stairs.

"I want to take the Frisbee! Or that guitar thing!"

"Don't touch filth," says the father of Freddy Ahmad, pushing him forward. "And don't be difficult. I need you to cooperate."

"Maybe I need *you* to cooperate," says Freddy, and although his father has a firm grip on his left hand and is tugging his arm, he manages to lean over and grab something with his fingers. It is only a book, stupid luck, but there's no way he's going to let go of it. He is six years and seven months old and tired of people telling him what to do. Last week he decided he wanted to be called Freddy instead of Faraj, which caused his father to say he would get a whacking, although he never does. His nanni said she would have a heart attack, but he knows she is not going to die until he's married, she's said that so many times. Also, she is the best cook.

The door to AAA Best Price Electronics has three locks. His father fumbles with the keys. He spends so much time at the store, Freddy's mother says her husband might as well live there. He comes home only to sleep. But now he must go back because Dakshesh messed up the inventory count, whatever that is, and Freddy has to be with him because his mother has a client coming for a dress fitting.

The door sticks. His father pushes him inside.

"It smells like pee in here!"

"Be quiet, Faraj! You will have your mouth washed out with soap. It's the carpets that smell. Now go play on one of the game consoles. And don't be rough with it."

"I want a snack."

"Look in Dakshesh's desk. He is always eating."

Freddy goes to the battered desk and yanks on the drawer. Snickers bar! He takes a big bite and chews as he looks from one big-screen to the other. They're all playing the same dumb commercial about diapers for old people, ha ha. At school the kids think he's so lucky, getting to play the latest games, but the truth is Freddy isn't very good at them and just gets frustrated. He hates the store, hates the low ceiling tiles, the crowded aisles, the dopey guys who come in and ask his father or Dakshesh a million boring questions. He hates the way his father is always pleading with Mr. Bank Man on the telephone or screaming at suppliers. He wishes he could have just stayed home with Nanni, but she says America is making him too wild.

Freddy crawls under one of the display tables and sits among the cables. Maybe he'll get electrocuted—*zap!*—and his hair will become curly like Jerome's. Jerome says he knows a lot of famous baseball players, but Freddy is doubtful. Jerome once kissed Melanie in the schoolyard and she ran away to tell the teacher. Freddy is hoping Jerome will kiss him next, even though he will punch Jerome for doing it.

He eats the last bite of Snickers while still holding the book in his other hand. On the cover is a picture of two birds flying around some big flames. Maybe the birds will explode. He is an okay reader, but his teacher says he has trouble focusing. Anyway, it's much easier to imagine the story in a book. Like this one, which is probably about a boy who gets struck by lightning and when he wakes up in the morning he has turned into a T. rex. He smashes the house, then heads to the school, scaring the birds, starting fires, and mashing kids along the way.

He crawls out from under the table and goes to the glass door to look at people passing by. The dinosaurs take over the world and make people into their pets. Then a bunch of aliens come and start attacking the dinosaurs. And then everybody is dead except for the T. rex and his pet Jerome and they live in a mansion and eat junk food the rest of their lives.

"Okay, Faraj, we can go now. It's past your bedtime."

"It's past *your* bedtime."

"Such a mouth on you. Don't run ahead of me. The streets aren't safe at night."

His father unlocks the door to let them out. The sidewalk is crowded. Freddy would like to hang out with those guys eating pizza slices. He starts to walk, his father grabbing his unwilling hand. At the corner of Third Avenue a girl is sitting cross-legged on the ground. There is a spotted dog curled up beside her. The girl looks dirty. She has fallen asleep with her head against the post and her mouth open. In front of her is an open suitcase with a few coins in it. He wishes he had the nerve to grab the coins. Instead, he puts the book into it.

"Don't dawdle, Faraj."

His father yanks on his arm. The girl opens her eyes and smiles at him. Freddy sticks his tongue out. He doesn't really mean it, though.

When Clara Kahlo opens her eyes she sees a little boy putting something in her suitcase. She smiles at him, but right after, some guy leans down, trying to scoop up the coins. "Back off, motherfucker!" she shouts, and Molly starts barking and baring her teeth. Molly wouldn't hurt a fly, but she can look fierce, and the guy takes off down the sidewalk. Clara calms the dog with her voice and a kiss on the head, then scoops up the money, shoves it in the pouch around her neck, and latches the suitcase. When she stands up, Molly looks at her and whines.

"Okay, Moll, just hang on. I'll get us some breakfast. What do you think, Taco Bell or Wendy's?"

Her real name is Clara Andover but somebody gave her a street name after seeing some of her drawings. One leg has fallen asleep, so she practically has to limp into Wendy's to join the lineup. She gets two sausage, egg, and cheese biscuits, one coffee triple sugar and cream, and one free cup of water. Outside, Molly is dancing with excitement. Clara breaks up one biscuit, tells Molly to sit, and gives it to her in three bites. She holds out the cup and Molly laps until it's empty.

It's always a good night when the cops don't rouse them, but now they need to move on. They turn onto 15th Street so that Molly can squat on the square of grass surrounding a tree. Clara uses a plastic bag to scoop it, having discovered it's the small rules that can screw you over. They reach the south end of Union Square, where she sees Red and Jasper busking. She takes up her own spot on the low brick wall that surrounds a bronze statue of some guy on a horse. Molly lies down, resting one paw over her eyes.

Inside the suitcase is the book she vaguely remembers some kid dropping in. She takes it out and has a good look. It's easy to pull off the cover and then start separating the pages, which are already coming apart. She dismantles the entire book, leaving her with a nice pile of small, type-covered leaves. Book pages are really great for drawing on. From the suitcase she pulls out a dollar-store box of coloured markers and, using the suitcase as a lap desk, gets down to work. On the first leaf she draws the heavy outline of a bird in flight. Birds are what she draws best, but on the next leaf she does a running rabbit. Then a turtle. Then another bird and a fox and a rat and a bird again. Every so often she chooses a different colour because some people won't buy a drawing if it doesn't match their bathroom or whatever. The square is getting busier with people on their way to work and kids going to school. A bunch of city workers in jumpsuits are walking single file across the street. She turns over the book cover and prints in large block letters. *$2 EACH.* She lays down two rows of drawings with the sign in the middle.

A few people look down, but most pass without noticing. She keeps drawing, putting the pictures in a pile beside her. Some prick steps on the rabbit. A couple of girls in school uniforms stop to look. A light breeze moves the pleats of their skirts. Clara smiles but keeps drawing.

"I like that bird," says the shorter girl, crouching to pull up a sock.

"I like the rabbit," says the other. "Too bad it's got a footprint on it."

"That'll probably come off," Clara says. She picks it up and rubs it against her sleeve. "See?"

"Oh, right. What do you think, Stace? Should we both get one?"

Clara goes back to drawing. She finishes the last one and puts it on the pile. The wind picks up, fluttering the corners of the leaves.

"We can put them in our lockers," says the short one.

"Cool. Let's do it. I hope I have some change."

They sling off their backpacks and start looking in the pockets. A leaf from the pile flutters up and lands on top of the fox. "I found my money," says the taller one. She gives it to Clara.

"Thanks. I really like your braid."

"Can you loan me two bucks?" the shorter one asks her friend. And now the wind picks up and a few leaves slide along the sidewalk.

"Oh, shit," Clara says. "I usually have some stones for weights." She opens her suitcase to look.

"Hey, I found some change," the shorter one says, and just then a gust lifts all the drawings into the air.

"Wow," says the taller girl.

The leaves somersault in the air. Some rise, rush forward, and get caught in the low branches of trees. Others swoop down again and skid across the pavement. A few plaster themselves against fire hydrants, light poles, legs. A large group appears to rise as a flock and soar over the trees toward Broadway.

"Well, fuck me," says Clara.

Half a dozen leaves separate and disappear down 13th Street. The rest keep rising. A small group has reached Fifth Avenue; they tumble over the roof of the New School. One leaf does a figure eight and spirals down toward a woman exiting the CVS Pharmacy. The woman has long white hair, piercing blue eyes, and skin that looks leathery from exposure to the outdoors. As she reaches for it, a honking limousine makes her pull back. The breeze from the limousine causes the leaf to rise straight up and then arc back down until it is fanning against the woman's face. She grabs it and holds it out. On it is a drawing of a dog or wolf or fox. She looks at the printed lines underneath and starts to laugh and, holding up her hands, lets the paper go so that it rises up and over the traffic and keeps going, higher and higher, until it disappears into the clouds.

MUSWELL HILL

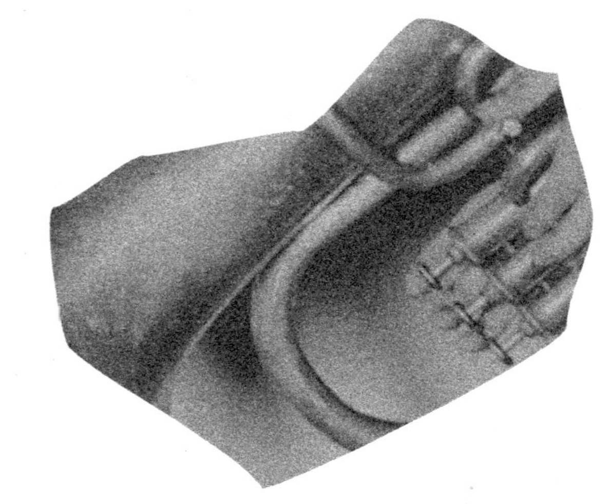

MISS BINGHAM HAS MOVED OUT. I DID NOT CARE FOR MISS Bingham, no more today than I did three years ago at the start of her degree. For one thing, she is fat. I cannot tolerate double chins and stomach rolls on a young person. (My own age is a different matter.) For another, she has a laugh like a donkey's bray that expresses both her insecurity and the naïveté of her rural origins. But like others before her, Miss Bingham has graduated and so has just now left to take up a position—in her case as some sort of nursing assistant in the hinterlands of Yorkshire. Let me record here for posterity: On August 29, 1978, Miss Tessa Bingham left the premises.

More to the point, she has vacated the coveted top room of the house. Coveted by me, that is. I have lived here for nine years and have looked upon the succeeding inhabitants of that room with envy and also disdain, for none of them has deserved it as much as I do. But the room with the slanted wall (for it sits just beneath the roof) is five pounds a week more than the other two, and my budget has not allowed for the expense.

Until now. For just this month I was promoted to assistant manager of the Bloomsbury branch of BestBrit ticket kiosks, which requires me, beyond my previous duty of manning the desk, to make sure the operation runs smoothly. Ordering and delivery of tickets, regular updating of signage, staffing schedule—all this now falls to me. I become second only to the manageress, about whom I remain mum. The point here being that I can at last afford the top room and it is only a matter of approaching Mrs. P. at the appropriate time. Then I shall literally move up in the world.

My first salvo: a bouquet of flowers. Tomorrow I shall bring one home and present them to Mrs. P. Like all women, she is bound to be foolishly touched by the gesture.

My other name for Mrs. P., only to myself, is Mrs. Not Tonight Dear. She is friendly to me of course, very good about making all tenants feel at home. She has a natural touch with people that I can only marvel at. No, it is for the long-suffering Mr. P. that I call her that, he of the reedy voice and weak chin and unfortunate taste for the bottle. When he's in his nines, Mr. P. must sleep on the parlour sofa, which he always makes up before the children wake in the morning.

But I drift. There is time enough for such details of the life of this little row house in Muswell Hill.

Let me speak of the curvaceous sensuality of the euphonium. The kiss of the mouthpiece, the generously open horn. Yet how is it that the instrument to which I am so devoted remains unappreciated? After all, it is smaller than the tuba, not ridiculous like the American sousaphone. I give this afternoon as the latest example. In order to practise I must wait for the house to be empty. Contrary to what many think, the instrument does not have to be loud; indeed, it can purr like a cat. But I understand that not everyone delights in the sound of repeated scales and tricky phrases and other exercises to make the tongue and fingers nimble. Today I had the early shift and returned home by four, so I brought the instrument down to the parlour and began to practise. I was just starting a series of quick eighth notes, triplets, and trills demanding tremendous breath control when in burst Mrs. P. and her two urchins, eight- and ten-year-old boys.

It is true that I was rather deshabille, wearing only a shirt, a pair of perfectly ironed boxer shorts, and argyle socks, and that to be seen like this was naturally an embarrassment to me. Still, neither the instrument nor the attire was cause for those children to point and mock and make various indecent noises, slapping their own rear ends. Mrs. P. scolded them, but I could see the half-smile of amusement on her own horsey face.

That last comment was cruel. I do not wish to lower myself to the level of those inadequately washed children. While it is true that Mrs. P. has a somewhat equine visage, she is not unattractive for a woman of thirty-five or so. If she is a horse, she is a handsome horse.

No doubt wishing to compensate, Mrs. P. offered me tea. I condescended, only retreating upstairs first to put away the euphonium and pull on my trousers. She did not set the pot in the parlour but on the kitchen table, along with a plate of biscuits that had to be defended from the urchins' grubby hands. Not wishing to waste her time on the likes of me, Mrs. P. proceeded to put away her shopping while chatting on about the usual trivia: a broken window in the high street, a female mannequin left naked in the window of the charity shop being ogled by schoolboys. Any new plays of interest? she asked me, knowing that my position required the most up-to-date knowledge. I was pleased to tell her of the new and rather lurid Tennessee Williams, *Vieux Carré*, which had transferred from Nottingham to the Piccadilly. The play had failed in New York due to a misguided production, and wasn't it ironic that it took the superiority of English theatre to bring an American play to life.

Mrs. P: And what did you think of the play?

Myself: But I never go to the theatre. I much prefer the cinema.

It was at this moment I made the decision to thrust my sword for the kill and ask her about my taking the top room. But just then came the front door banging open and Mr. P. dragging his overcoat and briefcase into the kitchen.

What a hideous day, he said. Another business almost pulled out. I practically had to get on my knees and beg. In the end I reduced their rent by twenty-five percent, which means no profit at all. Is that tea hot? I'm parched. Ah, I didn't see you, old chap. Still playing the big tuba? How's the Christmas concert shaping up?

I gave Mr. P. one point for his reference to the concert and deducted three for calling my instrument a tuba. He collapsed onto the chair and swallowed half a cup of tea in one go. Mrs. P. looked at him with a mixture of pity and dislike, but when he looked up, she smiled sympathetically, the good housewife.

I extracted myself and went up to my room to listen to the BBC.

When I first arrived in England, it was a struggle to stay alive. To fend off hunger. It is hard to believe, looking at myself in the mirror, how thin I was then. Doing odd jobs that nobody else wanted. Carrying, cleaning, scraping, mucking out. And then the first regular job in the butchering plant, poorly paid, unpleasant work but a steady paycheque. Any free time I had was spent on improving my speech, beating the foreigner out of me. Learning how to be English. One might say I performed my own *Pygmalion*, being both professor and student. Only I never fell in love with myself, that's for certain.

London has become a giant dustbin. Garbage in the streets. One can hardly see the architecture for the Wimpy burger places and the tourist shops full of bobble-headed queens.

This morning I arrived at the kiosk to find a grizzled man urinating on the step. It used to be just the hippies and now it is the homeless, and I don't know which smell worse. When I came to London, the city was still struggling to get out from under the war, but it had pride nevertheless. People knew how to get on with it. Now everyone whines for what he believes is owed to him.

Later in the day a gentleman in a new double-breasted bespoke suit wanted tickets for a musical. I sent him to *Kismet* at the Shaftesbury. Streets of Baghdad. Evil Wazirs. That ought to remind him of his compatriots in the city.

It will be useful, perhaps, to preface the recounting of a certain incident with a description of the house. Muswell Hill has many like it. Bruised red brick. Little touches of ornament, long darkened with soot. A ground-floor vestibule, a parlour vaguely in green and yellow, with furniture bought two decades ago on the instalment plan, a rather stuffy dining room and its adjacent kitchen with a door leading to the small back garden. On the second floor the family's two bedrooms as well as the WC. The separate bath on the other side of the hall. The narrower third floor with just two bedrooms, mine and Miss Smythe's. And between them the narrow stairs to the top room.

I put on my robe, draped my towel over my arm, carried my back scrubber beneath my other arm, and proceeded down one flight to the bath. Opening the door, I had a glorious view of Miss Rosemary Smythe in the nude. Apparently having just exited the shower, she was drying one leg, which was raised so that the heel of her foot rested on the tub's edge. Miss Smythe, an accounting student, is sometimes privately referred to by myself as the Mouse. Her voice is so quiet as to be inaudible. When she is surprised, she squeaks.

It is not hard to imagine how alarmed Miss Smythe was on seeing me glaring at her while brandishing my scrubber as if it were a sword. She squeaked several times, pulling up her towel. I closed the door but slowly, not for a longer view of the Mouse's pale and freckled body but to prolong the embarrassment she deserved for not latching the door.

Miss Smythe! I growled. Her mousey apologies could barely be heard through the door. I did not leave but stood there until she came out, hustling quickly by, squeaking constantly, and not stopping until she was up a flight and behind the safety of her own door.

It strikes me that I must demand the top floor before Miss Smythe gets a chance. Although in truth I do not think she has the squeak for it.

Last night I had a dream. But I despise people who insist on recounting their dreams, as if there could be nothing more fascinating. So you shall not find me putting down mine. I will say only that it was terrible and bloody and there are floorboards beneath which one does not want to look.

Mrs. P. made an unkind remark to me this morning, and I thank her for it.

I was late to get up, having forgotten to wind my alarm clock. Hurrying to prepare myself for the workday, I saw that arriving at the kiosk on time was going to be very close. I rushed down the stairs, taking them two at a time.

Let me admit to having an unusual gait when descending stairs, turning my rather large feet to one side. I suspect this is due to some fear of falling that must have originated in my earliest years. As a boy I was frequently mocked for it, just one more excuse for bringing out the cruelty of children. This morning as I came down, this minor peculiarity, no doubt exaggerated by speed, may have taken on the appearance of something appropriate for a pantomime comic, even Chaplinesque. I did not begrudge Mrs. P.'s little laugh from the bottom of the stairs, where she was taking the urchins' jackets from their hooks. No, it was her words that followed.

So energetic! she said. Why, I've never seen you so ambitious of a morning.

I could feel my eyes bulging with effort as I reached the bottom of the stairs. With little time or breath to do more than garble some words about being late, I tugged on my galoshes and overcoat, and snatched my umbrella from the stand. Mrs. P. opened the door for me.

By the time I got off the underground it was raining. My umbrella went up. As I passed Russell Square I thought of Mrs. P.'s words. Ambitious! Little did she know the ambition that I had. It was my ambition (the word ringing in my ears) to finish the detective novel I have been writing for several years. A book to take its place among the works of Wilkie Collins, Arthur Conan Doyle, and Raymond Chandler. When the young people of this country were flooding Carnaby Street and putting on ridiculous clothes, I was studying the rope, the knife, and the gun. It is true I have not worked on the manuscript for several weeks, focusing my attention on the euphonium. A worthwhile endeavour, certainly, but it will not derail my "ambitious" plans, to use Mrs. P.'s word. Yes, it is her thoughtless remark that will send me again to my desk, though it is no more than a folding table at the end of the bed. Here I will roll another sheet of paper into the old Remington and begin to type again, starting from where I left off. It will not be a long book; the great detective novels rarely are. The point is to bring both honour and innovation to the tradition. And I do so with my own Detective Cyril Helmsworth and his words that will one day be recognizable to all. Well, well, says Detective Helmsworth, here's a bit of interesting stuff.

Ambition, Mrs. P.? Oh, I have ambition enough. Soaring ambition!

Let me recount this late afternoon's conversation. In cold-blooded detail.

I came in from the blustery outdoors, removed my galoshes, and went straight up to my room. Changing into my robe, I descended again to the bathroom to shower, shaved for the second time, and put a drop or two of aftershave on my neck. Upstairs again, I dressed in the newest of my three suits (its two-year anniversary having recently passed). I chose the tie with little green hummingbirds on it that Mrs. P. once complimented. Then I stood in the hall, waiting for the sound of the front door. Soon it was rattling and then the urchins were bursting into the house while Mrs. P. shouted at them to remove their shoes.

I waited for the children to disappear into their room and for the whistle of the kettle. Then I descended to the kitchen.

Mrs. P., if I might have a word.

Oh dear, what have the boys done now. Not another dead mouse in your pocket, I hope.

No, no, they are dear children to be sure.

That is a relief, anyway. Would you like a cuppa?

Thank you kindly, no. I've come to speak with you about the living arrangements.

That sounds even more dire. Should I sit down?

It is nothing like that. It's about the top room. In the house, I mean.

It *is* a nice room, isn't it? What with that view of the trees and back gardens and the charm of the slanted roof. Such very good light. And of course the privacy.

Yes, it is rather nice. That is why I wish to speak to you. As you are no doubt aware, I have been living in this house going on ten years—

Is it really that long? How absolutely frightening.

Yes, well. As I was saying, or about to say, I have recently received a promotion at work with a commensurate raise, if modest, in salary.

Good for you!

Thank you. I feel confident of being able to pay the higher rent required for the top room. I know it is possible that Miss Smythe has already said something to you about the matter, but I wish to point out my considerable seniority, both in number of years in residence and in age, which I believe bestows upon me the privilege of a first offer.

How you speak, sir! I almost feel as if I am reading Trollope. Miss Smythe has said nothing about it. I believe she is satisfied with her room.

Very good then.

Unfortunately, it is already taken.

Taken?

You see, when Tessa gave me her notice I put an advert on several bulletin boards, including one or two at the university. That's what I usually do, it only takes a phone call. And a young man came to see it this morning while you were at work. He is very recently arrived from Canada. Doing his year-abroad sort of thing at the University of London. University College, I believe. Apparently he couldn't find anything remotely affordable near the school or really anywhere in the city. He liked the room very much. He called it picturesque.

Did he?

I suppose if one is from Canada, one is used to looking out upon the tundra. That's meant to be a joke. He gave me first and last months' rent, which if I'm being strictly honest went immediately to pay several outstanding bills. Between you and me, I raised it another five pounds. He has already left a small duffle bag and a portable electric typewriter.

An electric!

I know you yourself prefer the reliable old machines, but I suppose the young must be up-to-date. I do wish you had spoken earlier, I certainly would have saved it for you. He does seem a nice young man, though. I'm sure you'll get along swimmingly.

Yes. Good. Excellent. No doubt we will indeed get along swimmingly, I muttered, backing out of the kitchen. I smiled and apologized for bothering her before climbing the stairs again.

Mrs. P., you fishy-smelling bitch!

On reflection, I feel some shame on having written that last sentence. I thought of simply scrolling back the sheet and xxxing out the words, but then these pages would not be an accurate reflection of my momentary thoughts, for good or ill. Mrs. P. can be ironical, even sharp-tongued at times, but that is a reflection of her intelligence. Given the dull-wittedness of most Britons, I ought to praise rather than criticize her. Nor has she ever wished me harm, even if I am the occasional object of gentle fun. No, the person I ought to be cursing is myself for not having asked her to give me the room weeks earlier. Hesitation ought to be my name. In fact I do not believe I have yet named myself. I thereby dub myself "Mr. Hesitation" and shall henceforth be known as such.

After work, I lugged my instrument case to the Crouch End Playing Field to practise. I was still somewhat upset with myself. Proper embouchure is difficult when one is sulking; I made noise, not music. A boy, walking behind his parents, stuck out his backside and pretended to join me.

In my room again, I brought out the portable ironing board from under the bed and proceeded to press my shirts, trousers, and briefs. I consider ironing to be a most soothing activity. The glide of the iron, the pulse of the steam. Perhaps the young people of today should drop their Buddhist meditation and psychoanalysis and iron their clothes instead. After a while I went down to use the WC, sitting there a few minutes, gazing at the old postcards that Mrs. P. has framed and placed on the opposite wall. Places, she says, that she would like to visit and increasingly wonders whether she ever will. The Charles Bridge in Prague. The Alfama district of Lisbon. The Broadway lights of New York City. I was just departing when I heard someone struggling with a key in the front door. The lock is sensitive; it requires one to pull at the same time that one turns the key. Of course all the regular residents know this, and so I stood there listening until suddenly the door crashed open. Then came the sound of something heavy—luggage—being dragged over the threshold.

The Canadian! Quickly but silently I exited the WC and made my way back upstairs to my room. Lurking just behind the closed door, I listened to a series of thuds, up the first flight of stairs, the second, until it was in front of my own room. I thought I could detect the sound of panting. Then the thudding began again, up the final stairway, scraping along the walls, up to the top room. The door opened, a struggle ensued, and it shut again.

He has arrived.

I told myself to go up, knock, offer a bright smile of welcome. But I didn't know if I could pull off an acting job that demanded the talent of an Olivier. I stayed put. From long experience I know there is always an adjustment period when a new resident arrives. Routines must be established to avoid conflicts over the use of the shower, WC, and kitchen. There needs to be an unspoken understanding, expressed through body language, of when to be social and when to pass silently. Then there is noise, cleaning up after oneself, etc. All is upended. I hardly know whether I have the strength for it anymore. And yet, what choice do I have?

The BestBrit ticket kiosk in Bloomsbury is wedged between a barber shop and a shoe store. It is no wider than twelve feet. The façade of blue wood painted with red trim and faux-leaded windows gives it the air of a hobbit's pub. Inside, it is all business: a scuffed linoleum floor, a rack of pamphlets advertising various entertainments, a board of magnetic letters showing the day's discounted tickets (usually some long-running tripe or recent production eviscerated by the critics). At the far end there is a grill behind which yours truly sits on a stool not intended for someone of mature girth. Behind me are the pigeon holes containing the tickets. Twice a day a courier arrives with new batches which must be sorted, while the expired tickets are bundled up for return to head office. A telephone on the wall is strictly intended for calling the other branches when our own does not have seats for a requested show. While I can state unequivocally that it has never been used by me for a single personal call, I cannot vouch for others. It is rumoured that some employees will hold back tickets to a popular show, waiting for a customer to slip them an extra tenner. If I saw a fellow employee do such a thing, I would denounce him to head office *tout de suite.*

Surely it is nobody's ambition to smile at dithering American, German, Japanese, and Australian tourists who can't decide whether to see *Evita* or *Annie.* But unlike the youth of today, all of whom consider themselves special and "gifted," I knew from the earliest age that to survive was as good as to prosper. Arriving in this country, I spent a year hosing down the floors of a slaughterhouse and tipping the barrels of offal into an incinerator. The smell of that burning will never be purged from my nostrils. After that I operated a newspaper-bundling machine. I delivered for a chemist shop on a bicycle in all weather, I nailed on roofing shingles until my arms ached so that I could hardly lift them, I dug basements feeling as if I were digging my own grave. A job not good enough for me, not satisfying enough, not *creative* enough? Never did I consider such things. So now I smile and talk about what good reviews Alan Howard is getting in *Wild Oats* at the National. Am I polite to customers, do I try to satisfy their needs? Certainly. Do I judge my own worth by the job that puts food in my mouth? What a ridiculous idea.

This evening a knock on the door. I put on my dressing gown. And there he was, the young Canadian in all his glory. He is not quite what I imagined, not some six-foot-tall, broad-shouldered lumberjack with a black beard and a hearty laugh. Instead, he is a mere boy, slightly plump, no more than five foot six. He wore a corduroy jacket, just purchased on Charing Cross Road in the misguided belief that it will make him look like an Oxford man. Glasses, a mop of curly hair, and a name (he introduced himself) like that of a Jewish character in an American situation comedy.

He seemed eager to please, like an anxious cocker spaniel, mentioning that he was "just upstairs" and would be happy to loan me anything I might need. What exactly? Toothpaste? Books of Canadian verse about sled dogs? He assured me that he would be a most quiet resident, intending to spend most of his time writing.

Ah, writing, I said. And may I enquire as to what sort of writing?

Plays, he said. My intention is to become a playwright. That's why I chose London for my year abroad. To see a ton of plays, to soak up the influence. Do you ever go to the theatre?

Well, occasionally.

That's great. That's amazing. That's swell. Because I've just arrived and don't know anyone. It would be great to have a friend for going to the theatre. Maybe talking about it afterwards over a drink—

I do not have much free time, I'm sorry to say. You see, I have a little writing project of my own. Not so noble as the theatre, but still something that amuses me.

And do you think the young Canadian asked me what my project was? Of course he did not. He is far too self-involved to even register what I said. Well, he went on, perhaps sometime. And while he was at the door, did I know how to turn up the heat? He was surprised by the autumn weather here, how damp and chilly it already was. Mr. and Mrs. P. seemed to have retired to their room already.

This is not the suburbs of Philadelphia, I said with a tone of restrained indignation. There is no giant furnace wastefully blasting hot air throughout the entire house. We do not have central heating.

Oh, I didn't realize. I'm sorry to offend—

Look in the front closet. I believe there is a small electric heater that will take the chill out of the air. But do not leave it on all night; electricity is very dear. Tomorrow you can go to the chemist and get yourself a hot-water bottle.

Seriously? Do they still make them?

At this I smiled coldly and closed the door.

***

It has been announced by Buckingham Palace that Prince Andrew will join the Royal Navy. There are some who worship the royal family, as if they were a combination of film star and Greek god, and yet others seethe with hatred at the very thought of them. I myself feel little, except to think that Charles is a tad ridiculous, the Queen Mother something of a sourpuss, and that the dame herself has an unenviable task in keeping them all in line.

The real point is the utility of the royals. They can be marched about on special occasions. They are excellent at cutting ribbons and launching ships. They help us to forget the imbeciles who really run this country. May our dull, inbred royal family reign forever.

On Sunday afternoon I went as usual to the Odeon Cinema on the high street of Muswell Hill. It is a mere twelve-minute walk. I would never go all the way to Piccadilly Circus (perhaps better called Piccadilly Zoo); therefore, what I see depends on what not-quite-new film has been sent to the hinterlands.

There is a simple reason I prefer motion pictures over the theatre. Credibility. Whenever I go to a play, I must believe that the artificial trees are real, that the kitchen actually works, that a few yards of contained mud is a battlefield. I must convince myself that the actors are not bellowing the same lines they said yesterday and the day before and twice on days with a matinee. We are expected to have the make-believe capacities of children at a Punch and Judy show. In a motion picture a mountain is actually a mountain, a horse a horse. If it is a model or some form of special effect, I cannot tell. To me, King Kong is real. The actors do not have to declaim to the cheap seats but mumble, whisper, shed a single tear.

I admit to considering American actors—Jimmy Cagney, Henry Fonda, Spencer Tracy—to be the finest in film. I tip my hat to the upstart country's classic Hollywood stars. I am less enamoured of the pictures of more recent times—*Five Easy Pieces, Taxi Driver*—but even here I recognize the superiority of the American product. Yet I am increasingly worried about the state of American cinema. This week's film was the much-acclaimed *Annie Hall.* It concerns a disagreeable insect of a man who spends his time whining about the privileges of his life. For a love interest there is an overly thin, overly tall woman who dresses like a hobo and speaks like someone who is mentally deficient. Lauren Bacall, Bette Davis, where have you gone?

I look to the cinema to escape from the mundane world, but this time I walked home in a foul mood. As I hung up my overcoat I heard Mrs. P. laughing. There she was in the parlour, serving tea and chocolate biscuits to the young Canadian. Well, I thought, it hasn't taken him long to work his way into her good graces. Will *he* be the house favourite now?

Ah, you are home from the cinema, she said. How was the film?

Execrable. Where is Mr. P. and the little ones, if I might ask?

Flying a new kite on the Heath.

What was the film? asked the young Canadian in his blunt way. I told him. He said, I think Woody Allen is a genius. A great comic hero of our times. He captures what it means to be a modern urban man.

If that is true, I replied, then the modern urban man is doomed.

I went upstairs, feeling much lighter.

London has become a hotbed of international intrigue. A Bulgarian dissident named Georgi Markov was assassinated on Waterloo Bridge. Stabbed with a poison-tipped umbrella. Even here one sees the influence of British style, for surely this is an idea straight out of Ian Fleming. Meanwhile, the German terrorist Astrid Proll has been arrested here. One imagines her as a lurid Bond Woman, wearing a bikini and pointing a machine gun. Despite my repulsion for disorder, I do find it exciting to imagine all these spies and assassins running about this crumbling city.

Incidentally, my digestive problems have returned. They have given me frightful wind. I try to stay out of common spaces.

The detective novel goes swimmingly. I find it remarkably easy to find something suspicious in each character, to give them a burning reason for wishing somebody dead. Nor do I find it difficult to imagine anyone capable of dropping poison into a cup of tea, or running a knife across a neck, or swinging a mallet over and over. It only takes the right series of events—disappointments, humiliations, little hatreds—to build until one transcends the person one believes himself to be and becomes something else entirely. What fun!

Taking my hands from the keys of the Remington, I felt creatively satisfied and materially peckish. Expecting to find the kitchen deserted at this hour of the evening, I made my way downstairs with the object of securing a tin of sardines and a box of crackers from my designated larder. With my story still running pleasantly in my mind, I did not hear the voices before stepping into the kitchen to find Mrs. P. and the young Canadian at the table. All of us were startled and Mrs. P. even looked embarrassed, the result of which was her greeting me with exaggerated pleasure. The young Canadian, she said, was just telling her about a play called *Bent* that he had seen at the Royal Court. He was describing the opening scene of two homosexuals in robes chatting lightly about amusing trifles. It seemed to take place in the present day, at least until the arrival at the door of two Nazi SS officers. Brilliantly disorienting, said the young man.

And tell us, Mrs. P. addressed myself, what have you heard about the play in your professional capacity?

I'm sorry, said I coolly, but BestBrit never carries tickets for the Royal Court Theatre. It is all too well known for staging left-wing propaganda. (Well, if *I* had my way, we certainly wouldn't carry them.) I then excused myself. It was only when I was back in my room again that I realized I had not retrieved my snack.

I was on my way to the shower, wearing only a robe and slippers and bathing cap, when Mrs. P. approached me in the hall. I do not enjoy being accosted in this vulnerable condition, but Mrs. P. did not notice at all, getting quite close and speaking in a softer than usual voice.

Dear sir, she crooned, you are so prominently employed in the theatre business.

I do not, said I, exaggerate my position.

Yet it gives you such an advantage! You see, there's a play that is a great success at the Savoy just now.

Don't you think I know it, madam? *Whose Life Is It Anyway?* has made quite the star out of Mr. Tom Conti in the lead role. Every hour of the day customers harangue me for tickets.

Yes, of course you know all about it from the inside. Well, our young Canadian friend mentioned to me how eager he is to see it. As you know, he dreams of being a playwright himself.

So I have been informed on numerous occasions.

It's just that this is his first time living away from home. And I thought, how nice if I—or rather, if you—might procure for him a ticket. Just think what a kind gesture that would be.

I see very clearly. You are not the first, nor will you be the last, to approach me for coveted tickets. I cannot be bribed, Mrs. P. I am not corruptible.

I do not doubt that for a moment. But I recall your once saying that a few tickets for a popular show may arrive with the day's delivery.

Yes, that is true. Held back by the theatre until the day of performance. Ours is the flagship kiosk, the head of the fleet, you might say. But not many, four or six or eight at most. They are gone within the hour.

What a position of responsibility you have! But say you were to get tickets tomorrow morning for the evening performance? It is my understanding that our young friend would be free to come by.

I looked hard at her. Being several inches taller and six stone heavier gives me something of an advantage. I raised my gaze upward, as if consulting heaven itself. Mrs. P. held her breath.

I am wondering, said I, whether you are planning to bake one of your famous chocolate streusel cakes any time soon?

Why, I was planning to make one tomorrow. In fact, I was thinking of making an extra one if you'd care to have it.

I cleared my throat. A monetary bribe was out of the question. But a cake is a different matter. I said, There might be a ticket for the young man.

Wonderful! And here Mrs. P. tenderly grasped my arm. There is just one thing, she said. I believe that he is hoping to take a friend. If it would be possible to hold *two* tickets—

A friendship established already! What a likeable fellow he must be. Please ask him to pick them up at the kiosk before 4 p.m.

You are a godsend.

For a moment I thought she was going to stretch upward and kiss me. But she merely squeezed my arm and hurried down the stairs with the energy of a girl.

As I have already made clear in these pages, I am no devotee of theatrical artifice. And here is a play where the main character is onstage every second, in a hospital bed. Yet I thought, why not go and see a hit play? After all, I read the reviews in order to better serve my customers. Why not judge for myself? And if I happen to spy the young Canadian and his newfound friend? And see who that friend happens to be?

And so I kept the last available ticket for myself. Only when I made my way to the seat did I realize it was in the last row. Not such a bad perch, however, to see others below me. Before the lights went down, I used a pair of opera glasses (left at the kiosk and never claimed) to scan the audience. But I could not see the young man. I cursed myself for not having taken note of his seat numbers. And then, just as the lights were dimming, I spotted his curly hair and corduroy jacket in the third row of the orchestra. And who was with him? A woman certainly. With a kerchief over her hair. Several inches taller than him. But she did not turn and so I could not catch her profile. The theatre became dark.

How impatient I was during the confounded play. This Conti fellow, supposedly paralyzed from the neck down, speechified endlessly. At other times, as the secondary characters discussed his case, he seemed to genuinely fall asleep. The audience lapped it up like cream while I waited impatiently for intermission. As soon as the lights went up, I put the glasses to my eyes and searched along the third row, but the seats were already empty. I would have to go down and find them.

The aisles quickly filled with people desperate for a drink. I could not imagine paying good money on a regular basis to be subjected to such pushing and pulling. Sometimes my bulk can be handy for pushing through crowds, but the stairs were too narrow for such bullying and I could only shuffle after the person in front of me. At last I reached the lobby; the young Canadian and his friend were nowhere to be seen. Some people had stepped out onto the Strand to smoke or get a breath of air and I followed. But no. The bell began sounding. I made my agonizing way back up to the seat. Using my glasses again, I caught sight of them down below once more. He had his face turned toward her and was speaking with great earnestness. But the woman did not move.

The lights went down as act two began. Tom Conti grew weaker yet growled in his bed, demanding the right to die. I wanted to shout: Let him! Let him have it! And when, in the end, he became still, his last breath spent, the audience wept buckets. There was a long moment of sobbing and then furious applause. The people in the row before me rose as one to give the actor a standing ovation.

I tried to make a rush for the stairs but could not remove myself from the row without climbing over the back of the seat, an impossible athletic feat. The audience demanded to see Tom Conti and called him back, standing now and looking exhausted. The house lights came up at last and people started to move.

There's no point in recounting the rest. By the time I got down, the young Canadian and his female companion were long gone. A total waste of an evening.

Last night I came down to prepare my dinner. As the family always eats at about half past six, I wait until eight to have the kitchen to myself. Often I can hear the telly in the living room, the bursts of recorded laughter demanding the viewer join in Pavlovian response.

But as I approached the kitchen, I smelled something quite exquisite. It drew me like an enchanter's spell. Standing by the stove was the young Canadian, frying up three small and perfect lamb chops. Lamb is far too dear and I never buy it, nor does the family. He turned and smiled at me, seemingly oblivious of his privilege. Perhaps in Canada one has lamb every weeknight and caviar on the weekends.

The young man began to talk about the "old-fashioned" butcher shop where he chose his chops and watched them get wrapped in paper and tied with string. Apparently, he has only seen pre-packaged meat in gigantic suburban supermarkets.

I had been planning to make myself a plate of eggs and chips. Instead, I quickly grabbed a few slices of ham from the refrigerator, a couple of pieces of bread, some leaves of iceberg lettuce, and a few remaining stewed prunes. I retreated to my room like the British evacuation of Dunkirk, although there was no way I could convince myself that a retreat was really a victory.

I could not stop thinking of those chops. Not just how they must have tasted (although I did indeed think of that), but what they signified. And so I decided to orchestrate a meeting with the young Canadian, he coming up the stairs as I was going down.

I was just going down to make a cup of tea, I said pleasantly.

I bought an electric kettle for my room. Why don't you come up. I've even got some chocolate.

It's possible that my face gave me away. His *own* kettle? Never had it occurred to me to strike out for such independence. I recovered and accepted with a smile. Did my young friend need a few minutes to put his *chambre* in order? Not at all, I should come right in. And so I followed him up the stairs, his blue-jeaned buttocks wagging before me.

I prepared myself for the sort of student dorm room seen in American movies: heaps of clothing, marijuana cigarettes and beer bottles on the desk, a left-behind brassiere hanging from the bedstead. And was surprised to see a room kept neat as a pin. The bed was well made, pens and paper neatly placed on the wooden table beside the electric Smith Corona typewriter, books stood in the bookcase. His student papers were organized on a small wooden stand with one shelf reserved for his toiletrics, all set in a row.

I have to say that the impression of the room itself, which I had desired for so long, was almost overwhelming. There was, despite the neatness, a slight bohemian feel to it, with the beads hanging around the wall mirror, the incense holder on the windowsill, and the whiff of patchouli in the air. I noticed that the pages beside the typewriter were for a play, with speakers' names and dialogue and handwritten corrections between the typewritten lines. I was overcome with the unpleasant feeling that the room did not rightfully belong to me as I had always believed, and that it had found its true inhabitant in this young, artistic soul. He turned his desk chair around and offered it to me.

From there I watched him make an absolute hash of the tea. He put in the underboiled water first, then a single teabag which he stirred about with the end of a pencil. Immediately he poured two mugs. He was unguarded to an almost shocking degree and assumed it only natural that a recent acquaintance would be fascinated by the details of his life. I heard that he is the third son—the "baby"—of the family, treated as a precious treasure. That the worst part of his childhood was the chest cold he suffered every winter—formative, however, for allowing him to stay home and make up stories with cut-out paper figures. His father was a successful manufacturer of dentures and his home had a swimming pool and tennis court. As a teenager, he brought in some bricks and boards to make shelves for his Penguin paperbacks and pretend he was living in a garret. He showed me a photograph of a plump girl in a bathing suit—the high school sweetheart who broke his delicate heart.

I thought it might take some coaxing to get the name of the play he was working on. But of course it took none at all. My play, he said, is called *Chekhov and Mandelbaum*. I tried to take on an expression of wonder and delight, to signify the vast possibilities suggested by such a title. He told me that next week was the season-opening party of the University College Drama Society. Perhaps they would be interested in putting it on. Did I think it might be possible?

How could they not be? I assured him, when in truth I was certain that nothing of interest could come of a mere boy who'd had such a coddled upbringing.

The young Canadian looked at me as if I were his best friend. He put his hand on his heart. And then he said, Mrs. P. thinks it's really good.

There is nothing I dislike more than a weeknight rehearsal of the Muswell Hill Brass Orchestra. I am required to take my euphonium in its equally heavy case to work. Imagine lugging such a thing to the Underground, down the steps of the Northern Line, getting onto the train, finding a place to put it down, trying not to miss the Warren Street stop, fighting one's way back up to the surface. In the kiosk itself there is just enough room to shove it beside the stool if I move over, making it difficult to reach for tickets in the farthest pigeon holes.

The conductor of our orchestra, Maestro Stilwell, was seduced away from the Notting Hill Serenaders three years ago, requiring each of us to pay an additional sixty quid toward his honorarium. Maestro Stilwell (he prefers to be called "Greg" but I refuse) doesn't much look the part, being rather short and egg-shaped. His hair, or what's left of it, is long, however. And he does act the part, for he is quite the demanding tyrant and sometimes yells or throws his baton as if it were a poison dart. Part of being a conductor is assessing the talent. Until now I have always been relegated to second chair, with Judy Tunnelworth taking first. But this season he has called for a re-evaluation of all players and has not yet assigned the euphonium solo in "Carnival of Venice," to be played at the Christmas concert. Of course Judy has the advantage and, as a result, her attitude toward me is one of condescending cheerfulness. How frequently she finds a reason to mention her music degree from Cardiff! What I want to say to her is, Did your degree help you to become a travel agent? But despite her advantages (she plays a top-of-the-line Getzen), I believe the maestro has been noticing my improvement. At the last rehearsal he even complimented my glissando, which caused her beady eyes to narrow. He has announced that the solo parts will not be officially assigned until very close to the performance date, sparking what he hopes will be a "good-natured and fruitful rivalry." Good-natured—ha! But fruitful, yes, judging by my increased practice time and improved wind.

Talent cannot be purchased, Judy Tunnelworth. Watch your neck, I say. For I am breathing down it!

Today three letters arrived by post for the young Canadian. I have become adept at identifying the senders by their return addresses, the young man himself having mentioned his correspondents to me. One is from his mother (an elegant hand from a time when civilization still understood the value of penmanship), one from his older brother in Vancouver, and one from a friend who cannot resist drawing immature cartoons on the back of the envelope. The house rule is that whoever finds the letters beneath the door slot puts them on the vestibule table by the coat rack. Today I heard the letters fall and so I picked them up, put the bills for the family on the table, and decided to leave the young man's missives on the doorstep of the top room. It never hurts to ingratiate oneself—a lesson I learned long ago.

I trudged up the stairs, prepared to lay the letters down by the door, when to my surprise I spied an object already there. It was a stuffed animal of the teddy variety but small enough to sit in one's palm. A note was tucked under its arm. Ought I to read the note? Yes, no—I went back and forth.

Reader, I read it. Here is what it said:

It is sad that you have no one to talk to at night. So I am here to keep you company. And you can tell me anything. I'm very discreet!

The note was unsigned. Interesting, I thought, very interesting. Well, I can be as discreet as teddy. I brought the letters back downstairs and left them on the vestibule table.

The detective novel moves on apace. I have beefed up the part of the alluring Miss Amelia Rattlesbone, who may be as deadly as she is beautiful. The secret of a good novel is understanding and even empathizing with one's villain. For nobody considers himself evil, but quite the opposite. We are all heroes of our own story.

First there was a bread strike which caused people to hoard loaves. Now there is a BBC strike and the lorry drivers may be next. England is turning into France. Soon we will be forced to wear berets and discuss Jean-Paul Sartre. God spare us.

Today on my way home I did my shopping at Sainsbury's. There were only two loaves left and I took one. Also a package of spaghetti, a cabbage, some pudding cups, sausages. I carried the paper bag in my arms and on reaching the house fumbled for my keys at the front door. Over the bag of groceries I looked through the front window and saw—

Our young Canadian friend. Sitting back on the sofa with a strange, intense look on his face. Hitching myself up onto the doorstep I saw Mrs. P., kneeling before him. What exactly she was doing I could not tell. But I could easily imagine. And I was shocked, even indignant. I have sat on that very sofa!

And then I thought of Mr. P. The cuckold. Yes, he is a poor provider. Yes, he has a problem with alcohol. But does he deserve this? Unless Mrs. P. was doing something else—removing a splinter, say. Whatever was going on, I decided it best for my own sake not to interrupt. I stashed my bag on the porch and went twice round the block, rather agitated in the blood. When I returned they were gone. I went inside and put away my groceries.

On the way back to the staircase I paused to look into the parlour, at the spot where the young Canadian had been sitting. I gingerly approached the sofa, put my hand out, leaned over, thought better of it, and took myself upstairs.

Today on the Broadway I saw Mr. P. with the urchins. Frankly, I have never paid the boys much attention. Children are an annoyance as they pass through the various stages of development and never remind me of my own childhood, which can be hardly given that name.

They were sitting on a bench outside Barclays Bank, sloppily consuming ice cream cones. The older one was mocking the younger for "licking like a baby" and proceeded to demonstrate by stealing licks all around his brother's cone. How tempted I was to slap the older boy on the back of his head.

Mr. P. was leaning on a lamp-post, smoking a cigarette. He

is not supposed to smoke and has promised Mrs. P. that he will stop, especially around the children. I sometimes wonder whether he smokes because she doesn't wish him to. In any case, his little act of defiance makes Mr. P. appear more manly, for he is a droop-shouldered, unprepossessing fellow. Catching sight of me, he gave out a mild greeting.

Bit chilly for ice cream, he smiled, but the boys insisted.

And how are you, Mr. P.?

You know, hanging on by the fingernails. He gave a dry little laugh.

During my time in the house, Mr. P. has embarked on three different financial enterprises. In the first he maintained several dozen condom-dispensing machines in bars and clubs. In the second he imported perfumes with names like Camel No. 5. In this latest he has borrowed from Mrs. P.'s aged parents to lease the entire floor of an office building in Stoke Newington. The floor has been divided into separate offices (Mr. P. doing much of the work himself), which are then rented by the month to even smaller hopeful entrepreneurs who can make use of the secretary and central phone service and boardroom. Mr. P. proceeded to tell me that only four of the twelve offices were currently rented, not enough to even cover his costs. I know that he keeps one for himself, going there directly from the pub when he's had too many even for the sofa.

Finally the younger boy (is he a bit slow?) caught on to the ice cream trick. He tried to push his brother away, but the older boy pushed back and the younger one dropped his cone onto the sidewalk. He started to cry.

For heaven's sake, said Mr. P., stubbing out his cigarette. That's a bloody waste, isn't it?

Last night Judy Tunnelworth held her annual Halloween party for members of the band. While I do not generally enjoy parties, I've always believed that it is necessary to show oneself as a good fellow. Besides, such a gathering would give me a chance to ingratiate myself with those who might influence the maestro's decision on first euphonium. Harold Liss, for example, the band's best cornet player, who happens to be the maestro's second cousin. The maestro himself never comes to parties, perhaps in the belief that a conductor is like a military general who needs to stand apart from his troops. Quite right in my opinion.

For a costume this year I decided on John Wayne playing Rooster Cogburn in *True Grit*. This necessitated my finding a blue-jean shirt, leather vest, pink bandana, and of course an eye patch and cowboy hat. My size is not so very far off the Duke's at that stage of his life, making me a fair likeness. Admittedly it was a touch embarrassing to walk down the stairs and have Mrs. P. make a little whoop when she saw me. Or to ride the Underground, although there were plenty of ghouls and busty nurses and even a Charlie Chaplin I rather admired until I realized he was being represented by a female.

Judy Tunnelworth lives in a flat in Chelsea. I arrived a good ten minutes past the hour, five minutes later than last year, but still turned out to be the first. She let me in and went back to putting on her witch makeup. (Well chosen, Judy!) I sat on the sofa and ate a canapé while looking around at the "adorable" decor—pillows with musical phrases stitched on them, curtains with clefs and flats, a framed print of Andy Warhol's garish Beethoven. Finally the others arrived in a rush and made for the bar like camels racing to an oasis. Someone put on a record—some primitive jazz—and then the shoes went off and the dancing began. Harold Liss, dressed in a skeleton outfit, was impossible to approach due to his frantic and dangerous gyrations. It did not please me to see him occasionally running his hands over a hypnotically moving Judy Tunnelworth. Any attempt would have been useless in this scene of rank hedonism. Pretending to hold a six-shooter in each hand, I made my way out of the flat.

* * *

After supper a knock on the door. Mrs. P. in a rather giddy state. Would I care to come downstairs to the parlour? The young Canadian had finished his play and they were going to do a reading of it. Would I please be so kind as to participate?

They seem to have mistaken me for some degenerate member of the Bloomsbury Group. Nevertheless, I agreed, if only to hear Mrs. P. call me a jolly good sport. I followed her down the stairs to find both our young friend and Miss Smythe. The children were in bed, and Mr. P., not caring to take a part, had gone to the pub. We sat about while the young Canadian handed out copies. Before he had a chance to assign parts, Mrs. P. casually mentioned that she would play the love interest, even though Miss Smythe would have been a more appropriate choice for playing a college girl. Instead, she got the mother. The author naturally took on the role of Mandelbaum, the young would-be writer. I was given the Russian author himself, Anton Chekhov.

I hope to do the great man justice, said I, trying out my Russian accent. The others applauded.

To give a feeling of the play, I shall quote the first line: I'm either going to kill myself or move to Winnipeg. Apparently the word *Winnipeg* is always funny. Now I shall give the briefest of summaries. A young man is having difficulties with his girlfriend, whom he suspects is sleeping with someone else, another student who has already won the "Jackman Prize." His mother, meanwhile, is pressuring him to drop the idea of becoming a writer and go to medical school. While Mandelbaum is pacing about his room in emotional agony, he cries out, What would Chekhov do? There is a crashing sound in the closet and a moment later the long-dead author himself pulls himself into the room, several objects from the closet falling after him. Much of the rest of the play is a conversation between the two of them in which Chekhov offers advice to the lovelorn. There are also several encounters with the mother and the college girl and one climactic scene when the college girl comes over and the two go to bed (watched over by the salaciously interested Mr. Chekhov), only to be pounced on by the mother. It ends with the young man and the Russian sitting on the edge of his bed, shaking their heads at the absurdity of life that we poor humans cannot get enough of.

I certainly know enough to recognize a mash-up of Neil Simon, Samuel Beckett, Chekhov, and *Play It Again, Sam.* Yet I must admit to having enjoyed myself, and when it was all over we stood and applauded enthusiastically while our young Canadian friend got up and, blushing, took a bow. I did not mind showering him with such approval, given the unlikelihood of his script going beyond this room. And then I noticed something quite oddly touching. Mrs. P. with bright tears in her eyes.

Today is the thirtieth anniversary of my wedding to Agnes.

She was from St. Ives. Small and skinny but with large eyes. She worked in a shop and would make my sandwich at lunch break. So what do you do in the evenings? she asked. Who doesn't like going to the pictures? she said. Somehow we had a plan to see *Red River.* And then, sitting in the dark, her hand was in mine.

Almost before I knew it, we were involved. I was excited and terrified. I'd had a plan to pull myself up by the bootstraps, and a woman wasn't in it. But Agnes had a plan of her own and I cannot blame her for it. She was trying to escape her father, a brutal man. Suddenly we had a ring, a wedding, and a three-day honeymoon in Torquay. The bus trip there made Agnes nauseous so she went into a station to get herself a Lucozade drink to settle her stomach. Exhausted, I closed my eyes and fell asleep, only to open them again to the countryside rolling past and an empty seat beside me. She'd never returned to the bus. I went to Torquay on my own. Three months later I received a letter with no return address, an apology but also a warning not to look for her. She enclosed the ring, which I thought was good of her. I've no resentment; she was like an inoculation, making me immune to the powers of other women.

Speaking of stomach upsets, in the middle of the afternoon today I had to come home from work. No doubt it was the Italian meatball sandwich I had for lunch. I know very well that exotic foods roil my innards something terrible and yet I had a momentary desire for a little culinary adventure. It is always a mistake to step out of my routine. One cannot deal with the public in a small kiosk while suffering from such a problem. I did rather pity Mr. Ratchmule, who had to replace me. There was quite a look on his face as he came in.

At home I doused myself with bicarbonate of soda and went to my room to lie down. And then above me through the ceiling came a steady thumping. Which grew faster. *Thump thump thump thump*. I knew very well what it was: the beast with two backs! I lay there trying not to move as the sound grew louder and more frantic. And then it stopped. I continued to lie there and foolishly drifted off to sleep, for if I had stayed awake I could have seen who came down the steps from the top room. I cannot be sure it was Mrs. P. rather than some pasty undergraduate picked up at uni by the young Canadian. I lay there feeling my disappointment, the silence broken only by the sad sound of my innards, much like the deflating of a balloon.

And who do you think happened to be passing by the kiosk? None other than Judy Tunnelworth, pretending she had forgotten where I worked. She was dressed in a cloth coat with a fox collar, no doubt having brought it out of the mothballs as soon as the temperature dropped. How good to see you! she chirped. What a fascinating neighbourhood you work in. She looked about with feigned interest, as if visiting a mausoleum. And don't you think the band is coming along well? I believe the maestro has really hit his stride. And you know, I really think it's a toss-up for the "Carnival" solo, either one of us could play it.

I'd never heard her ramble on so idiotically. I just listened suspiciously, although when a customer came in to pick up a telephone order, I switched involuntarily into the subservient clerk, displeased that Judy was a witness. After the man left she said, Oh, what a nice poster for *The Music Man*. That's a show I'd rather like to see. I hear it's quite the sold-out smash. I don't suppose you have some tickets set aside?

And there it was. The reason for her passing by. Did I withhold the ticket? No, I did not. For one, I wanted to show her that indeed I had the power to pull a rabbit out of a hat. And for another, I made sure to give her a seat with an obstructed view, tucked at the back of the orchestra just behind a balcony pillar. How immensely satisfying was the thought of her checking the fox-collar coat, buying a special program, showing her ticket to the usher, and halting as she saw her seat.

But she was not the only visitor to appear. A while later I sold four tickets to *Deathtrap*, a play I have not seen but that, I admit, intrigues me as it is a mystery as well as a machine for making money. I turned to put some newly arrived tickets into the pigeon holes when somebody cleared his throat. And as I turned, smiling, who did I see but our young Canadian friend. He had the beginning of a beard, a patchy thing like the coat of a malnourished rat. And did he want something from me? No, he did not. He was merely in the neighbourhood, having gone to his philosophy class at University College with a Professor Wollheim. Had I heard of him? he asked. Of course I had not, why would I? Yet I felt almost touched by his coming by simply to be friendly. He began to speak of the National Theatre, which he had attended three times in the last two weeks. A brutal complex on the other side of the Thames, yet so lively and interesting. Three theatres of different styles and sizes! Bookshops and restaurants and bars! Cheap student tickets! He had seen Congreve's *The Double Dealer* and Chekhov's *The Cherry Orchard*. He praised to the skies Dorothy

Tutin's performance as Lady Plyant in the former and Madame Ranyevskaya in the latter. There was nothing, he said, like English acting, and I could not help but feel a little nationalistic pride for my adopted country.

So seduced was I by his genial enthusiasm, his apparent pleasure at seeing me, that it was some time before doubt began to creep in. Perhaps he believed that I heard his bed shaking overhead. Was he covering up, ingratiating himself so that I wouldn't tell Mr. P.?

If I had heard it, I would not tell. But when the realization came to me, I cut him off. Terribly sorry, I said, but I have a lot of work to do. And as if on cue, the door opened and a Japanese woman came in holding a lapdog. The young Canadian looked more saddened than anything else, but he mumbled a goodbye and left. I tried to feel clever for having seen through him, but still a melancholy mood settled over me that I could not shake for the rest of the day.

Today Mrs. P. was sporting her very first pair of blue jeans. Very youthful she looked, despite her slightly broad behind. It isn't hard to guess why she bought them. The urchins teased her and she swatted them away, blushing. Mr. P. returned from work, or rather from a detour to the pub. She turned to face him, eyebrows raised as if asking what he thought of her new look.

He said: That shoe importer decided not to take the office after all. Only then did he look at his wife. What's for dinner? he asked.

Of course there are some who do not consider the detective novel to be high literature. That bothers me not at all. There is a reason that many of the greatest movies are based on crime novels—*The Maltese Falcon, The Big Sleep, Strangers on a Train.* Indeed, these and many other films have been a great influence on me and I am convinced that my own story would translate splendidly to celluloid. Let others struggle with the absurdities of James Joyce or Virginia Woolf. Give me the question of motive, the mystery of evil, the desire to unravel the world and to make it whole again.

I must report on drama of the real-life variety.

As I trudged home from the tube, it began to rain, a very cold rain, and I was thoroughly chilled by the time I got home. I wanted to head straight into the shower, but as soon as the door of the house opened, I could tell that a great upheaval was going on. Mrs. P. came hurrying down the stairs with hair dishevelled, tucking her blouse back into her skirt. Apparently Mr. P. had come home unexpectedly, only to find Mrs. P. up in the top room. When I came in, they were on the landing of the stairs. Mr. P. was shouting—a frightening voice which was very unlike him. They moved into the bedroom, closing the door, but their voices were more than audible. He demanded to know whether she was "involved" with the young Canadian. She denied it. She called it a "stupid notion." She said he must have better things to worry about, such as not going bankrupt. Yes, the young man and she were very friendly. She might even say they had become friends. Was she not allowed to have a friend? Someone who actually read books and went to the theatre and had dreams of accomplishing something? Of course she could have friends, he said. And didn't he hope to accomplish something, to make a go of his own business? And what about the two of them? They hadn't been intimate in months. The thought of sleeping with a man who was drunk every night, she said, did not appeal to her. There was a crash, and for a moment I thought he had struck her, or she him. Later I found out that one of them had backed into the table lamp, one of a matched pair given by her parents, and it had shattered.

Even I, who dislikes children, was glad the urchins were not in the house. I retreated into my own room and turned on the radio. The next time I saw them all was two hours later, the family calmly having dinner (breaded sole and Brussels sprouts) at the table.

This morning I was surprised by a knock on the door. It was Miss Smythe. She asked if she might step in. I did not like others in my room but felt I had to allow it. Behind my closed door she confided her plan to leave the premises this very weekend. I do not like drama, she said whispering loudly. This was always a decent home. But the things going on now—well, it's just too much.

You must look after yourself, I said, nodding with sympathy. I think it is a wise decision.

Will you leave, too?

Ah, but I have a thicker skin. I will try to weather the storm. Perhaps I can even be of some use.

Suit yourself, she said, a little disapprovingly, and slipped out of the room.

And so good riddance to Miss Smythe.

I do not know the outcome of that argument in the bedroom, only that a semblance of peace has returned to the house. When Mr. P. and the young Canadian pass, they greet one another solemnly. But now I realize the truth, that both the middle-aged and the younger man are cowards. They are afraid of confrontation. The only brave person in this domestic catastrophe is Mrs. P. She takes care of the children, stands up to her husband but is not without sympathy for him, keeps the young Canadian from fleeing the premises. Meanwhile, life lurches onward. I go to the kiosk, I come back to find the young man and Mrs. P. intensely conversing in the kitchen, breaking off when they see me. The children return home, are nagged into doing their homework, are fed and bathed. I clatter the keys on the Remington, heady with the thought of soon reaching the end of my novel. I practise the euphonium. There is still no decision on who will play the solo on "Carnival of Venice," and if looks could kill, Judy Tunnelworth and I would both be pushing up daisies.

* * *

Our young Canadian friend has found a director for *Chekhov and Mandelbaum*. He is another visiting student, a young American from Chicago. A homosexual. And the play will be performed in the university's experimental "black box" theatre, which is nothing more than a converted squash court.

The young Canadian has been encouraged in this endeavour by Mrs. P., who is perhaps as thrilled as the playwright himself. I cannot imagine having someone in my corner in this way, but his success—minor though it undoubtedly is—has spurred me on to write the very last page of my novel. Yes, it is done. Now I need only make copies and send them to the publishers on the wings of her majesty's postal service.

Miss Smythe has unceremoniously departed and there is no sign that Mrs. P. is trying to rent out the empty room, even though a stack of unpaid bills is piled on the vestibule table. Mrs. P. continues her part-time job as a secretary in a dentist's office while Mr. P.'s enterprise struggles on. Strangely, they have stopped fighting over money. Nor does she complain when, after the children are upstairs, he goes off to the pub. This week she spent the evenings in the living room watching a BBC adaptation of *Crime and Punishment* with our young Canadian friend. Of course she asked me to join them, but I did not think the invitation was genuine and I declined. I do, however, wonder how my young friend feels, watching the poor Raskolnikov suffer over his guilty conscience.

It is not often that I go to the pub. And when I do, it is in the late afternoon, when the place is quiet and I can drink my beer in peace. But I worked only a half day on Wednesday and decided it had been too long since I had indulged in this most English of habits. I was reaching the bottom of my glass when who should come in but our young Canadian friend. I saw him enter hesitantly through the door, squinting in the half-light and then twitching his nose in reaction to the pipe smoke. There is nothing special about our local, but to someone from Canada, where they drink in saloons and spit on the floor, it must look like the best of jolly old England. Seeing me at the bar, he broke into a smile of relief. What a coincidence, he said, which immediately made me suspicious. The bartender came up and, as the Canadian had no idea what to order, the man poured him a Bass. The young Canadian put it to his lips, leaving a touch of foam upon them, and pronounced it "magnificent." The bartender nodded and went to the other end so he could watch the darts.

I quickly realized that our young friend is not much of a drinker, for it didn't take long before the ale began to loosen his tongue. Did he make a grand confession? No, he did not. But he asked me, did I ever feel like I was slowly drowning but couldn't get myself to swim to shore? Or that I was a bird too afraid to leave its cage? Then he laughed and said it seemed a very long time ago that he was back in Canada, hoping to have the most memorable time of his life.

After that he merely gazed into his glass as gloomily as a pub regular. And I realized that he was no happier than anyone else in this little soap opera of ours.

On my folding table I have placed a series of stick-on labels from the stationers'. On each one is typed the name and address of a publisher—Penguin Books, Faber & Faber, Macmillan, Macdonald & Co., Allen & Unwin, Hodder & Stoughton, etc. On the bedspread are laid out seventeen photomechanical copies of *Murder Most Morbid*. On each manuscript is an individually typed "cover letter," as they say in the business, describing my book in the most praising terms. Next to the bed is a tower of cardboard mailing boxes and a roll of packing tape. This evening my task is to put the manuscripts into the boxes, package them up, and stick on the labels. And tomorrow I will borrow the urchins' wagon and make the trip to the post office. And then—destiny!

Returning home from the wagon, having had an arduous journey with the mailing boxes toppling over several times, I was surprised to find the entire P. family playing the game of Monopoly. And was even more astonished to see them joined by the young Canadian. All apparently having a fine time, except for the youngest boy, who was sulking about having to pay some tax or other.

Mrs. P. looked up and asked if I'd care to join in, a ridiculous suggestion, as one must play from the start. So I merely watched awhile and waited for a suitable lull to announce the annual Muswell Hill Brass Orchestra Christmas Concert, to be performed in the auditorium of Creighton Comprehensive School. I sincerely hoped the family would be able to attend as in previous years, and added that our young Canadian friend was most especially welcome to partake of this annual tradition.

Shoot, he said, I'd love to but I'm going with D. to Italy for the holidays. We'll be gone by then.

D. is his American homosexual friend. I was frankly disappointed but I kept smiling, at least until Mrs. P. spoke up.

Oh, what a shame. I haven't had a chance to mention it but I must stay with Mummy and Daddy in Portsmouth. Mummy's got to be in hospital a few days and you know how helpless Daddy is on his own. But you boys can have some lovely time alone with your father. He can take you to the concert.

Mr. P. stared at her. He looked quite dumbfounded. At last he spoke.

Shouldn't we all go with you?

You know there isn't room in their pokey house. And then my mother will be recovering and the boys would be too rambunctious.

What about Christmas morning? asked the younger urchin.

I will be back on the twenty-fourth, just in time for Christmas dinner *and* Christmas morning. You see? It has all worked out.

And you, she said, looking at me, shall have a wonderfully attentive audience, won't he, boys?

At that the older boy put his lips to his bare arm and blew, making a rude noise. And they all fell about laughing.

I shall tear the metaphorical bandage off quickly, to get the pain over with. Judy Tunnelworth has been chosen as soloist. At yesterday's rehearsal, the maestro had the entire band play the work twice, with each of us taking the part in turn. And while I would admit that Judy was technically superior, there was little doubt in my mind as to who played with more feeling. All I could do was smile like an imbecile and, when the rehearsal was over, congratulate her. How smug she was, saying that her old professors at Cardiff would be so proud of her. But I shall play my lesser part, knowing that glory will not be showered upon me this time.

And so I trudged home, carrying the heavy euphonium case, as snow began to fall. Approaching the house, I saw the young Canadian standing in the street, arms outstretched, head tilted back, and a look of joyful abandon on his face. He told me he had spent two hours walking in Highgate Wood.

All very picturesque, I'm sure. I knocked my galoshes together, muttering about the bloody weather, and went inside.

The young Canadian is excited to be leaving for Italy. He invited me to his room, where I saw his ridiculously large knapsack packed and waiting by the door. He spread out a map to show me the route he was planning to take. They would land in Rome, spend a night in Bologna, head to Milan, and fly back from Venice. The art they would see! The ruins! The wine they would drink!

Meanwhile, Mr. P. sulks about Mrs. P. going to see her parents. He doesn't usually drink at home, but I saw him take a flask from his jacket pocket and bring it quickly to his lips. Later I was in the toilet, trousers at my ankles, when I heard them outside the door. Mr. P. suggested that perhaps they could all go somewhere in the spring.

But you hate to travel, Mrs. P. said brightly.

From the *Finchley Examiner*:

This weekend the Muswell Hill Brass Orchestra performed its annual concert in the auditorium of Creighton Comprehensive School, a cavernous space smelling faintly of egg salad. The audience of forty hearty souls kept on their coats and hats as the thermostat had been turned down for the holidays. Nevertheless, the orchestra members looked splendid in formal black, instruments gleaming under the fluorescent lights. Conductor Gregory Stilwell led them in an unsurprising program including Liszt's Hungarian Rhapsody Number 2, *the second movement of Shostakovich's Tenth Symphony, and the well-worn chestnut* Carnival of Venice. *If anything roused the audience from their hibernatory stupor, it was the encore, a medley of popular Beatles tunes. And yet these amateur groups truly are the musical heartbeat of our nation. Our collective Lonely Hearts Club Band.*

Those who cannot play write reviews!

Two days before Christmas and I have the house to myself. The young Canadian has gone to Italy, Mrs. P. to see her mother, and Mr. P. has taken the urchins to a panto. I used this luxury of solitude to take a long bath, first scrubbing the tub of course, and then coming down in my robe to make a soft egg and toast. While I was eating in the kitchen, the mail slot opened and several letters dropped to the mat. I myself rarely get mail but I rose to sort through it anyway. Two for the departed Miss Smythe, who has not left a forwarding address. Mr. P.'s sporting paper. Three bills. A few flyers. A letter to me from none other than Penguin Books, in the corner the symbol of the famous bird in its oval.

The first response to my novel! Let the bidding wars begin! Or so ran my fantasy, only to evaporate upon opening. A form letter.

Rest assured your submission was seriously evaluated... Without a moment's hesitation I tore the letter into a dozen pieces. Seething with anger, I gathered up the pieces along with the flyers to shove into the bin and noticed a postcard tucked among the bills.

One side showed a photograph of the Eiffel Tower. Postcards by their nature are not private and so naturally I turn it over. *Paris is beautiful! Weather crummy but who cares? Love the cafés! Met some great people. See you soon, D.* My first thought was that the writer is profligate with his exclamation points. My second was to register who the writer was: the young American homosexual director. The very person our friend is supposed to be travelling with in Italy! Now, *that* is an appropriate exclamation point. If our friend is not with the American, then just who exactly *is* his companion?

The answer is obvious. I'm surprised I did not guess this subterfuge earlier. And the postcard—I waved it in the air like a winning lottery ticket—is red-hot evidence.

The question is what to do with it? Should I slip it discreetly underneath my young friend's door? Or hold on to it until I can give the card to him myself, showing what a loyal friend he has in me? Or do I leave it on the vestibule table for Mr. P. to find when he returns home?

I slipped it into the pocket of my robe.

I took it out again.

I put it back in.

My toes positively tingled. I finished lunch, washed my dishes, then started up the stairs before returning to the vestibule, where I placed the postcard on the table. Who am I to change the course of human history?

Mr. P. has seen the postcard.

I happened to be on the landing of the stairs, where I had planted myself and waited with one shoelace undone. The kids burst into the house, tossing their coats and boots and shouting for a snack, followed by Mr. P. in his overcoat. I bent down to tie my shoe, which admittedly took some physical effort as I generally use a footstool in my room for the purpose. Mr. P. hung up his coat, removed his scarf and boots, and only then noticed the card. He picked it up and examined the image before turning it over. It seemed to take him an inordinately long time to read. He turned it over again and then back, reading it again. A look came over him, the look of a man who has been informed that his death sentence would not be commuted after all. He ran his hand over his face. The urchins were screaming for him to make them cheese toasties, and he answered and walked toward the kitchen.

But what has been the result? Nothing. Mrs. P. arrived home on the day before Christmas as promised, to be smothered at the door by the urchins. Mr. P. smiled a little and gave her a peck on the cheek and they immediately began dinner preparations. And then four days later the young Canadian returned, dragging his backpack and carrying a new poster for his room. He picked up his mail, and I watched him shuffle through it, his face blanching as he encountered the postcard. He looked quickly around and then headed up the stairs, barely greeting me as he passed.

But as I say, nothing. Mr. P. is going to the pub more often—most evenings in fact. He ends up sleeping on the sofa or at his office, if he's capable of driving there. There have been some intense, whispered conversations between Mrs. P. and the young Canadian. Now it is a new year, 1979, and all's right with the world!

It has been almost a month since I have written here. A result of further rejections of my manuscript. I know that one day, one day— In truth, I don't know anything of the kind. Perhaps the novel is worth less than the paper it is typed on. Perhaps I should be like frustrated writers in Hollywood movies and toss my typewriter through a window or into the sea.

In the news: the gravediggers of Liverpool are on strike and, as a result, dozens of funerals have been delayed. I wonder what is being done with the corpses. Kept in cold storage? I myself was a gravedigger once, a job whose memory I have managed to supress until this news has stirred it up again. Fifteen years old, spade cutting into the clayey soil. The electric clang when hitting a rock that sent vibrations up one's arms. I did not strike for higher wages nor ask for longer breaks. I kept my head down. I swallowed my bile. I hoped I was not digging a hole for myself.

This Friday will see the "world premiere" of *Chekhov and Mandelbaum.* Those are the very words on the mimeographed poster, one having been taped to a kitchen cupboard door by Mrs. P. It is to be performed Friday, Saturday, Sunday afternoon, and again Sunday evening. Rehearsals began two and a half weeks ago, which means our young Canadian friend has not been home much. Every so often we run into one another and he breathlessly catches me up on the latest details. Chekhov is being played by a second-year Russian major who has grown a goatee and is trying to learn how to keep a lorgnette on his nose. The real trouble has been the actor playing Mandelbaum. He keeps trying to sound Jewish by imitating American TV shows and as a result sounds to the young Canadian like an offensive parody. Meanwhile, the set is being built, the actors are trying to get "off book," while last-minute rewrites keep changing the final script. Our playwright fears a disaster in the making.

He has given me an opening-night ticket. In fact, he offered me two and for a moment I considered asking Judy Tunnelworth, to show her my connection to people in the arts. But I quickly came to my senses and, besides, she might well have refused. He also gave Mrs. P. two tickets, hoping Mr. P. might also fill a seat. Clearly an artist has no shame. However, Mr. P. politely declined and so Mrs. P. will take her friend Francine instead. Apparently the woman has been complaining that Mrs. P. has neglected her for months.

I shall report all.

* * *

The University College's theatre is indeed a converted squash court, a concrete box sitting behind the college building. The interior has been painted black, with a grid of lights hoisted to the ceiling and eight rows of seats installed. I took one at the back so I could keep an eye on things. Mrs. P. and her friend came in shortly after and the space was too small for us not to nod at one another. Then came students and some older people who no doubt knew the actors, and perhaps also a professor or two. Our young Canadian friend poked his head in to see that most of the seats were filled.

The lights dimmed to black. They came up again upon the simple set, an ugly sofa and two armchairs, a coffee table with books on it. Stretched out on the sofa with a book over his face was a young man, just as in the script we had read in the living room. Not in the script was the deep snore which elicited a few titters from the audience.

The young man roused himself, the book falling to the floor. He picked it up and looked at the cover. Anton Chekhov? he said. I could not have fallen asleep to Anton Chekhov! And right in the middle of reading *Lady with Lapdog...*

And so on. The young man began to lament his failing relationship with a young woman with the improbable name of Sophie Sackenheim and wondered what Chekhov would do. Chekhov, a man known for his great success with women, matched with an extreme reluctance for commitment. And then came the crash in the closet, startling the young man (and us), followed by Chekhov himself stumbling out.

A superb morning! said the author. The cathedral bells are pealing. Just now I saw a raven circling overhead like an omen. Ah well, one must die. Meanwhile, I spent two kopecks on these sunflower seeds, and how can one be melancholy with sunflower seeds?

I'm never smoking weed again, said the young man.

Eventually the young woman showed up, played by a comely undergraduate with flowing locks. She had arrived to break things off, but Mandelbaum, with encouragement from Chekhov (invisible to her of course), tried to work his rhetorical charm. He attempted to convince her that her happiness lay in their union, he denigrated other men, he promised her pleasures untold, and when none of that worked he threatened to kill himself, at least until he remembered that there was no gun present in the first act that could then go off in the third. In the end, of course, she said her goodbye, gave him one last kiss, and was gone.

There are consolations, my friend, said Chekhov, putting his arm around Mandelbaum's shoulder. The young man asked what they were. Chekhov began a list. Small dogs. Sunflower seeds. Birds on the telegraph wire. Comfortable boots. The distant sound of a balalaika. Books. Rain tapping on the roof. Lying half-awake in bed. Friendship. Death.

The great Russian then bowed as he retreated backwards into the closet and was gone. Of course there was one more speech from Mandelbaum, delivered standing, then sitting, and finally lying on the floor. The stage lights dimmed and were extinguished.

The last thing our young Canadian friend needs is a boost to his carefully nurtured ego, but I must admit to having enjoyed his little play. Derivative yes, naive certainly, but smart nevertheless and even a touch—a very small touch—moving. In any case, *Chekhov and Mandelbaum* has been declared a success. That means a mostly positive review in the student newspaper and a near sold-out run, adding up to a total audience of fewer than two hundred thirty people. Then came the closing-night party that sounds as if it was a regular bacchanalia. It seems unfair that Mrs. P. was not invited, considering the encouragement she gave to the playwright, and she spent the hours he was away sitting in the back garden in the dark. Did she perhaps fear the allure of the young actress in the cast, she of the flowing locks?

It turns out that our young Canadian friend is not the only successful *artiste* in this house. My manuscript—my *book*—has been accepted by BlackNail Publishing. True, it is not a big house. And has previously specialized in regional tourist guides and books of confessional poetry with images of roses on their covers. But that only means that *Murder Most Morbid* will be an important book for them. Really, I am too giddy for words.

Here I am, wishing to revel in my own impending literary triumph, and the house is in turmoil. For it seems that Mrs. P.'s excessive praise of our young friend's play was too much for Mr. P. He finally found the courage to confront her about the Christmas vacation, claiming the postcard as evidence of betrayal. And Mrs. P., usually so able, found herself dumbfounded for a moment. Eventually she managed to wave the accusation away, claiming that the young Canadian had two friends with the same name.

Mr. P. did not believe her. And now he alternates between angry outbursts and pathetic begging. Mrs. P. looks as if she is near the end of her strength. The urchins seem unaware and make their usual noise, but one never knows, and for once my dislike of children is second to a growing concern.

And what is the result? Our young Canadian friend, himself looking like a cornered hare, has gone looking for a new home. He tells me, without a confession, that it is the only way to end these intolerable conditions. And now he has found a room in another house, closer to the university, not so nice a room but he says it will do. He is to move out on Friday. All he needs, he confides to me, is the courage to tell Mrs. P.

Mrs. P. knows. From my room I can hear her screaming. I do not know how to characterize the sound. It is more animal than human.

* * *

Mrs. P. has crawled into the back of her bedroom closet. She will not come out. Nor does she speak, but only sobs. The children have been sent to a neighbour. Mr. P. looks truly frightened by her behaviour. Every hour he goes into the bedroom and talks quietly, asking her to come out. He brings her a cup of tea that she doesn't drink, a bun that she won't eat.

He and I meet on the stairway. No better? I ask quietly.

Worse if anything. I fear she will harm herself. I don't know what to do.

The young Canadian has not seen any of this, for he has been at the university all day. He has volunteered to work backstage on another play, and because he will be late he has made arrangements to sleep on the dorm-room floor of his American friend. The day after tomorrow he is to leave for his new room. His backpack is half-packed, his posters taken down from the walls. Mrs. P. spends the entire night in the closet. Mr. P. does not sleep.

My own night's rest is fitful at best, and in the morning (my day off) I hear a key in the lock and know that the young Canadian has come home. Mr. P., dressed in a suit and tie, is waiting for him. He asks the young man into the parlour. I cannot hear the conversation, their voices are too low—although at one point the young man says, No, that isn't right. I can't. Mr. P.'s voice remains low as they talk for another hour. I cannot go down to the kitchen to make my breakfast for fear of intruding. At last they rise from their chairs. They stand in the vestibule for another moment and then Mr. P. puts his hand on the young man's shoulder. He lets go, picks up a small valise, and leaves the house.

The young Canadian remains standing by the door. Then he comes up the stairs, head down, seemingly unaware of my presence on the landing. He keeps going up and along the hall until he is standing before the door of the master bedroom. He appears to be—what is the term?—hyperventilating. I think he will keel over. But he opens the bedroom door, goes inside, and shuts it behind him.

A week has gone by and I do not know what to make of things. On the surface all seems quite as usual. Yesterday I came home to find the young Canadian helping the older urchin with a science project in the kitchen, measuring the ingredients for a model rocket. But in the evening he waited until the family (that is, Mrs. P. and the urchins) were finished dinner before making his own.

Today when I passed the young man on the stairs, he asked me to his room for a cup of tea. As he poured water into the pot (his tea-making technique having improved), he asked what I thought of Margaret Thatcher's chances of winning the election. I told him I thought she was the only real man among the candidates. He laid out some plain biscuits. And as we sat he began to talk about Mrs. P., almost as if he were telling me about someone I had never met. She has a sharp intellect that has been underused for too long, he said. She can read a novel or play with surprising insight that comes partly from her experience of life. From her he has learned how strong a person can seem so that one doesn't see the vulnerability.

But he also told me something quite surprising, looking upward as he spoke. He said that he'd been looking forward to moving out of the house, that he'd discovered something he never would have suspected, that love could be a prison. And then he looked at me and smiled and said he didn't understand how a woman politician could hold the views that Margaret Thatcher had.

A few minutes later we were standing again. At the door the young Canadian told me that his school term was almost over and he would be going home in another month. Had he mentioned that his older brother was getting married? He was to be best man. He said this as if it were most remarkable, and then he smiled and said good day and gently shut the door after me.

***

It turns out that BlackNail Publishing is made up of scoundrels and thieves. In order to publish my book, they require a contribution of twenty-five hundred pounds, payable immediately. They are nothing but a vanity press. I tore up the contract and flushed the pieces in the toilet, only to cause it to back up.

I cleaned up and went to bed, calling in sick to work. At last I got up but did not dress, going downstairs in my robe to scrounge a meal from what few provisions I had left. I believe the young Canadian sensed my misery, which admittedly could not have been difficult. In a cheerful voice he asked whether I might see a play with him that evening. Not long ago I would have been eager to go, hoping that a few delicious secrets might come my way. But now I did not care. However, when I said no, he asked again, saying he felt the need for company and I would be doing him a great favour. And so I agreed.

Of course my thought was that he hoped I might acquire for us some coveted West End tickets. But in fact he already had them, and for some small suburban theatre I'd never heard of, the New End. He did not tell me the name of the show and nor did I ask, so I was in the dark until we were standing outside looking at the poster for *A Day in Hollywood / A Night in the Ukraine.* I asked nothing; we went inside and took our seats. The first half turned out to be a spoof of American musicals from the thirties and forties, filled with song and dance. An amusing trifle, it lifted my spirits a little. But the second half was something else altogether. It was as if we had gone back in time to the days of vaudeville, when those famous Jewish siblings the Marx Brothers used to ad-lib their way through the most absurd of plots. Here was Groucho, Chico, and Harpo, or rather actors doing precise and yet exuberant impressions of them. One moment Groucho was crossing the stage in his crouching, long-legged walk, the next Harpo was reaching to shake someone's hand so they would somehow end up holding the comedian's leg in the air. Chico had the exact Italian-restaurant accent and even sat down at a piano to "shoot" the keys. Before long I was guffawing along with the rest of the audience until my eyes filled with tears.

When we came out of the theatre I felt wrung out and, yes, better. Perhaps my young friend did, too. He really is a decent fellow.

An almost eerie calm has fallen over the house. The urchins get off to school in the morning. Mrs. P. goes to her part-time job or has a cup of tea with the young Canadian, who then leaves for the university. The urchins are picked up by their father, who spends an hour or two with them before dropping them back in time for dinner. At the table there is the usual talk and nonsense between the urchins and their mother. After they are in bed Mrs. P. will watch a television program alone or with the young Canadian, or perhaps they will sit and read before going off to their respective bedrooms. I have never seen them kiss or hold hands or sneak from one room to another. There is an almost resigned melancholy about them.

The young Canadian has told me he is writing a new play but not what it is about. As for me, my literary ambitions have been snuffed out. Perhaps it is for the best. I go to the cinema every Sunday, I practise the euphonium with greater diligence. I have even started to attend the occasional play, having decided I shall be better informed to serve my customers.

I have not yet mentioned the upcoming spring concert parade. Nor that Judy Tunnelworth has become engaged to the first trombonist and likes to show off her little ring. Well, let her have her happiness, for it is rarely lasting.

Our young friend has been taking advantage of his last days, going to the National or the Royal Shakespeare Theatre, sometimes with Mrs. P. and sometimes with friends from the drama society.

For him this is a mere stopping place, an adventure, a story one day to be told about the year abroad. But for us—for the likes of Mrs. P. and myself—it is where we will end our lives. And when our young friend is out, I sometimes hear Mrs. P. quietly weeping in her room. She always emerges dry-eyed and smiling. Just today she asked me what I thought of the naturist beach that has opened in Brighton. Mrs. P., I said to her, I have no interest in lying on a flinty shore while pear-shaped women and bandy-legged men strut about. There is nothing, I said, natural about nakedness. Give me a nicely tailored suit, a dress with good lines. Now, *that* is something to look at.

Mrs. P. laughed and touched my arm. You do so cheer me up, she said.

It is not my intention to be cheerful, I replied.

Yes, I know. That's exactly what does it.

And now I report on the spring concert parade. On the second Saturday of May we took up our positions at a small corner park—the cornets, the baritones and euphoniums, the flugelhorns, the E-flat and B-flat basses, the trombones and timpani. Civilians have no idea of the discipline it takes to march in time while playing. The maestro raised his baton, and then a young boy, the maestro's own son, led us into the street. People stopped with their shopping bags and wheeled carts or looked at us through bus windows. For the most part they were smiling. And why wouldn't they? What can lift the heart more easily than a marching band?

But here is the thing. *I* was playing *first* euphonium. That is right, the maestro chose me. All of that practising paid off. And Judy Tunnelworth was quite gracious about it. Well done, you, she said, flashing her ring.

And so we marched. And whom did I see standing in front of Barclays Bank? None other than the young Canadian. He was grinning at me and giving the thumbs up, and I played with gusto as I stepped past.

* * *

The postcards and posters have been removed from the walls, this time for good. The overstuffed backpack and duffle bag are resting by the front door.

Today the boys are with their father. They have already said their goodbyes to the young man by invading his room in the morning and tossing confetti over him. Mrs. P. is driving him to Heathrow. He and I said our goodbye at the door. He was smiling, but I could feel the brimming emotion as his voice choked up. He reached out his hand, took mine, and then pulled me in for a hug. Steady on! I said, patting him on the back. Then I watched them get into Mrs. P.'s little car and putter away.

It has been three weeks since I have last written. Somehow my original purpose in beginning these pages has evaporated. What was it? To vent my frustrations? To scheme about getting the top room? To record the imbecility of my fellow man? I no longer remember.

Mr. P. has not moved back in. Returning has not proved to be possible—by agreement on both sides, or perhaps the pretense of an agreement. As is the decision that the urchins should remain in the house with their mother. They are desperately looking forward to the end of school and seem even more crazed than usual. Sometimes they stay over with Mr. P., which for some reason they call "camping out."

A few days ago Mrs. P. lugged several cans of paint up to the top room. She scraped off the old wallpaper, patched holes, and transformed the room with "Sunflower Yellow." She was quite surprised when I came up to assist her, rolling up my trouser legs and tying a handkerchief on my head. She had the radio on and we talked only a little as we worked, the brushes making a pleasant *wush*. And when we were done, we both stood by the doorway to admire our handiwork.

Isn't it cheerful? Mrs. P. said. Perhaps a little too cheerful for my taste, but I didn't say so.

The next day a truck delivered a new bed frame and mattress and dresser and mirror. Mrs. P. asked me to help her take down the curtains and put up modern blinds, a fussy job.

I know how long you've wanted the top room, she said as we stood there once more. Look at it now, fresh as anything. I can keep the rent as it is for the first year, anyway.

Very thoughtful of you, Mrs. P., I replied. But I have thought on it and believe that I am quite content just as I am.

Oh, she said, clearly surprised. And perhaps a little disappointed. Only then did I realize that she was, at least in part, doing all the work for me.

I'll put in an advert, she said. For the other room, too. We certainly do need the money.

And down to the telephone she went.

A new tenant has moved into the top room. He is a medical student from Romania doing some sort or residency here. Thirty years old, with a florid moustache and smelling of sausage. With squeaking boots. And a tenant also in the room next to mine, a woman of indeterminate age who has recently divorced. She and Mrs. P. have taken tea in the parlour twice and seem to be getting on like a house on fire. Mrs. P. has also enrolled in a summer extension course at the university and has a new pile of books on the kitchen table. She seems to enjoy studying and has begun musing about taking a degree. The other day a reading group she has somehow conjured up met in the back garden, where there was much argument and laughter. So the house has become busier once again, with traffic on the stairs and occasional waiting for the bath. But I do not mind. It is life after all. Indeed, I seem to find myself reinvigorated. I have started a new detective novel, which I am calling *The Mystery of Muswell Hill.* I have not decided yet who will die. Perhaps everyone. For that, of course, is inevitable.

THE MUSICIANERS

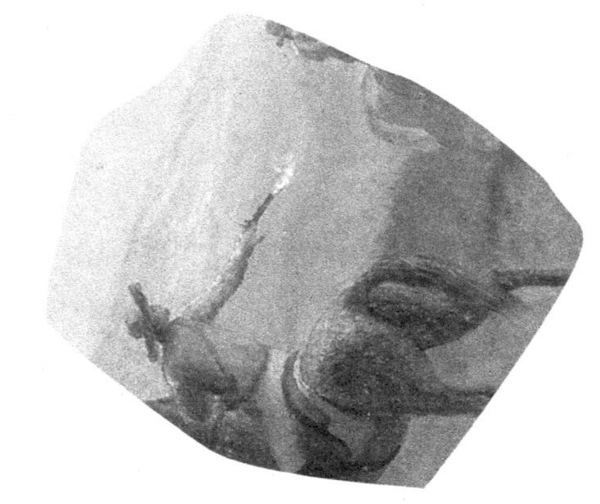

THE COW ROOTED IN GRASS. SHE RAISED HER KINKED TAIL, tufted like a fraying rope, and shat. Something at the edge of her vision made her look up.

"There's something out there," said the tall one.

The three men stopped. They'd been walking on land as flat as a skillet, so unchanging as to put a fellow used to mountains and valleys in a foul mood. As well as being tired and anxious for their lives, they were desperately hungry.

Each raised a hand to shade his eyes. Shirtless, they wore cotton overalls and three rather dusty bowlers. It was getting on in October, but some of the days had been hot and their shoulders and noses were burned, for they weren't used to being outdoors all day. Each carried his instrument. The short one had a strap on his guitar and the advantage of being able to carry it slung on his back. The tall one carried his fiddle in a flour sack, the bow tapping against it when he walked. The third, of middle height, had no way to carry his banjo other than to hold it by the neck in one hand or the other, depending on which was the least cramped.

"I think it's a cow," said the last one, walking again. "Unless I'm seeing a mirage, if that's what you call it."

"A mirage is something you see in the desert," said the tall fiddle player. "You can't see a mirage in the fucking prairies."

"How do you know? I remember that time you were convinced you saw a sea serpent in the French Broad River."

“I never said just a sea serpent. I said maybe a whale or maybe a dolphin. I had the excuse of being drunk. And it *was* something. A dead body. Easy to misidentify.”

“That *is* a cow,” said the shortest and youngest. “An honest-to-god cow.”

“Even you’ve seen a cow before. I wish I hadn’t lost my cravat. It’s bad enough wearing these overalls. But it’s hard to look dressy without a cravat.”

“Isn’t anybody here to impress,” said the banjo player. “Unless you’ve taken a shine to that cow. She is a pretty one with that white stripe down the centre of her nose. And she’s got the sort of backside you prefer.”

“That isn’t even worth a chuckle. I happen to look good in a cravat, it sets off my long neck. And why do we have to have *purple* overalls? We look like damn circus clowns.”

“I’d take the work,” said the banjo player. “Nothing wrong with a circus orchestra. Better than a minstrel show. Though I do remember one of them hawkers trying to sell his bottles of Kickapoo medicine. He said that if you take one spoon a day it would keep you regular in the morning, awake in the afternoon, and bucking all night. He said ‘bucking’ but people knew what he meant.”

“That isn’t funny either,” said the fiddler. “But if you think you’re no better than a medicine show performer, then by all means join one. In fact, you’d fit right in.”

“Are you insulting my pa? I’m proud of what I am.”

“I was referring to your ability, not your heritage.”

“Anyway, Black or white, you can’t call him ‘pa’ if you never met him,” said the short one. “And you can go ahead and insult *my* father as much as you want. Course he might be dead. Irish prick.”

“We could have told that from your flaming hair,” said the banjo player.

“You still haven’t told us why these overalls are purple,” said the fiddler.

"I'd call them mauve," said the banjo player.

"And I'd call you a horse's ass, Douglas, if I could bother. Come on, Jimmy. You went into the store in Bismarck and bought them. Don't evade the question, as the lawyer said to the highwayman. Why are these overalls purple?"

"All right, Moses, I'll tell you. They were discounted. Something wrong with the dye. They were half price."

"They ought to put that on our tombstone," said Douglas, the banjo player. "*They were half price*. Which I imagine they'll be able to do sooner than later."

"Now you shut up," said the fiddler, Moses. "I've been putting some effort into not thinking about that."

"Thinking about being killed, you mean? Don't know why."

"Maybe we'll starve to death first," said Jimmy. "I'm not kidding."

"We gone without for as long as you," said Douglas. "In fact I've been thinking what it would be like chewing on the head of my own banjo."

"What kind of skin is it?" asked Jimmy. "Groundhog?"

"Cat. A catskin makes a good banjo head."

"My cat, General Grant, disappeared last January," said Moses. "Are you telling me that banjo head *is* General Grant?"

"It was winter. I couldn't find any groundhog."

"Purrs pretty good when you play her," said Jimmy.

"You bastard, Douglas."

"Yes, I am. And so are you, Moses. And Jimmy, too. Our mother gave birth to nothing but. That really is a nice-looking cow. Pretty eyes. Wait, look behind it. Isn't that...?"

"Isn't that what?" asked Moses, still sounding miffed. "Isn't that a pile of cow dung? I hate when you don't finish your sentences."

"That big mound. It's like the picture I saw in the newspaper. It's a marker. A border marker. We've reached Canada."

The three increased their pace as much as they could, given how tired they were and how knotted up their stomachs. The cow evidently disliked being rushed at and trotted a few feet to the side. They reached the mound, which was taller than Moses, and put the flats of their hands on it as if it were some ancient religious site offering good fortune.

Douglas took two steps past the mound. "See that? He can't get me now. I'm in another country. I'm under the protection of the king. I'm safe. He isn't going to bring any vigilante justice across the border."

"I hope you're right," Moses said.

"You don't think I am? *Now* you tell me? After all these days? You're saying he might..."

"There you go, not finishing your sentence. I'm saying that I don't know. If he's smart he won't. The problem is he's not smart. That's a lesson I learned a long time ago. Don't cross stupid people."

"Come here, pretty cow," said Jimmy. He took a slow step toward it.

"You've got a funny look on your face, brother," said Moses.

"Do I?" He unslung his guitar and laid it on the stubble.

"Why you taking off your guitar?" said Douglas. "You got to squat?"

Jimmy didn't answer. He slipped two fingers into the pocket on the smock of his overalls and drew something out.

"Where'd you get a Barlow knife?" asked Moses.

"Come here, cow. Nice cow. Good cow."

"You're not serious, Jimmy," said Douglas. "That cow belongs to somebody. We just crossed into Canada. We're trying to stay out of foreign jails. And not get strung up. I'm sure we'll find something to eat soon. Besides, you could hardly kill a toad with that little knife. Let's keep moving."

Jimmy began to breathe in quick gulps. Then he started to run, shouting, toward the cow. The other two watched wide-eyed as their younger brother jumped onto the back of the animal and plunged the knife's three-inch blade into her shoulder. A spurt of blood hit him in the face as the cow bellowed and started to kick out her hind legs. Jimmy pulled out the knife and stuck it in again and again and again, until the darkening blood soaked the cow's hide and made her slippery to hold on to and he began sliding sideways. He managed to clamp his legs and put the knife in lower, grunting with the effort. The cow hopped in a circle, eyes wild. Jimmy fell off. The animal screamed and tried to run but her legs buckled. She dropped to her knees, whimpering, as bubbles of blood sprouted from her nostrils.

Jimmy got himself up off the ground. He was covered, arms and shoulders and face, the front of his overalls streaked black. The three of them stood and watched the cow die. She kept blinking and snorting and trying to stay upright on her knees. Finally she tipped over. Her legs kicked and shivered and stopped.

"Jesus, Jimmy," said Moses. "I wondered where that knife went to."

With no trees nearby, it took them a good three hours to find enough wood for a fire, half of which came from a broken-down fence and most of the rest branches blown in from God knows where. The sun was already down. Moses carried the matches in a brass cylinder hung around his neck along with a six-pointed silver star that had been left behind by his father, a dealer in religious goods. Jimmy was best at getting a fire started, using some dry, mossy stuff to start it off.

They cut strips from the cow and lay them right on the fire as they had nothing to hold them up. The fat sizzled and popped and the meat flared and burned. They pulled out the strips, swearing from the heat on their fingers, and could not stop themselves from eating too quickly, burning their mouths.

"If only we had us some salt," said Moses, chewing and blowing in alternation.

"You just reminded me," Douglas said. He pulled a small bottle from his pocket, pulled the cork, and dabbed it on his meat.

"What is exactly is that?"

"Hot chili sauce. Got it from that Mexican I used to drink with. Told me he couldn't eat gringo food without it."

"Chili sauce? Jimmy's got a knife and you've got chili sauce? What else are you two carrying that I don't know about? A goldfish in a bowl? A piano?"

"Very unlikely," Douglas said.

"I've got nothing else," Jimmy added.

"Oh, you've got something more, Jimmy," said Moses. "You're carrying murder in your heart. As we have just been witness to."

"That weren't murder," he said, pulling another strip from the fire and then dancing it between his hands.

"Then what was it, I'd like to know."

"That was butchering."

"That's true," said Douglas. "Killing a cow isn't a homicide."

"Besides," Jimmy said, "it just came over me, it was the hunger. What do you call it? Instinct. It's not as if I don't feel guilty, eating the thing. Never did me any harm."

"She did have pretty eyes," Douglas said, chewing. "But she's also good eating. A shame I'm almost stuffed."

Jimmy wiped his hands on his overalls, which were stiff from the dried blood. He scratched at the streaks on his face, then stepped away from the fire and lay on his back to look up. "Sure are a lot of stars. Never seen so many."

The others kicked back, too, their instruments by their sides like spouses. The night was chilly, but they didn't want to waste the wood they had left.

Jimmy yawned and said, "One thing about Ma, she made sure we slept on feather mattresses. I miss the house in Asheville. I miss that feather mattress."

"Keep your eyes open," Moses said. "Maybe next you'll be able to kill us a giant chicken."

"Fuck you, Mose."

"You sleep well yourself, little brother."

They put their bowlers over their faces.

In the morning they built the fire up out from the embers and ate a meaty breakfast. Knowing the cow would start going bad in the day's heat, they cooked enough for lunch and supper, too. Now they found themselves with a powerful thirst, but Douglas discovered a slough behind an almost invisible slope.

"It's still got about three inches of water in it," he called. "And about three hundred jiggers."

"This time of year?" said Moses. "What sort of a place is hatching mosquitoes all year long?"

The other two came over to look. There was a flat bottom of mud underneath the clear water. Jimmy asked, "You think it'll make us sick?"

"Maybe," Douglas said. "But not drinking it might make us dead."

They decided to risk it, leaning down and carefully scooping handfuls of water, trying not to stir up the muck.

"Tastes a tad funky," said Douglas.

"Spoke the connoisseur," Moses said. "You maybe drink only bottled Perrier water from gay Paris?"

"You're making that up. Nobody puts water in bottles."

They waited but did not get sick. And so they decided to spend the day there, recovering some of their strength before moving on to look for civilization "or what passes for it in a British outpost," Moses said. They ate and drank and lay about and had enough wood left for a small fire to cheer themselves up for a while when it grew dark again.

"For the first time since we left, I feel like sawing out a tune," Moses said. The others watched the light flickering over him as he untied the flour sack to pull out his fiddle. He sat cross-legged on the ground and ran the bow scratchily over the strings as he tuned up. Then he started a slow, droning "Bonaparte's Retreat." After he'd played it a couple of times, Douglas picked up his banjo and began to thump the rhythm, picking up the occasional melody note.

Jimmy just kept looking at the fire. "I wonder what happens to a cow's soul when it dies," he said.

Moses switched to "The Eighth of January," quickening the beat. "According to the Hindus..."

"I wish you'd give me warning," Douglas said, catching up on his banjo.

"As I was saying, the Hindus believe..."

A growl. Moses stopped playing but Douglas must not have heard, because he kept on frailing.

Another growl. Douglas too stopped. "Shit," he said. They all had the same idea, which was to slide on their asses closer to the fire. More growls and teeth-gnashing followed, then a whimper. The sound of flesh being yanked from the bone.

"The cow," Moses said. "They're going after it."

"Wolves?" Douglas whispered.

Jimmy said, "Somebody stir up the fire so we can see. Use your banjo, Douglas."

"Why don't you use your guitar, since you don't seem to play it much."

"Shut up, the both of you. I've got a stick here." Moses poked at the remains of the fire, sending up sparks. Behind it they saw sleek, moving shapes. They were different sizes—small, large, and in between.

"Dogs," said Moses. "Gone wild. A pack of them. But just about as dangerous."

"There's more than enough cow left," Jimmy said. "I'm going to sleep."

"If you can sleep so sound, I guess you don't suffer a killer's guilty conscience."

"Did you partake of that cow or didn't you?"

"Don't be so touchy, Jimmy. I'm just joking on you, more or less."

"Yeah, well, you try being born last and see what it's like."

"Not sure how I can accomplish that."

"And being five foot four."

"Is that really all you are? I didn't know the Irish were a miniature race."

"Listen, fellas," Douglas said, "we've had two days of rest and eating. This is the best we've felt since leaving Asheville. Maybe we ought to just enjoy it."

"Not to mention," Moses said, "we've got the entertaining sounds of crazed dogs ripping the remaining flesh off a murdered cow."

"Fuck you again, Mose," Jimmy said.

Moses dreamed that a colossally fat man was sitting on his face. It was the fella who taught him his first licks on the fiddle when he was a kid—only the real man wasn't fat and the only thing he'd wanted from Moses in exchange was a pair of his mother's undergarments, preferably unwashed. Now Moses began to blink and he tried to draw breath but felt his throat being crushed.

It was in fact no fat man but the heel of a boot, as he realized on waking. The boot smelled like chicken shit. His hands came up and slapped at the leg attached to the boot. At last it lifted off, allowing him to draw a noisy breath.

Sputtering, he sat up. The other two roused themselves and looked over. The man was tall and bony and with a patch of straw-coloured hair atop his long-weathered face. His eyes gazing down on Moses were the colour of lake water.

"Who's that, Mose?" asked Douglas.

"How do I know who it is?" Moses growled as he rubbed his throat. "I've got no *Who's Who of Saskatchewan* on me." With some difficulty he got to his feet, picking up his bowler, which had been knocked into the dirt. All three of them saw the hay wagon behind the man, but what drew their attention was the massive beast yoked to it. A great, bushy head and cruel horns.

"Isn't that a buffalo?" Jimmy asked.

"It is," said the man, whose lilt gave him away as a Swede.

"There isn't any more buffaloes," Douglas said. "The cowboys shot them all years ago."

"There's this one," said the Swede.

"And it's tame?"

"I didn't interrupt my day to be talking about Brutus."

"Well, you named him well," Moses said. "I myself would be interested to know why you near crushed my windpipe."

The man looked at Moses without any change of expression. Then he walked back to the wagon. He pulled something from behind the seat and came back carrying a shotgun.

"You three marauders killed Cleopatra, my best milker. Just look at her."

Reluctantly the brothers turned. On the other side of their firepit they saw a carcass stripped bare but for a patch on its head.

"I admit that's a ghoulish sight," Douglas said. "But *we* didn't do it. Just Jimmy here murdered Cleopatra."

Jimmy stared at his brother. "Thanks a lot. You also going to tell him I was at Custer's last stand? You ate your share, both of you."

"Now, that's true," Moses said, softening his voice the way he always did when the brothers found themselves confronting any trouble. "She was a fine creature, anyone could see that. And we wouldn't have touched a hair on her if we hadn't been starving. But we came up from the United States of America and hadn't eaten for some two or three days. No law obliges a man to die of hunger, or ought to. Maybe we can work it off and pay you back."

The man wore an old but well-cared-for straw hat with a large brim. His eyebrows and lashes were so light as to be almost invisible and he had an unnaturally wide mouth with thin lips, which he now wiped with one hand. "'The robbed that smiles,'" he said, "'steals something from the thief.' I will control my anger."

"That is a relief, sir, and mighty Christian of you. I imagine that's the Bible you're quoting from."

"It's Shakespeare."

"Isn't that something, a Swede quoting Shakespeare. You don't have your own bard in Sweden?"

"I learned English by reading Shakespeare."

"Forsooth and by your liege." Moses pretended to bow.

The man didn't smile. Perhaps he was incapable of doing so. He looked all three brothers over. "If you have come from over the border, I am thinking that you are running from something or somebody."

"That's a good—"

"Shut up, Jimmy," Moses said, turning to the man. "What would we be running away from? We're just lowly musicianers, bit players on the theatrical stage of life. See, we've got our instruments here. And we're brothers."

"You do not look like brothers. That one in the middle is brown while the short one looks like a lit candle."

Moses laughed. "I've called him just about everything under the sun, but I hadn't thought of that. Lit candle. But you see, good sir, we've all got the same blessed mother. Just different fathers. Our ma runs a boarding house in Asheville. Perfectly respectable excepting perhaps for her own behaviour. But in her defence the woman is no whore. She is a seeker after love, a lonesome dove in search of her mate. She just never found him yet."

"Nor never will," said Douglas.

"You don't know that," protested Jimmy.

"I am not so interested in your mother as you all seem to think. Tell me your names."

"Moses Woltoff Clennan at your service," Moses said.

"I'm Douglas Dorchester Clennan."

"I'm James Boyle Clennan."

The man turned around and walked back toward the wagon. The brothers looked at one another in puzzlement. Was he going to leave them there? But the man pulled something else from the back of the wagon and came toward them again. He held an old grain sack in one hand and in the other a crude shovel made from a whittled branch and a short piece of weathered board nailed to the end. "You can walk behind. When Brutus shits, you put it in the sack. We need it for the vegetable garden next spring. You can put those music makers in the wagon."

"And where are we going exactly?" Moses asked.

The man didn't answer. He went back to the wagon and they followed. He got onto the seat and said sharply, *"Hem!"* The animal lumbered forward. They hurriedly put in their instruments. The animal had left a considerable pile where it had been standing, and Jimmy opened the sack while his two brothers pushed the shovel at one another. It ended up with Douglas. He scooped up a pile and tipped it in.

"Careful! You're dropping buffalo shit on me."

"Whatever you do," Moses said, "don't try sticking that Barlow knife into Brutus. I'm pretty sure a buffalo wouldn't like being tickled that way."

The brothers began walking behind the wagon.

The beast was in no hurry and the brothers could easily gather its turds while keeping up. The land wasn't as flat as first appeared but slowly rose to a field of stubble marked here and there with a circular hay bale. In the distance a farmhouse appeared and they began to argue whether or not they ought to have seen the smoking chimney from their campsite. It was a good while before they could see it clearly, made of fieldstone and chinked with plaster, two floors with a few small windows and a heavily slanted roof and a narrow front porch.

"That's a handsome house," Moses shouted up to the man.

"A bugger to build, it was."

"Windows seem a bit small," Douglas said. Jimmy smacked his arm and gave him a look. "Well, they are."

"Windows come in by train from the east. Expensive."

"Where's the station?" Moses asked, moving up alongside the wagon. "There a town near here?"

"Seven miles northwest."

"It got a name?" Jimmy asked.

"I don't expect they just call it 'Town,'" said Moses.

"Stevensville," said the man.

"You think there might be a call for some musicianers there? Listening or dancing."

"You can sing in Ukrainian? Or German?"

"Not that I'm aware of."

"Then I wouldn't think so." The ringing of a bell came from the house. "That would be breakfast."

"A delightful noise. I believe I smell coffee. Sir, you have the better of us since we don't know your name."

"Johansson."

"I should have guessed."

"Mose, the beast is shitting again."

Moses fell back and the brothers performed their task. They came upon the house, with its vegetable patch and pens. "*Sluta,* Brutus," said Johansson, and the buffalo came slowly to a halt. The man got down and unhitched the animal, which wandered a few feet away and started to graze.

"Old Brutus don't need to be penned?" Moses asked.

The man didn't bother answering. He headed for the pump and began to work its handle. There was a lump of lye soap in a tin box and he washed his hands and face, then put his head under. "See if you can get some of that dust and blood off yourselves," he said.

The water was painfully cold, but all three brothers were relieved to wash, working the pump for one another as they put their heads under and yelped. They scrubbed their ears and nostrils and the backs of their necks. Moses shook out his hair like a dog and wiped his eyes and saw three young women standing on the porch watching them.

"Well, I'll be," he said. "For once I'm at a loss for words."

The other two looked up. The women were close in age, all with their hair pulled back into a bun, high lace collars and wide petticoats, with a resemblance to one another but just as many differences.

"It's like we're characters in a story I'm making up in my head," Douglas said.

"Well, this isn't any story and you're sure no writer." Moses picked up his hat and put it on his head so he could remove it again as he stepped toward the porch. "The name's Moses," he said. "And these are my brothers, Douglas and Jimmy. We are very pleased to meet the offspring of our friend Johansson."

"You are not my friends," Johansson said, stepping up onto the porch. "And my daughters are perfectly capable of taking care of themselves. So you will mind your manners unless you want something broke."

"Enchanting," said Moses. "May we at least ask their names?"

"That's Desdemona, the one in the middle is Cordelia, and the short one is Juliet. Now let's go in and eat."

The three young women looked at the brothers, their faces inscrutable, and then went into the house, followed by their father.

"Not exactly your giggling schoolgirls," Moses said under his breath as he pulled his sack from the wagon.

"They're pretty, though," said Douglas, grabbing his banjo. "In a sturdy way."

"I don't care for having to sit at a table with this dried blood on my overalls," Jimmy said. He had to hop up and lean over the side of the wagon to get his guitar.

"Perhaps you should have thought about that before going for the poor animal's jugular."

"How could I have known we'd be invited for breakfast?"

"A gentleman is always ready for an invitation."

"I think maybe we ought to shut up," Douglas said.

Moses went in first through the admirably square door frame. The contrast between outside and an interior lit only by small windows rendered them temporarily sightless. Moses found himself bumping into one of the daughters, although which he couldn't tell. The brothers stood until they could see well enough to put their instruments in a corner and then discern two empty chairs and a barrel pulled up to the table. A little manoeuvring took place among them with the result that Jimmy, complaining of "always getting the short stick," had to perch on the barrel.

The oldest daughter took the percolator off the stove and poured coffee. "Blessed liquid," Moses said, bringing it to his lips. "Scalding hot and bitter as Hades, just the way I like it."

The middle sister, whose most obvious feature was a snub nose, passed around the biscuits. The youngest was fair like her father, her hair not pulled back so severely. She brought the pan of bacon and went back for the eggs. Only Moses declined the bacon.

"Our brother is a Hebrew," said Douglas. "According to some book he read, Jews don't partake of the cloven hoof."

"Thank you for speaking on my behalf, brother," Moses said. "I am so frequently tongue-tied."

"I've never seen a Jew before," said the eldest sister.

"You are Desdemona, yes?" Moses said. "As you see, I am a mere man. A finer figure than my brothers but otherwise quite mortal."

"You have seen one," Johansson said. "The fellow who runs the saloon in Stevensville."

"I've never been in the saloon, Pa, as if you didn't know that."

"These biscuits are sure solid," Jimmy said. "They give the teeth a good workout."

"I made them," said Juliet.

"Well, you all have a talent for the culinary arts," Moses said. "That is for certain."

"You're musicianers?" said the middle one, Cordelia. "We've

seen your instruments."

"That's correct, miss," said Douglas. "It's how we make our living."

"What sort of music do you play?"

Moses jumped in. "Reels, hornpipes, breakdowns," he said. "Waltzes, polkas, mazurkas, a jig or two. Good dance music. For the last three years there was a steady job in the Mount Pisgah Hotel in Asheville, which happens to be our home town. Touring in the off-season."

"We had good suits to go with these bowlers," Jimmy said.

"What happened to them?" Juliet asked.

"Left behind," Douglas answered. "On account of having to leave so—ow!"

Moses had kicked him hard under the table. "Bit your own tongue, did you, brother? We'd be happy to play for you all. We enjoy having us an audience of sympathetic toe-tappers."

"'If all the years were playing holidays,'" Johansson said, "'to sport would be as tedious as to work.' We've got too much to do, even if you did miss the harvest."

"We missed the harvest?" Moses said. "That is certainly a shame. We could have helped you, all right. Might I have a spot more of that delicious coffee?"

"It's roiled up my stomach," Douglas said. "I fear I'm going to have to excuse myself quick." He rose, pushing back his chair.

"Shithouse is out behind," Johansson said. "There's an Eaton's catalogue for paper but don't use any pages from farm implements."

They finished the meal in silence, a condition unfamiliar to the brothers. Johansson got up from the table, put on his boots, and went outside. The women began clearing the table. Desdemona folded up the tablecloth to shake it outside.

"Let me help you with that," Moses said.

"I've done it on my own up to now." Yet he had the sense that she was permitting him to follow her out. A sharp wind had come up, making the dust swirl over the path from the door. Moses came forward and briefly touched her hand as he took two corners of the cloth. She looked at him and they stepped away from each other like a pair of square-dance partners. The wind spiked, catching the cloth underneath and yanking it from both their hands. They stood watching as it rose into the air, folding and turning, moving up and away over the field.

"Isn't that a pretty sight," Moses said.

"Just staring isn't going to bring it back," she said, going after it.

The brothers were lined up by the pump before the Swede. "As I said, you missed the harvest," Johansson muttered.

"We're usually a little late when it comes to being useful," Douglas said.

"But there's still work. I am going into town to finish the sale of our wheat. The girls will tell you what to do."

"Their wish is our command." Moses looked over at the three sisters, who stood on the porch.

"You have a natural inclination to irritate," Johansson said, blinking his pale lashes.

"That's a pretty good read you got on our brother there," Jimmy said. "It usually takes people another day or so before the charm wears thin."

"We are ready to work," Douglas added. "You've been very decent to us. We want to be useful."

"I wonder whether musicianers can ever be useful." Johansson turned and, putting two fingers into his mouth, gave a sharp whistle. The buffalo, which had been grazing nearby, raised its head, swung its enormous body toward them, and began to trot. Johansson met the beast. "All right, all right," he said, rubbing the dark curls between its horns that looked to Moses like a poorly fitted wig. It willingly submitted to the yoke and then Johansson climbed into the wagon. *"Till staden,"* he said, and the animal began to move.

"Tame as our mother's bulldog," Moses said.

Juliet was holding an axe. She came over and stood before Jimmy. "You," she said. "Come."

She turned and started walking, and Jimmy, shrugging comically for his brothers' sake, went after her.

"If you really are writing this story," Moses said to Douglas, "you might consider giving the women more lines. They don't say much."

"How would I know what a woman would say?"

"Maybe there's a school where they teach you that sort of thing."

"You're pulling my leg. There's no such thing as a writing school."

Cordelia came forward and stood before Douglas. "It's laundry day," she said. "Maybe I won't feel like my arms are falling off afterwards if you do your share."

"It would be my pleasure to wash your, ah, things," Douglas said.

"You can wash our father's long johns. He wears them winter or summer. Don't dawdle now. We've got to get the baskets and take them down to the creek."

Douglas tromped up the porch stairs after her. Only the eldest sister was left. Moses was just an inch or so taller than her, which didn't give him quite the stature he would have liked. "You Swedes do grow tall. So what is it to be? I live to serve."

"Well, we've got the animals. Chickens and pigs."

"Feeding animals is a task I believe I can handle."

"And shovelling shit. Which I guess you're a natural at."

"I admire your wit, Miss Desdemona."

"That isn't wit, that's simple observation. Giddyap, now. The critters are hungry."

The sisters worked the brothers hard and, to one degree or

another, each of the men felt a certain embarrassment at not being quite up to their respective tasks. Juliet was an efficient wielder of the axe, splitting her logs with one swing. On his first try, Jimmy buried the axe in the dirt so close to his own foot that he shaved off a sliver of boot leather.

"Is this enough wood to last the winter?" he asked after a while, just to give himself a moment's break.

"Course not. What'd you use back in Ashyville or wherever you come from?"

"Coal. Got delivered to us, too."

"Well, there's no coal around here. The woodpile's only for the coldest days. Other times we burn corncobs or chips."

"Chips?"

"Dried cow dung gives off a good heat. Start swinging that axe or we'll never get done."

They worked for nearly an hour, until Juliet was glistening with sweat. She stopped and, to Jimmy's surprise, pulled her dress over her head. Underneath she wore a man's shirt and a pair of trousers rolled at the cuffs and held up by a rope belt.

"I don't think you're exactly like your sisters," he said.

"Why should I be? I'm a different person, aren't I? Anyway, I've always felt different. Worries Pa some, but he doesn't mind that I'm a good worker."

"It doesn't mean you're not pretty."

"Shut up with that talk." He could see her blush. "You're just trying to take a break. Start stacking or we'll be here till sundown."

The work that Desdemona put Moses to wasn't so hard; it was the smell he found difficult to tolerate. Not that he wasn't as familiar with bad odours as the next man, but there was a peculiar concentration to the smell of chicken shit that seared his nostrils and burned his throat. On the other hand, it was his stomach that turned from the more fecund odour of pig feces. He tried to keep his mind off them both by gazing at the sloe-eyed Desdemona.

There was nothing romantic about the way she scattered those chickens and slapped the hogs. They had one boar and three sows, each of whom had given birth to a litter in the spring, most being sold off. One of the sows had a second litter just two weeks ago, "cute little fellas" to Moses, which caused the young woman to snort loudly. One of them was notably smaller than the others, a double handful of pink with a couple of dark patches on his back. "Look at them all struggling for a spot at the soda fountain," Moses said. "And that little one keeps getting pushed aside. Can't you do something about it?"

"I can stave in its head."

"Come on now."

"You don't even eat pig, as I have been informed."

"That isn't the point. It's a living thing, isn't it? I don't see the value in letting it starve to death."

"All right then," she said, and opened the gate to enter the pen. She scooped up the runt, which began to squeal and paddle its little hoofs, and came out again. "Here you go," she said, pushing it into his hands.

"What am I supposed to do with it?"

"Feed it. I'll get you some mash and a wooden spoon, it's old enough. See what kind of nurturing instincts you have."

With that she picked up a bucket and walked toward the house. He cradled the runt in his arms. "There, there, little one, it's all right. Moses is going to talk care of you now. You know, I read there's a word that Jews use for food they can't eat. Treyf. Good a name as any, I'd say. So you like being scratched between the ears, do you? We best follow that beguiling woman so we can get you that mash. Let's go, Treyf."

On the way to the creek, they passed an old sod house. It leaned to one side and deep green moss grew on the front. "What you use that for?" Douglas asked.

"Nothing," said Cordelia. "Ma and Pa built it when they first came out. It was their first home together. Desdemona and I were born in it, though I don't remember."

"Can I take a look inside?"

"What for?"

But he was already putting down the basket of laundry. For a door there was a wooden board, rotting at the edges, leaning across the low opening. "We haven't got time for sightseeing," she said as he moved the board. It smelled damp inside and something—a mouse, maybe—scurried into hiding.

"I can just stand up without touching my head. It couldn't have been much fun for a couple of newlyweds. There's still a few jars in here, looks like beets, maybe. And hey, what's this tin box?"

She rushed forward to grab it from him. "Never mind. Just something I keep in here."

He put his hands up. "Sorry, I don't mean to pry. You've got a right to your privacy."

She held the box against her bosom, looking down at it and biting her lip. "Okay, maybe you can see. It's foolishness, that's all. I don't need my sisters teasing on me."

"They do that, too? Sometimes I think the purpose of siblings is to torture us."

She pried off the top and gave him the box. He stepped toward the doorway to get more light. "There isn't anything but postcards in here. San Francisco. New Orleans. Paris, France—I recognize that Eiffel Tower there. What's this one? It says Amsterdam on the other side. And this one comes all the way from Tokyo. So where'd you get these?"

"In town. They arrive at the hotel and nobody picks them up. Lance, the man behind the desk, saves them for me."

"He sweet on you, this Lance?"

"I don't know and wouldn't care if he was."

"You know, all right. But why do you want these, other than the fact they're kind of pretty? And why not keep them in the house?"

"Because I want to go to all these places. Or some of them, I don't even hardly care which. I want to see cities and go to the theatre and watch people strolling down the sidewalk with their fancy hats and umbrellas, nodding at one another. I want to hear them speak languages that don't make any sense and eat food the likes of which I never seen."

Douglas nodded. "You got what's called the wanderlust in you. I met a musicianer or three with the same itch, but never a woman before."

Suddenly she grabbed his hand and pressed it between her breasts. "Do you feel it?" she asked. "That's my heart beating. Just talking about it gets my pulse racing."

He did feel it, all right. Slowly he pulled his hand away.

"That's exactly what I've got," she said, ducking into the sunshine again. "I've got a bad case of the wanderlust."

The women took turns at the stove. This evening it was Juliet, who was the least able, judged by the ribbing she took from her sisters. The brothers sat in what already felt like their places and waited expectantly while Juliet stirred the pot on the stove with a large wooden spoon. She brought a taste up to her lips and frowned.

Jimmy got up and came to her side. He looked down into the pot, where he could see lima beans, cabbage, potato, and shreds of some pale meat.

"Your looking at it won't help," she said.

"What sort of meat is that?"

"Rabbit. I've got some traps."

"I don't know if the Hebrews eat rabbit, so maybe don't say anything about it to Moses. What's wrong with it?"

"Doesn't taste that good, is all."

"I've got something that might help."

He went over to Douglas. "Give me your bottle of chili sauce."

"Not a chance."

"Come on, I need it."

"Fine." He pulled it from the pocket of his overalls. "But don't use it all up."

Jimmy went back to the stove, keeping the little bottle close to his chest. Taking off the cap, he tapped in a generous amount. "Mix it up," he whispered.

"Don't be speaking suggestive words into my daughter's ear," Johansson said.

"He's not, Pa. If he was, I would have cuffed him one. Now bring these bowls to the table," she said to Jimmy. She brought the rest.

"It's good," Moses said, his spoon on its way back to the bowl.

"Has some taste for a change," Cordelia said. "What'd you do to it?"

"Just a little something extra," she said, smiling at Jimmy.

The musicianers were more polite eaters than most men. They didn't slurp and they wiped the corners of their mouths on their sleeves. When they wanted a hunk of bread or the jar of molasses, they said *If you would* and *Thank you kindly*. They knew how to make conversation, talking about a particular stew called gumbo made in the hotel dining room where they worked and then changing the subject to the latest fashions as seen in the streets of Asheville. Afterwards, as they cleared their plates, Moses said, "We'd be pleased to play some tunes for you. Most people like our music."

Johansson said, "'Is it not strange that sheep's guts should hale souls out of men's bodies?' But that is from *Much Ado About Nothing*. I prefer the tragedies and am going to continue our reading of *Othello*."

"Is that one of them lost Bible chapters?" Douglas asked.

"It's Shakespeare," Cordelia said. "Pa reads to us every night. We practically know them off by heart."

Moses was sent out by Desdemona to feed the piglet runt. He heard Johansson intoning in his accent, "'Villainous thoughts, Roderigo,'" as he walked in the remaining light to the pens, carrying the mash and a small spoon. He began whistling "Five Miles from Town," and when he looked over the fence the piglet scrambled toward him. It stopped short and looked up nearsightedly, blunt nose twitching.

"A pair of spectacles would suit you," Moses said, leaning over to slip a hand under the runt's belly.

The last hour of the day was spent in silence, the family and their three guests in the parlour. The women read their books or knitted in the lamplight. The three brothers sat or stood, doing nothing at all. Johansson was seated at a delicate-legged desk, the slanted top inlaid with fine marquetry depicting a winged cupid playing a flute. He opened a leather-bound ledger and used a stub of pencil to write the date. He scratched his chin and put the pencil on the paper again. *Three* musiker *come today. They ate Cleopatra.*

Someone passed a little wind. Everyone was careful not to register it on their faces.

Johansson stood up. "It is time for bed. You three will sleep in the attic. The ceiling is low and you must watch your *huvud*. The ladder is at the end of the upstairs hall. There are blankets up there and you can take one of the lamps. Also some old clothes that you can use. My daughters and I will be on the floor below. I am a light sleeper, just so you know."

They went up, Moses leading the way with the lamp, passing the two small bedrooms on the second floor to the crude ladder that rose up through a trap door. Immediately Moses clanged his skull on a rafter. The roof was so low even Jimmy, sneezing from the dust, had to move with bent knees. There were a couple of old steamer trunks and a straw-filled mattress. Douglas, still snickering at his older brother, smacked his head on a slanted wall.

They found the blankets and spread them out, then stripped to their shorts. They got into bed, Jimmy in the middle with his head at the other end. "I'm glad to get out of these overalls," he said. "The blood made them stiff as I don't know what."

"A corpse, perhaps," said Moses. "Speaking of your recent slaughter, I once met a man who ate no meat. It was on account of a book he read by some Russian. This Russian believed that killing innocent animals prevented us from reaching our highest spiritual capacity."

"Do you think it's possible?" Jimmy asked. "To reach your—what is it?—your highest spiritual capacity?"

"It's an interesting question, little half-brother. Personally, I haven't met many people who have reached the third or fourth rung, never mind getting to the top."

"And I never met a Russian who wouldn't eat whatever was put in front of him," said Douglas. "Nor drink, neither."

"The truth is that by my calculation," Moses said, "your average person commits some little sin every seventeen minutes."

"Your hairy leg's touching my chin, Mose," Jimmy said.

"Can I interrupt this edifying conversation for a moment?" asked Douglas. "We ought to be thinking about our situation, not the state of mankind's soul. This place has some advantages, I admit. Food. Company. A roof over our heads."

"A *low* roof," Moses yawned.

"I'm sticking to my point. Which is that we're awfully close to the border. That seems to me a mite dangerous, considering who we're running from. And we've got no way of earning any money without a place to play. And Johansson here won't even let us play for our own pleasure."

"I believe that's three points," Moses said. "If there's many more, I'm going to be asleep before you reach the end."

"You could get yourself a job in vaudeville," Douglas said. "Moses Woltoff Clennan, the Human Interrupter. I'm trying to reach my conclusion, which is that if we got ourselves to a city, maybe we could find work. Worst comes to worst, we play on a street corner for tips."

"But is the city a place where you can reach your spiritual

capacity?" Jimmy asked.

"We've moved on from that topic," Moses said. "Douglas, you are making sense for a change. The only problem is that there isn't any big city nearby. We'd have to go all the way to Winnipeg, but that's at least five hundred miles east. Calgary is almost as far in the other direction and it seems to me I heard the place burned down. We used up our money taking the train to Bismarck."

"That wasn't even the right train," Jimmy said.

"Now, let's not start pointing fingers again. As our ma likes to say, you start that and somebody's going to lose an eye. We want to travel to a city, we'd have to hop a freight car."

"We've done it plenty of times before," Douglas said. "And we only ended up in jail twice."

"Or," Jimmy said, "we could just stay here awhile longer. Maybe work on our spiritual—"

"I don't want to hear it, Jimmy. If we did stay here we could get up our strength, having square meals and such. There's also a good argument for it."

"Let me get this straight. You and Jimmy think we ought to stay here even though we might get found."

"I think it's worth the risk, for a while anyway." Moses said.

Douglas sighed. "Well, even though this country had no revolution, I believe it is a democracy of some kind. I give in to the majority."

"Only thing," Moses went on, "there has to be no canoodling with the sisters. I believe that Johansson means business. He's got a shotgun on the wall and a knife on his belt. I wouldn't be surprised if he decided to gut the three of us for the actions of one. Agreed?"

"Agreed."

"Agreed."

"I bet you're both thinking the same thing I am," said Moses.

"That the other two can't be trusted?" asked Douglas.

"I was thinking that a person ought to abstain anyway if he

wants to reach his higher capacity," Jimmy said.

"Let me give you a tip for starting," Moses said. "Don't go murdering any more livestock."

"Come on now."

"Hush, you two," Douglas said. "Let's get some sleep."

Each settled into his place. Then there was silence but for deep breathing. An owl hooted in the distance, but none of them heard it.

The brothers were woken in the early morning by the pounding of a broom against their floor from below. They got up and searched the trunk for clothes, finding three serviceable pairs of herringbone trousers—two inches short for Moses, three inches long for Jimmy, who rolled them up. Also shirts and vests not unlike what they had worn while performing at the hotel in Asheville.

After breakfast they set to work again. And the next day and the next. Moses was cheered by the way the little pig now recognized him, squealing with what he called "porcine love" upon seeing Moses' shadow fall over the pen. After eating, the runt would invariably fall asleep in his lap. "Gosh," he said to Desdemona, "the bugger is a little stove of heat."

Meanwhile, Douglas—who had never before shown any entrepreneurial tendency—came up with a scheme for making them some money. It wasn't one that old Johansson was likely to approve of any more than music, but it had the advantage of not making any noise.

"You got an empty sod house," Douglas said to Cordelia. "You got corn. Isn't any reason we can't make us some corn liquor. There's good money to be made. People get tired of paying saloon prices."

They were moving that fall's jars of pickled vegetables into the root cellar. "I believe there's laws against it," Cordelia said.

"Course there is. Ignoring the law is step number one. Our

uncle Cyrus had a still up near Pilgrim's Knob. He was known for the quality of his product, which I believe we can reproduce, though we won't have his mountain water. What do you say?"

"I've got to think. Pa's against drinking."

"That is no surprise. Your pa doesn't seem to take to anything that might give a person pleasure, unless you count cracking your head on that Shakespit fellow. And I never heard of anyone who was against music but in favour of liquor. I believe he'd prefer to remain ignorant of the endeavour. There's a few things we need—metal pots, some stovepipe, various odds and ends. You might have it all in the kitchen and the barn. Then we'll need the ingredients—sugar, corn meal, yeast. More than you've got in the larder, so you'll have to get some at the store. You got empty jars. This can work, Cordelia. We can make money, you and your sisters and us, too."

Cordelia sat on the root-cellar step and tapped the air out of her cheek with her hand to help her think. "I like the idea of making some money, though I'm not sure what I'd do with it."

"Maybe we could do something together," Douglas ventured, trying to make eyes at her.

She didn't look back at him. "The idea scares me. But it's also kind of exciting. Life is such a routine. Every day's the same unless there's a twister or hailstorm or some other natural disaster. But we've got to be careful. And secret."

Douglas put his finger to his lips.

Juliet took Jimmy to check her wire snares. There were seventeen of them, laid out on uncultivated land, that she visited every second day. They found two rabbits, one strangled as it struggled to get loose, its eyes bugging out. The other one had been caught by a front foot and was alive but weak, kicking feebly when they approached. "Sometimes they chew their own leg off, which don't do them much good," Juliet said. She spoke softly to the animal, put one hand gently on its head, and quickly broke its neck.

Jimmy turned his head at the last moment but still heard the crack, like a twig underfoot. He said, "Did you ever wonder if you could reach a higher spiritual capacity?"

"You mean like becoming a preacher?"

"Not exactly."

"I know nine ways to cook a rabbit," she said, resetting the trap and tying the rabbit to her rope belt next to the other one. "Rabbit stew we already had. There's roasted with potatoes, there's rabbit pie, there's fried rabbit..."

They walked back to the house. Moses had his fiddle out and was sitting on the rocking chair while Douglas was on the bench under the window with his banjo. "Go get your guitar," Moses said. "We're going to play us some tunes before we forget how."

"Good idea," Jimmy said. He practically ran into the house and up the stairs to the ladder. In the band his job was to play rhythm, not very showy, but he loved it when the pulse of a tune took over his body and mind. His guitar was leaning in a corner of the attic, a slot-head, Chicago-made Regal his mother had garnished from a boarder who couldn't pay his rent. The top was all scratched up and someone had carved an erect penis on the back, but Jimmy had immediately fallen in love with that guitar. His mother said, "Learn to play and your brothers won't be half as mean to you."

Now he grabbed it by the neck and scrambled back down. He sat on the top step of the porch, half-turned to face his brothers, and started tuning up. "What we going to play?" he asked.

"I'm thinking we can start with 'Possum Up a Gum Stump,'" Moses said.

He put his bow to the strings and set the beat with his four potatoes, when Johansson's voice called, "What are you doing here?"

Moses stopped. "Respectfully, sir, we thought to indulge ourselves now that the work was done. And perhaps to give pleasure to whoever might be in earshot."

"I still see the sun up," Johansson said. "You boys have some fence-mending to do."

"I don't suppose you're using that as a figure of speech."

Douglas said, "I've got an ache in my hands from not playing." But he laid down his banjo as Johansson gave them instructions and told them where to go. They set off to the far field with a roll of barbed wire, a pair of wire cutters, a hammer and nails. It took almost half an hour of walking to reach the place where the fence was down.

"I guess we should get it over with," Jimmy said.

"What's the hurry?" asked Moses. "I say we study it awhile. You rush into a job, you just have to do it again." He fished in his pocket and came up with a tightly rolled stick of tobacco and a box of safety matches.

"Where'd you get that?" Douglas asked. "I haven't seen a smoke since we left Minnesota."

"Found it in this here shirt. Must have belonged to a hired hand since old Johansson would never partake. Wonder what happened to the man. Buried under one of these little mounds they call a hill around here. Since Jimmy is trying to cut out the vices, Douglas can share it with me."

"Thanks, Moses."

"While you two are enjoying yourselves, I'm going to dig out that rotten post," Jimmy said.

"Good," Moses mumbled with the cigarette in his mouth. "It'll give us something to watch." He lit it with a match and inhaled deeply, immediately breaking into a violent fit of coughing as he dropped the match. "Even older than I thought. And making me dizzy enough to wonder if it's regular tobacco."

"Fellas..." Jimmy said.

"It's my turn." Douglas reached out. "No changing your mind."

"Don't worry, I don't want it all for myself."

"I said, fellas, I think your match lit the grass on fire."

Moses and Douglas looked down. Indeed there was smoke rising from the stubble between them.

"Shit's creek," Moses said. "We've got to do something. Here, take out your wangs and piss on it."

"You aren't serious?" Douglas said, but Moses was already unbuttoning his trousers. The other two did the same and they stood in a small circle aiming for the burning patch.

"Douglas, you're splashing me," said Jimmy.

"Which is also a waste," Moses said. "But it looks to be out. Douglas, stamp on the patch with your boot."

"No, thank you. You can put *your* boot on our piss."

"Well, I guess it's out good enough."

The three of them stood there with trousers open. A sound made them all look up. To the south some hundred yards away was a trail of men and women walking their horses. The horses were loaded with blankets and pots and skins and rifles. There were children, too. Some of them turned their heads to look at the brothers as they passed.

"Indians," Moses sniffed.

"I wonder why they don't come over," Jimmy said.

"They're looking at us holding our dicks. Would you come over?"

"Douglas is right," Moses said. "They aren't likely to want any part of our story. Can't say I blame them."

The brothers buttoned up their trousers. They watched the line move toward the lowering sun and then they got to work.

"Today we go to *kyrka*," Johansson said, putting down his coffee cup.

"That's church, is it?" Douglas asked. "Must be Sunday. I lost track of the days. Truth is, I'm not even sure what month it is."

"You've got the century all right, then," Moses said.

"Don't make me look stupid," Douglas whispered, glancing at Cordelia.

"Oh, it was me doing that."

"Excuse me for being impertinent, Mr. Johansson," Jimmy

said. "I had the impression you weren't such a believer. No saying grace before meals, I suppose. Preferring that Shakespeare fella."

All three daughters made a sound with their lips.

"You don't have to be a believer to go to church," Desdemona said, imitating her father's accent.

"It's good discipline for the wayward mind," came from Cordelia.

Juliet intoned, "'However wickedness outstrips men, it has no wings to fly from God.' *Henry V*, right, Pa?"

The man's face showed nothing. "I'll hitch up Brutus for the ride to town," he said, rising. "You clean this table up quick. And I expect you all to behave."

The brothers proved a nuisance and were sent by the sisters to ready themselves. Upstairs they put on their vests and brushed off their bowlers. Moses had found a comb in the trunk and wet it in the basin to slick down his hair. "Can't say I'm looking forward to sitting on a hard pew and being told that I'm going to hell," he said. "Not to mention out-of-tune hymn singing. But I don't mind having a look-see round the town."

"Maybe Johansson isn't right about there being no call for music making," Douglas said. "Wouldn't hurt to ask at the saloon."

"Or sample their wares," Moses added. "You ready there, Jimmy? Why, I've never seen a vainer peacock when it comes to gussying up."

"What are you talking about? You've hogged that little mirror the whole time."

"Maybe so, but now there's no time for you. Let's go, boys. We got to have some salve applied to our souls."

The beast didn't walk much faster than a man, and the brothers found themselves jostled like Mexican jumping beans, in Moses' words. The women sat looking forward and talked among themselves, refusing to turn around no matter how coaxed. It was almost an hour before some buildings became visible and a good stretch longer before they passed the first outlying shack where a couple of very dirty children stared at them while a dog half-strangled itself trying to break its rope so it might have the pleasure of destroying them. Then came some farmers' stalls selling corn and baked goods and a blacksmith's shop and a stable. The road led right into the main street, one block of wooden buildings, all single-storey but for the hotel and saloon, although there were a few false second and third storeys, no more than wooden flats raised to make the place look grander. There was a barber shop with a white-and-red-painted pole outside, a corner bank built of stone, a general supply store, a Chinese restaurant. Behind the main street could be seen three church steeples while to the north was a grain elevator and the roof of the train station. A grizzled man was asleep on a bench in front of the telegraph office, a woman swept the dust out through the saloon doors, and a fellow in broken-down boots was yelling at a goat refusing to budge.

"Why, Kansas City hasn't got anything on this," Moses said. "Clearly I wasn't excited enough about coming here."

"I wouldn't mind some chow mein," Jimmy said.

"I wouldn't mind getting a decent shave," Douglas added.

Johansson turned up a side street, passed a few modest houses, turned again, and came to the church with the tallest steeple. There was already a line of wagons and carriages, horses and mules. Some of the horses didn't like the smell of Brutus and pulled at their traces. Johansson didn't bother tying up the animal but brought it a bucket of water and an armful of hay. The women brushed off their dresses and the men fell in behind as they entered the church. The pews were mostly full and every person turned to look at them.

"You're just in time, brother Johansson," said the preacher up front. "For your favourite part, I mean. My sermon."

People laughed. Johansson said nothing, just slid into the last pew. The others followed.

"Today," said the preacher, "I know that all of you are breathing a sigh of relief. Your crops are in, your seed is separated from the chaff. You've had a respectable harvest. No drought, no late storms to rot your bales. You're feeling that you did a lot of things right, that your bounty is because of what good farming people you are, what smart decisions you have made. But let me tell you, my friends, you aren't responsible for anything but your hard work. You know who is responsible and that's our Lord and Saviour. And don't think that the danger is passed, that all is well. Because there's always danger, in fact there's more danger now than ever. At this very moment when you're feeling so satisfied and content, the serpent is raising its head. It's a-crawling and a-slithering across your field and into your house. It's finding your bedroom and winding its way up the bedpost, the leg of your child's cot, it's opening its wide mouth and showing its glistening fangs..."

"Jesus Christ," said Douglas.

"That'd be the fella on the other side," said Moses.

"That, my friends," said the preacher, appearing to look to the back row, "is the fate awaiting you if you don't go home today and *cut* off that serpent's head. And now let us sing 'A Mighty Fortress Is Our God.'"

They came out of the church to a sky of roiling clouds. The men held their hats and stood at a distance while the women talked in clutches, and the children, tired of being well-behaved, threw themselves about. Feeling like outsiders, the brothers shuffled to the side of the church where the wagons and animals had been left.

"Why, that was about the most cheerful and edifying hour I've ever spent," Moses said. "Now what's keeping us here?"

They stood beside the buffalo, who regarded them with a placid eye. "I expect the old man is talking wheat prices or some such subject which is an endless fascination to farmers," said Douglas. "It's probably more than he speaks the rest of the week."

"What d'you imagine Brutus here is thinking about?" Jimmy asked.

"He's wondering if you got that Barlow knife on you," Moses said. "Whether or not he'll have to protect his balls. I wonder if we might take a stroll around town. Talk to the saloon keeper about playing there. He'll be closed Sunday but the man should still be there, considering there's nowhere else to go."

"I don't think we should be wandering off," Douglas said. "We ought to stay on Johansson's good side, seeing as he's giving us room and board."

"You figure we're on his good side at the moment? Oh-oh. Looks like someone's coming over with the hope of saving our miserable souls."

The other two turned to see the preacher approaching with a purposeful stride. He wore a buttoned-up white shirt with the sleeves rolled, starched trousers, and old but well-polished boots.

"You think he knows something about reaching your spiritual capacity?" Jimmy asked.

"Not if he's like every other preacher I've met," Moses said. "He's a good-looking man, though, with an impressive head of hair. Knows it, too."

The three nodded like ducks on a river as the preacher came up to them. "Sir," Jimmy said, "you put a storm of thoughts in my head."

The preacher smiled benevolently and then, swivelling on his foot, pulled back his right arm and propelled it forward, his fist cracking Moses' jaw. The brother went down like a shot deer.

"What the heck did you do that for?" Douglas asked.

"I really am sorry," the preacher said. He bent down and grabbed Moses under the arms to help him back onto his wobbling legs. A line of blood trickled from his split lower lip. "This is not in the usual line of a religious man," said the preacher, "but sometimes it's necessary." He then jabbed Moses in the stomach, causing him to bend over gasping.

"All right, that's enough now," Douglas said, stepping between them. Jimmy joined him. "You better step away."

"I'm not going to do it again," the preacher said. "And I am nothing if not a man of my word."

Moses threw up and then tried to draw breath. Jimmy grabbed his arm and helped him to slowly straighten up. "That...wasn't... fair," he managed to say. "I have to...protect my...hands."

"He's a fiddler," Jimmy said, by way of explanation.

"I know what he is, and you two as well. I know all about you. And I understand the attraction that a musicianer might hold for a young woman like Desdemona. But I have taken to calling on her these last three months and I would ask you to respect my position as her suitor."

"I...respect your position as a...son-of-a-bitch."

None of them had realized it had started to rain, but now the drops struck hard, like diamonds falling from a height. The preacher, whose actions had been hidden from his congregation, walked back to the front of his church just as people began to come around the side to fetch their wagons and buggies. Moses rubbed his jaw and said, "I don't much care for that man's preaching but I do have to admire his right hook."

"Looks like you made yourself an enemy," Douglas said. "I was hoping we might avoid that for a while. You going to stay away from her?"

"What's life without a little risk." At that moment a newspaper came blowing wetly toward them and plastered itself against Moses' legs. "The world is treating me like a trash dump," he said, peeling it off. He held it up and all three brothers read the headline, or as much of it remained on the torn sheet—

Three Musicianers Wanted for Killing of

Just then Johansson called out to them. He'd come around the side and was climbing up behind Brutus. The women were close behind him.

"That isn't the kind of fame we'd been hoping for," Jimmy said.

* * *

It took Cordelia less time than Douglas had expected to gather all the parts needed for the still. Even with some money put away, she couldn't get the ingredients in the quantities he wanted, afraid of arousing suspicion. That meant they could only make a small batch to start. They stood in the sod house, looking down on the pot and the coil and the firewood and the bags and boxes. "Is that all of it?" she asked.

"I think so. Now all we have to do is put it together. I thought I knew how from seeing my uncle's, but looking at it leaves me with a few questions. If you don't do it right, there's the chance of an explosion. And then there's the possibility of poisoning your customers. Maybe I should ask my brothers for help."

She grabbed his arm. "You can't be asking them for everything."

"But we don't keep secrets from one another."

"You sure about that? How do you know they tell you everything?"

Douglas looked down at her hand still on his arm. A load of possibilities were going round in his mind. "Maybe this isn't such a good idea."

She let her arm drop. "So we won't make any money. And I won't ever see Paris and Istanbul and the mountains of Peru. Men are a disappointing species, and that is a fact." She turned on her heel, ducked her head, and went out.

"That stings," he said, going after her. "Hold up, Cordelia! We'll do it then, and all by ourselves."

Moses had never even had a dog, and now this little pig wanted only to follow loyally at his heels. If he leaned down to scratch its belly, the ridiculous thing grunted as if in ecstasy. When he had some new chore to do, he took the pig along with him. It always kept nearby, snuffling, snorting, or sneezing, like a strange child talking to itself in a made-up language.

Done for the day, he slipped into the house to get his fiddle sack. He wasn't one to feel down, but that preacher's punch had taken the air out of him and he needed something to lift his spirits again. This time he'd walk farther from the house so old man Johansson couldn't go all sour on him. He passed the outhouse and kept going till he found a few spindly trees not worth the effort of turning into firewood and stood behind them. The pig rooted around. "See what you think of these, Treyf," he said, setting his hat back on his head. He played "New Five Cents" and "Grasshopper on a Sweet Potato Vine." The pig proved equally indifferent to them

Just as he was starting up "June Apple," Moses saw someone coming around the outhouse. Desdemona. She must have seen him, because she was walking straight toward the trees. Maybe he had forgotten some chore he was supposed to do. Or she was going to tell him that she was engaged to that fraudulent preacher. "That man ought to be selling patent medicine," he said to Treyf, who responded with a toot. One thing that men and beasts shared in common, Moses thought, was the pleasure of passing wind.

As she grew closer, her hands behind her back, he found her expression impossible to read. But he stepped around the trees as she came up to him. "Let me just say, Desdemona, that I'm sorry for whatever I done. My imperfections are legion, just ask anybody in Asheville. But my intentions are—"

"I've got something," she said.

"What?"

"It's behind my back."

"Am I supposed to guess? What if I get it right? You've got a rutabaga? Some hard candy? I sure hope it isn't a lady's pistol."

"No, it's this."

She brought out a mandolin. It had a slim neck and a pretty headstock and its pear-shaped back was made from strips of yellow maple alternating with dark rosewood.

"Now, where'd you get that taterbug?"

"It belonged to my ma. But she died when I was little and I don't remember ever hearing it played. I don't even know what it's supposed to sound like."

"Like a mosquito in your ear, to some folks. But it can sound pretty nice. You're holding it like a dead goose. Let me take a look."

She handed it to him and he turned it over in his hands, looked through the strings into the sound hole. "Says on the label it's made by the Vega Company of Boston, Mass. There's a plectrum rattling around inside it, I'll get it out and then tune her up."

He turned it upside down and gave the mandolin a vigorous shake until the small triangle fell into the stubble at their feet. He plucked his own fiddle for the notes, then worked the mandolin's tuning knobs, holding it slightly away in case, he said, a string decided to break and take out his eye. "It's easier to play these things sitting down," he said, crouching to strum it. "Not bad. Now, I'm no raggedy-rag, mud-stepping mandolin player, but I should be able to squeeze out a tune."

He started to play, picking the strings with the plectrum and dancing his fingers on the neck.

Desdemona clapped like a little girl. "Show me," she said, tucking her dress beneath her as she sat cross-legged beside him. The pig came up and tried to climb onto her lap.

"Get over, Treyf. Here, hold it like this. That's right. Now take the plectrum between your finger and your thumb. More like this. Hold it with the neck pointing sort of up but not too high and keep your hand loose, don't strangle it. Now see if you can make that plectrum go up and down across the strings."

She got out a few uneven notes, then missed the string altogether, then dropped the plectrum. "It's hard," she said.

"Course it is. A person isn't born playing music. But you sure look good holding it."

She picked up the plectrum and started again. "Teach me a

tune," she said. "Something easy to start."

"All right. First tune I fiddled was 'Boil 'Em Cabbage Down.' That ought to do."

"How can you get along in this world and not know how to shoot a gun?"

Jimmy looked at the rifle in Juliet's hands. It made him nervous, as guns had always done. He was not about to tell her that he did shoot a gun—once. That he'd done it with his eyes closed and the shooting of that gun was the reason he and Moses and Douglas weren't in North Carolina anymore.

"It never came up," he said.

"Well, if you want to be useful around here, you got to learn. Today we're going to get us some groundhog. They got dark meat but taste mild if you cut out the glands and cook them right."

He looked over the scrabbly earth and saw what looked like holes here and there. "Do we do something to get them to come out? Make their love call, maybe?"

"I'd like to hear you do that. Nah, they'll just come out on their own if you wait a while. Then you shoot. You've got to move slowly so as not to scare them back down. They've got good eyesight, too. Look down the barrel. Squeeze the trigger slow. There's going to be kickback, so stay loose or you'll get hurt. Now go ahead and take it."

He did as he was told. They turned and waited. It wasn't three minutes before a twitching nose could be seen. Then the groundhog scrambled halfway out, using its claws to pull itself up. Sniffed the air.

"Now?" he whispered.

"Wait for it to come all the way out. You want to see its fat body before you shoot."

The groundhog emerged, darted forward, stopped. It began to nip at the remaining grass. Jimmy wanted to miss deliberately but was afraid of what Juliet would think of him. He decided to try for a close shot that wouldn't make him look too bad. Squinting with one eye, he sighted the animal's rump, then moved the barrel an inch to the right. The kick knocked him backwards and the noise made his ears clang.

"Bull's eye!" Juliet whooped. "And I forgot to tell you that gun shoots to the left. Let's go get it." She jumped into the air, kicking her feet, and began walking toward the groundhog.

Jimmy followed. "Is it really dead?" he said glumly.

"It isn't sleeping. If we're lucky it's a mother and now the little ones'll starve, too. Tell you what, let's go celebrate with a swim in the creek."

It seemed as if killing things was turning out to be one of his few talents. He didn't feel much like swimming but he followed her anyway. Following her was what he seemed to do now. They got to the bank and she started to unbutton her dress. He turned.

"You don't have to look the other way," she said.

So he turned back and watched her remove several underlayers until she was standing there naked. She had a furious patch of black hair between her legs.

"I didn't say you could stare. You coming or what?"

He fell over trying to pull off his boot. His own patch of hair was red as a rooster's comb. He saw her looking at it.

"I've seen the way you moon over me," she said. "You're in love with me, aren't you, Jimmy?"

He felt the blush rising from his neck up to his face. "Yes, ma'am," he said.

"I thought so. Desdemona said no man would ever love a tomboy squirt like me, but I knew she was wrong. I knew it."

She skipped down the bank and into the water, hooting with pleasure.

The sun slipping past the western edge of the world. A storm in the distance, a streak of lightning.

A man on a horse.

The man held himself wearily, his Stetson pulled hard over his ears. The horse's mouth foaming. "I smell me a river," the man said. "Going to get us both a drink. Soon as I see what we've got here."

He dismounted and looked at the skeletal remains of a cow, some of the ribs scattered. The ashes from a fire nearby. He kicked at it, raising dust, then got back onto the horse. They reached the creek and he got down again, leading the horse by the reins. He let it drink, filling his own canteen. He knocked the dust off his clothes, took off his hat, and poured a trickle over his head. He ran his tongue over his gold tooth.

"They're around here, all right. I can smell them. Finish your drinking. We'll find them soon enough and then we'll do what we set out for."

On Saturday morning Johansson hitched Brutus to the wagon and loaded two hogs into the back. He planned to swap them for one of Schevenko's cows to replace the one the brothers had dined on. There were a few Swedes in these parts but far more Ukrainians, and Johansson had learned some words of the language to make trading easier. The farmer had two married daughters with new babies, and the sisters decided to go along so they could coo over the little ones. At least, Desdemona and Cordelia wanted to, and they made Juliet come, too.

The brothers watched the wagon pull away, leaving a small whirlwind of dust. Moses stroked the piglet in his arms and said, "Say goodbye to your aunt and uncle piggies and don't think upon their fate. You see, boys, this creature isn't the least concerned. How much we care for our own flimsy lives and how little for the lives of others."

"That pig makes you deep," noted Douglas.

"It is a well-known fact that of all the farm animals, a pig is the most likely to induce philosophizing."

"What you suppose we're supposed to do while they're gone?"

Jimmy asked.

"How quickly they have broken you, youngster. Already you've got no will of your own. I aim to see about making some money with our God-given talents. That is, I'm going to hoof it into town and talk to that saloon owner about playing there."

"That's quite a ways," Douglas observed.

"If you two come with me and we bring our instruments, we might get a chance to play then and there, seeing as it's Saturday. What do you say?"

The other two agreed. They put on their vests and hats and took a long drink of water and a biscuit from the kitchen. Then they set out, instruments in hand. Moses had to put the pig back in the pen so it wouldn't follow him. They saw nothing for the first five miles but a small family graveyard and a dead snake. The sun wasn't overly warm but the ground was hard, and it was becoming an unspoken contest, which brother would be the first to start complaining. One of them might have given in if the sound of wheels didn't make them turn. They saw a boy driving a donkey cart. Douglas put two fingers in his mouth and whistled while Jimmy waved his hands.

"You really think he's likely to miss us?" Moses asked.

The boy brought the cart to a halt. He looked about twelve and had a crossed eye that must have made him the object of cruel ridicule among the other children. "W-w-where you g-g-going?" the boy said.

His troubles were clearly compounded. "Marrakesh," said Moses. "We hear it's nice this time of year."

"We're going to town," Douglas said. "Sure would be nice if you could give us a lift."

"I can t-take one of y-y-you. Nellie won't p-p-p-pull any more."

"We could draw lots," Jimmy said. "Or we could ask the boy to pick a number from one to ten..."

Moses stepped up into the cart. "I'll get the negotiations underway. Everything will be all sorted out by the time you two get there."

The boy flicked the reins and the mule started up, causing Moses to fall back into the seat. Douglas shouted after them, "Don't you run up a tab and drink up our earnings before we even play a note."

The boy's name was Vernon Pritchett and he'd been an orphan since the age of six, when his folks were killed in a cyclone. Vernon himself had been lifted up in his bed and set down again half a mile away, still sleeping. Nobody had adopted him, or rather everybody had, for he was passed from one household to another every few days. The boy enjoyed recounting the various unusual deaths in the area. There was the farmer who stood in his field shouting obscenities at the sky for raining too late to do any good. The apothecary's wife who got struck by lightning. There was the fat man who liked taking baths in the muddy bottom of a slough, only to get sucked all the way under. The bride who decided on her wedding night that she'd married the wrong man and jumped out the second-storey bedroom window, impaling herself on an upturned harrow.

As the boy's stories got more gruesome, his stutter lessened.

"The demise of your own kin has given you a morbid cast of mind," Moses said.

"Yes, sir," said the boy. "And then there was the man who tried to rescue a baby..."

Moses wasn't so sure he wouldn't rather be walking. When they reached town the boy pulled up the donkey before the saloon. "What's the name of the owner?" Moses asked as he got down.

"Mister F-F-Fefferman. He ain't always f-f-friendly."

"I've dealt with plenty like him. Thank you, young Vernon, for the ride and the heavenly roll call. When we earn some money, I will be sure to give you a bob or two."

One of the saloon doors was propped open by a spittoon to

air the place out. Inside it was considerably more refined than Moses had expected, with red-checked cloths on the tables, the floor swept clean, and no lingering odour of piss or vomit. No sign of whores, either, just a couple of solitary drinkers, one at the bar and the other at a table reading what looked like a very old newspaper. The proprietor himself was wiping down the bar. Moses had never walked into a saloon and *not* seen the proprietor doing the same. The man wore a small cap and had wire glasses and a well-trimmed beard. Wearing a hat indoors, Moses knew, was a habit of the Jewish race. Perhaps they had other such inverse habits, such as men pissing while sitting down or eating soup with a knife.

He hadn't realized that Vernon was behind him until the boy said, "Mr. F., th-th-this here's a m-m-m-usicianer."

"Mr. Fefferman, I believe," Moses said.

"Thank you for reminding me," said the man.

"Me and my two brothers, who are promenading in this direction as we speak, make up a fine string band. We play music that is good for listening or dancing or even ignoring if desired. Our sound makes people thirsty for drink and increases profits. We are looking for a place to play."

The man took off his glasses and began to clean them with the same rag. "And what would you need to be paid?"

"Our usual rate is a dollar apiece and two drinks each and anything we can make in the hat."

"I can do a dollar for the three of you."

"You drive a hard bargain, sir. I expect you'll start to get busy in another hour or two. We can start then—"

Behind him came the sound of jangling spurs. Moses turned and got only a half glimpse of a man in a Stetson and a long coat wiping the dust from his face before he dropped to his knees. He crawled under the cloth hanging over the nearest table. The proprietor had no doubt seen every sort of behaviour imaginable, for he said nothing. Beneath the table dangled two legs that Moses realized belonged to the boy, Vernon.

"W-w-what you doing und-d-d-er there?" asked Vernon.

"*Shhh.* Act like I'm not here. Does the man who just come in have a moustache? Curled at the ends in an expression of comical vanity?"

"Why, he d-d-d-oes. H-how did you—"

"Never mind!" Moses hissed.

The man's spurs jangled as he walked up to the bar.

"What can I get you?" asked Fefferman.

"Bourbon."

"I haven't got bourbon. I got whisky."

"That'll do."

Sound of a glass on the bar, the cork being pulled from a bottle. Swallowing.

"Another."

"I better see some money."

"I've got American dollar bills."

"Good enough. Here you go."

Sound of a hork and a spit. "I'm looking for some men."

"That so."

"Three brothers, only they don't look like brothers. Musicianers."

"We had a Salvation Army brass band come through a while back. Not too fond of the sound myself. We might get more music if the town council starts up that parsnip festival they've been talking about, but in my opinion that particular vegetable is not favoured enough to be so honoured."

"You do talk a lot. What's the kid eating from that bowl, anyway? It's awful red."

"Borscht. Very popular around here. Now, the beet—that is a vegetable that deserves a festival."

Give me a bowl, then. And some bread."

The man was a noisy eater. Moses listened to the slurping while feeling his lower half going numb.

Fefferman said, "You want a room, maybe? We got a nice one available. Actually, they are all available. Clean sheets."

"You got whores?"

"This is not Gomorrah."

"Then I prefer to sleep with my horse." Sound of coins. "I'll be back."

Moses saw dusty alligator boots go past the table. He waited for the sound of spurs to recede before crawling out again. "My leg feels petrified," he said. "And now the tingles are coming on. Mr. Fefferman, you've got a cool head on your shoulders. I appreciate you not giving me away."

"Wouldn't have done me any good and I would have just had to clean up the mess. Guess you won't be making music here after all. Which brother is he after?"

"Well, the youngest of us pulled the trigger, but I imagine any of us would do."

"But Mr. M-M-Moses," said Vernon, his mouth red with borscht. "There's th-three of you and only wha-wha-one of him."

Moses put his hat back on his head. "Those odds aren't as good as they sound on paper."

They were gratified to find the three sisters sitting on the porch with a lamp, waiting for them. As the brothers entered the circle of light, Moses said, "I feel like we've come to the promised land."

"Where have you been?" Desdemona asked. "We thought maybe you run off for good."

"We took a stroll and got a little lost," Douglas said.

Now Cordelia stepped forward. "We know you're lying. Vernon Pritchett come by in his donkey cart and told us about the man. Said he looked like a gunslinger. Had an evil glint in his eye."

"I guess we should've asked Vernon to take an oath of silence," Jimmy said, waving away a moth. "No use keeping it to ourselves now."

"Keeping what to yourselves?" asked Juliet.

"It wasn't our fault," Douglas said. "Who knew he'd take it so hard? Well, maybe it's a little bit Jimmy's fault."

"It isn't! This damn moth thinks *I'm* the lantern."

Desdemona stamped her foot. "No swearing, thank you. And this is no way to tell us."

All three men looked abashed. "I'll do the telling," Moses said. "My brothers just end up tying themselves in knots. We did us some touring last winter and spring. Virginia, Kentucky, Tennessee. Playing for dances, for teas, for whoever would hire us. Then we worked our way back to Asheville for the summer season. Elevation of the town makes it cooler, you see. And there's the view of the mountains. It's a genteel place and lots of wealthy people come in eager to spend their money."

"You sound like a tourist brochure," said Douglas. "We found ourselves a job in a hotel on Haywood Street, and another playing dances on an open-air stage by the river. At night we slept on our mama's porch as she had the rooms rented out."

"I suspect," Moses said, "that she was having a dalliance with a man come all the way from India. But we figured she was too old to give us another brother."

"You are straying off the subject," Jimmy said. "As part of the summer festivities the city council decided to have a music contest. Naturally, we put our names in, hoping to win the fifty dollars. That's when this cowboy-looking fella approached us. We'd all noticed him watching us play the last week or so. Brand-new Stetson and boots, always freshly barber-shaved. Big ugly dog at his heels."

"I never seen a dog slobber more," Moses said. "Looked like it wanted to eat somebody's leg. This fella was the only man in town that wore a holster and gun like it was the frontier. Finally he came up to us and said he played the concertina. Wanted to join our band for the contest and maybe stay on. Said he'd been working real hard at it. Naturally, we weren't too keen to have another player to have to split our earnings. Plus we're a string band. I'm something of a purist in these matters, and no wheezing squeezebox—"

"All right, Mose, don't go flogging that horse again," Douglas said. "This man said his name was Jack Endicott, like we ought to have heard of him. We didn't see much choice, given the way he liked to rest his hand on that gun, but to let him come play with us in the hotel restaurant the next day. Give him a tryout. So he came and he brought that ugly dog with him. I mean, the thing had warts."

"That fella couldn't keep time," Jimmy said.

"That's for sure," Moses said. "Always half a beat behind. Then he'd race to catch up and get ahead of us. And he made that thing sound like a cat having its innards removed. Remember his face? It got red as a wailing babe with the effort. He had his tongue sticking out in concentration, which was not a pretty sight for a diner."

"I felt kind of bad for him," Douglas said. "Trying so hard. But he just wasn't born to it. So Moses came up with a plan."

"Let me tell it, then. We told Jack Endicott that we drew a pretty high number and wouldn't be playing in the contest until around eight in the evening. In fact we drew number seventeen and got to play around six. The contest was held in this building on Patton Street and it was packed with people. We played 'Shaking Down the Acorns.'"

"No we didn't," Douglas said. "We played 'Hell Broke Loose in Georgia.'"

"It doesn't matter to us," said Cordelia.

"Whatever we played," Jimmy said, "we rang that last note and got out of there quick. When Endicott showed up, we were nowhere to be seen. But then we were declared the winner and had to come back around ten to get our prize. Everyone was clapping and hollering as we got our money and a nice ribbon, too."

"That felt awfully good," Moses said.

"But there he was," Douglas went on. "In the front row, glaring at us. With that damn dog sitting at his feet, ready to tear our throats out."

"They looked right ready for murder all right, both of them," Moses said. "In fact Endicott told everyone he saw that he was going to come after us. Overnight we got as famous for our upcoming demise as we did for winning. When we showed up at the restaurant the next day, the owner says, 'I hear I've got to find myself a new band.'"

"Ma told us we ought to go and reason with the man," Douglas said. "She said to flatter him, hand over part of the money, tell him he can join the band, and then get the hell out of town. Pardon our ma's language. We didn't have a better idea so we went to his hotel."

"One of the city's less reputable places," Moses said.

"A whorehouse," said Jimmy.

"Only partly a whorehouse," said Douglas. "There was also card playing."

"This is longer than *King Lear*," said Desdemona. "Only more of a farce."

"So we got to the hotel," Moses said. "And up to his room on the second floor. The door wasn't locked, so we got the idea of just peeking in. Maybe we'd get some other idea how to deal with this. And there was Endicott asleep in his bed, the covers pulled up. On the table by the door lay his pistol. Douglas here knocked over the cowboy's boots with his own big feet and the man woke straight up. He saw us and his face looked as angry as a hornet. He shouted out, 'Kill them!' And who emerged from underneath the covers but that big, ugly, slobbering dog. It took one look with bloodshot eyes, started to growl and bare its teeth, and then it sprang right for us."

"Jimmy shot it," Douglas said. "To give him credit, he was the only one of us who thought to pick up the gun."

"What sort of man lets a dog sleep in his bed?" Moses asked. "That alone has to make you wonder."

"I swear, I don't like killing things," Jimmy said. "I've just had a string of bad circumstances."

"Well, he shot that dog, and Jack Endicott started bawling. He's holding the dead weight of it and crying like a girl. We took the opportunity to bolt. But we knew we couldn't stay in Asheville, or anywhere nearby. That we had to go somewhere he couldn't reach us, at least for a few months. So we headed north."

"Northwest, as it turned out," said Douglas. "On account of Moses' inability to read a train schedule."

"I can read a train schedule as well as the next man. It had a piece ripped out. Anyway, we figured that Endicott wouldn't cross the border. We had this image of a line of Canadian Mounted Police protecting us, which was perhaps a little naive."

"Before we even got to the border we ran out of money," Douglas said. "So we started walking. And walking. And then Jimmy saw your cow, may she rest in peace."

"So I guess it turns out this Jack Endicott doesn't care about any border," Juliet said. "And now he's here and looking for you."

"That's about the size of it," Jimmy said. "Shoot, I think I swallowed that moth."

They stopped talking, all of them. The porch creaked under Moses' foot.

At last Desdemona said, "Wash up and go to bed. I guess we're mixed up in this, too."

The brothers weren't given any chores in the morning and so they passed some time up in the attic, playing rummy with a set of cards Moses found in the trunk.

"I never seen a pack of cards that wasn't greasy," Moses said. "They must make new ones, but damned if I ever saw one."

"I wish I won every so often," Jimmy said, picking up his hand.

"Problem is you telegraph what you've got with every twitch of your youthfully ratty face."

"Maybe you should hold off the insults," Douglas said, "given the fact we are likely to die in the next day or two. It isn't going to take Endicott long to find out where we are."

"Well, I don't see any point in trying to run," Moses said, picking up a card. "He's got a horse and we've got flat feet. What I'm more concerned about at the moment is old Johansson not putting us to work."

"You think he's planning on giving us the heave-ho?" Jimmy asked. "Then we'll be homeless *and* about to die."

"That's what the cowboy novels call a cruel turn of fate."

They heard someone slide open the trap door. Desdemona's upper half appeared. "Pa wants to talk to you."

"If he wants money for our room and board," Moses said, "tell him we'll pay next week. Get it, boys? Next week..."

The other two shook their heads. Desdemona retreated and they put down the cards and went down the ladder and then the stairs. Johansson was sitting at his usual place at the table while the sisters were standing. "You wanting to speak to us, Mr. Johansson?" Douglas asked.

"I am thinking of this cowboy who is coming to get you, or so my daughters tell me. For reasons I don't understand, they feel some responsibility for you to stay alive. Or maybe it's because they've taken a shine to you, which only shows I have failed to raise them right. In any case, I believe there is nothing to be done but to face this Endicott. Maybe one or two of you won't be dead at the end of it."

"Very comforting words," Moses said. "Actually, I may have another idea how we might be saved."

"Why didn't you tell us before?" Jimmy asked.

"Just popped into my head. Happens sometimes with a man of my intelligence."

"Well, don't keep us waiting," Douglas said. "We could use a good laugh."

"All right. We hold a dance. Tomorrow night in your barn,

Mr. Johansson. Jack Endicott won't be able to resist hearing us one last time, and maybe trying to join in on that toy instrument of his. He won't try to kill us before then, and we'll be prepared when he arrives."

"Prepared to do what?" Desdemona asked.

"All right, so I've got half a plan. We just have to figure out the rest."

"Sounds like you're making up a story but can't come up with the big finish," Douglas said. "Which makes it a piss-poor story."

"Maybe," Cordelia said, "my sisters and I can come up with the finish."

"We're not fussy about whose idea it is," Jimmy said. "Anyway, if it's a good one, Moses will just claim it as his own."

"Enough with the funny business," Johansson said. "We'll hold this dance. But not tomorrow. Tonight. And we have a lot of work to do."

Johansson went to town to find Vernon Pritchett and send him in his donkey cart to every house and farm for twenty miles around, telling them there was a dance going to happen in Johansson's barn, entry ten cents (a penny for children), and to spread the word. Meanwhile, the others started to get the barn ready. They rolled hay bales to the side, strung up paper decorations, hung oil lamps so they wouldn't light the place on fire, brought out crates for sitting. The sisters started baking up a storm. Johansson returned, looked in on them, and turned around again to take care of the livestock.

"I hope people actually show up tonight," Douglas said, running a rake over the barn's dirt floor.

"I expect they will." Moses was up on a ladder, pushing back a hay bale with a pitchfork. "When's the last time they had an entertainment around here that didn't involve somebody speaking in tongues?"

"That reminds me, maybe the preacher will show up and you

can let him punch you in the nose again."

"I just thought of something," Jimmy said. "We need a dance caller."

"Taken care of," Moses said. "Vernon knows a woman at the feed store in town. Told me himself. I sent a note with old Johansson for the boy to give to her. As for the preacher, this time I won't be taken by surprise."

"I've never seen you win a fight, surprised or not," Douglas said. "But on another subject, maybe we ought to scratch out a list of tunes to play."

"Don't worry, I've got them all in my head."

"Maybe this time you could actually tell us the name of the next one before you start sawing away."

The barn door opened; it was Desdemona in a halo of late-afternoon light. "We've got a cold supper on the table," she said. "Come and eat before folks start showing up."

"Let's hope it's not our last supper," Douglas said.

Moses smiled. "That's a good one, brother. I should have thought of it myself."

The pickled fish was a Swedish specialty and not easy for the brothers to get down. They followed it with bread and copious amounts of coffee. Then the three, who had been working in their purple overalls, changed into trousers. They buttoned up their shirts and vests and found some string ties in the trunk and brushed their bowlers and passed around a comb. They picked up their instruments and left the house for the barn. An old swayback horse and rider were coming down the road, leading a mule burdened with various satchels and bundles. The man on the horse wore a tweed suit and cap and wire glasses.

"Rather citified," Moses said. "I hope he isn't a government employee come to collect the head tax."

"I believe that's only for Chinese," Douglas said.

"That doesn't seem fair," Jimmy said.

"Then you go up to him and insist on paying it," Moses said.

The man pulled on the reins and patted his horse on the neck before lowering himself with some difficulty, for it turned out that he had an artificial leg beneath his trousers. "Afternoon, gentlemen," he said, tipping his cap.

"And to you," Moses said. "Any chance you're lost? Looking for Philadelphia, say?"

"Ha ha, no sir. I'm travelling the country and heard there were some musicianers here. Finbine's the name, Julius Finbine, photographer at your service."

"You wanting to take our photograph?" Jimmy asked.

"That was my very thought," the man said with a smile. "I have first-rate equipment with me here, ideal for outdoor settings." He backed up to the mule and padded a large square box peeking up from one of the satchels. "Photographic postcards are very popular. Get several copies, send some to your friends and loved ones. Use them for promotion. And my rates are very reasonable. I'll send them to you within the month."

The brothers looked at one another. They hadn't been photographed since childhood, sitting with their mother, who held the infant Jimmy in her arms as they posed before a backdrop depicting the Parthenon.

Moses said, "The idea of being photographed with our instruments does appeal to my vanity."

"How reasonable?" Douglas asked. "Reasonable as in free? Because we haven't got any money."

The man's smile vanished. "Well, I'm sorry to hear of your straitened circumstances. You would have made an excellent subject." He tipped his cap and turned back to his horse.

"Now, hold on there, Julius Finbine," Moses said. "We've got a dance about to start in that there barn. People have to pay to come in, but we can let you come to the dance gratis. There will be plenty of opportunity for securing sittings for the next day. I believe it will be worth your while."

The man rubbed his chin. "I am here after all," he said, putting on his smile again. "I don't see why not."

"But you've got to hurry up and do it before people start coming."

"I am nothing if not efficient," the man said. Already he was setting a wooden tripod on the ground and then screwing the square black box onto it. Next came the cloth hood. Finally he prepared the flash, holding it up with one hand as he slipped his head beneath the fabric.

"Get closer together, please," came his muffled voice. "A little to your right so as to be centred before the house. That's it. Instruments in front of you. You must keep very still. One, two..."

Whoosh went the flash. Moses said, "That reminded me of a magician I once saw perform in Charlotte. Except we don't get to see any woman dressed like an Egyptian queen disappear behind a curtain. Fellas, looks like we have us some customers."

Three wagons were approaching.

"Tarnation," said Jimmy. "We've got no time to warm up."

"No," Moses said. "But we had our photograph taken. Now we are immortal."

Desdemona had already brought out three chairs for the musicianers, positioned at the far end of the barn, along with a jug of water and three mugs. They sat themselves as usual, Moses and his violin in the middle, the guitar to his right and the banjo to his left and both turned slightly toward him. He tuned by ear, then played a long note on his D string for the other two to match. Douglas' banjo, bought in a pawn shop in Corpus Christi, was an S. S. Stewart with most of the abalone inlay missing. He'd filled in the spaces with green house paint.

Cordelia and Juliet hurried into the barn. "They're coming fast," Cordelia said breathlessly. "Desdemona's dropping their dimes into a flour sifter and it sounds like hail on the roof!"

Just then a group of three appeared hesitantly in the doorway, like black paper cut-outs against the light outside. Behind them were two more. A family of seven, the mother holding a baby, were next, and all of them in their Sunday best.

"Time to let her go," Moses said. He sawed a quick four potatoes and launched into "Buffalo Gals." He persisted in his annoying habit of making Douglas and Jimmy figure out what the tune was, but now Jimmy started to boom-chuck the chords on his guitar and Douglas hit the main notes to underline the melody while pushing the rhythm with his downstrokes and thumb drone. When Moses next looked up, he saw twenty or more people watching and listening, some of them swaying to the music, others leaning close and talking into each other's ears. Past them all came a woman wearing long pigtails like a young girl, although she must have been past fifty. Immediately he knew she was the dance caller. Moses raised the head of his fiddle to give his brothers notice and brought the tune to a screeching halt like a train trying not to hit a cow on the tracks.

"You sound good, boys," the woman said. She wore a buckskin jacket and a pair of jodhpurs. "Let's bring the tempo down a notch or two for the first couple, so people don't trip over their feet while they get the hang of it."

"Yes, ma'am," Moses said, happy to respond to her authoritative tone. A dance caller had to know how to control things. She turned around, put her hands around her mouth, and told people to partner up and form circles of four. By now there were a good twenty-five or thirty souls in the barn, but some of them were sitting on hay bales or hanging back, along with some young kids and a few frail elderly who'd found a place to sit by their relatives. The orphan boy, Vernon Pritchett, had taken up a high place by climbing a tower of bales that went halfway to the rafters. Moses put bow to strings and started in on "Icy Mountain."

The woman started calling and the dancers raised their linked hands, moved to the centre of their circles and out again before separating into pairs. Juliet began to sell baked goods from behind a plank set over a couple of sawhorses, some children and a few adults already waiting with money in hand. Old Johansson had come in without the brothers noticing and now leaned against a stack of bales with his shotgun leaning discreetly beside him. That had been the daughters' simple and practical solution to the question of what to do once they had lured in the man with the Stetson and the curling moustache. Some of the dancers were getting mixed up and laughing, but overall they were moving like shapes in a kaleidoscope. When the dance ended, people clapped and the brothers smiled and took swigs of water from their mugs.

Cordelia joined Juliet to help her surreptitiously fill teacups with moonshine for the men who put their money down.

"Bow to your partner, bow to your corner, circle left and promenade..."

Rising dust from the moving feet made patterns in the lamplight. The old people nodded their heads or just watched with glassy eyes. Young children grew bolder and began to chase each other around the perimeter of the dance floor. A couple of teenage boys got in a pushing match and had to be separated. A young woman watched a certain young man ask somebody else to dance and broke into weeping.

They played "Half Past Four." Faces began shining with sweat. More people arrived. Babies fell asleep and got passed from hand to hand. A boy of five or six stood near Moses and would not take his eyes off the violin.

They played "Broken Down Gambler." Somebody knocked over a lamp that caught some loose straw, but Johansson rushed over to put it out with a bucket of water. There were whispers about fornication in the field behind the barn.

They played "Merriweather." A woman got the hiccups and couldn't stop. A boy playing with a knife jabbed himself in the thigh. A young woman slapped a not-quite-so-young man hard.

An elderly woman with a wrinkled apple-doll face announced that her granddaughter had just given birth to a boy out in the wagon.

They played "Ways of the World." Bats living under the roof swooped over the dancers' heads on their way out the barn door. The moon appeared. Three marriage proposals were proffered, two accepted, and the third poor soul laughed at so hard that he ran out and did not return.

The brothers took a break. Jimmy went to speak to Juliet while Moses and Douglas tried to beat each other to the outhouse. As they walked over the dry stalks, Moses looked up and said, "Damn, there's nothing finer than playing for a dance on a beautiful night." They reached the outhouse, and Douglas deferred to his older brother, who opened the door. There, with his trousers down and a few pages from the Eaton's catalogue crumpled in his hand, sat the preacher.

The preacher stared open-mouthed, aware of his disadvantage.

"Well, well," Moses said. "Don't you move, good sir. We don't want any glimpse of your dangling balls."

"Go on," Douglas said to his brother. "Give him back what he already gave to you. Aim for his chin."

"What if he moves suddenly? I could end up head-first down the hole. Let's think on this a moment."

Moses closed the door, jamming his foot against the bottom of it. They could hear the sound of a belt buckle and then the flimsy door rattled.

"All right," called the preacher from inside. "Let me out now. We're all good Christians here. You don't want to linger around this smell longer than you have to."

"First of all, I'm no Christian," Moses said. "Second of all, I'm not going to let you out until you swear on Mother Mary's head that you won't throw any more punches."

"Don't you worry. I'm done with Desdemona, anyway. I swear to it."

Moses hesitated a moment, then moved his foot and stepped back.

The door swung open and the preacher stepped out.

"You're really done with Desdemona?"

"Yes, sir. I've decided that I'm more partial to Cordelia. Plus she's younger, which is an advantage for child-bearing. And she don't wear trousers like the youngest."

"So it's Cordelia you're wanting?" Douglas asked.

"That's the Lord's truth."

"All right then." Douglas hit him in the jaw, sending him back into the outhouse door. The preacher slid slowly to the ground.

The two brothers looked down at him. "See what you done," Moses said. "He's blocking the door. Now neither of us can get in."

Douglas used his own boot to push the man to the side. "Problem solved."

The brothers did their business and headed back to the barn, where Jimmy was waiting impatiently. Moses picked up his fiddle and launched into "Sally Ann." The dancers were if anything more eager. And as they played one tune after another, it began to look as if Jack Endicott wouldn't show up. The brothers smiled at one another as they played. A few families with young ones began to say their goodbyes to friends and head for their wagons, but most did not want to miss even a single dance.

And then it came time for the final dance and they started to play the "Westphalia Waltz," "named for a podunk town in Texas that doesn't deserve such a pretty tune," Moses said to nobody in particular as he set his bow. He started to play, and only then, looking about so he might remember the hot faces moving in pairs over the dirt floor and the onlookers swaying along the sides, did he see Jack Endicott. Leaning against a pile of bales, his Stetson in his hand, his moustache curled to perfection, a piece of straw dangling from between his teeth.

"Looks like we got company after all," Moses said, even as he kept playing.

"What?" Douglas called, not being able to hear over their own music making.

"Endicott." Moses pointed with the scroll of his fiddle and the other two looked until they spotted him. Jack Endicott didn't look worked up. In fact he looked positively mild, and when some people moved out from in front of him, they could even see him tapping one of his alligator-skin boots. They extended the waltz, afraid to end it now that they'd seen him, but he just placed his Stetson carefully on his head, nodded to those around him, and walked casually out of the barn.

By this time Johansson had seen him, too, and had his shotgun in his hands. And so did young Vernon, who raced after the man and stood in the doorway watching him go. Moses signalled to the others and they brought the waltz to a close.

"That's it, everybody," said the caller. "You all get home safe now. Thanks for coming."

She came over to the band and shook their hands. "Head over to Desdemona," Moses said, "and tell her I said to give you a quarter of the take at the door."

"Much obliged, it'll come in handy."

She walked away. Vernon had been standing behind her, itching to say something, and now he ran up. He was squeezing the life out of his own cap. "He's g-g-gone," the boy said. "On h-h-his horse. Galloped away."

"Thanks, young fella. Now you go off to Desdemona yourself. Tell her she's to give you fifty cents."

"Yes, sir!"

Moses reached down to find his sack. He wiped off his fiddle with the end of his shirt and put it away. "Looks like that's it, boys. Jack Endicott just wanted to hear himself some music."

Jimmy stood up and stretched. "Don't you think three thousand miles is a little far to come?"

"Well, we *are* a pretty good band," Douglas said.

"Let's go to bed," Moses yawned. "Tonight we get to sleep like musicianers."

The sun was up long before anyone woke in the house. Desdemona got up first and turned the coffee grinder as if in a trance. Sensing her presence below, Moses roused himself and pulled on his clothes. He came down and did not speak to her before going outside and putting his head under the pump. He shook dog-like and went back in, sitting himself at the table. Desdemona put a mug of steaming coffee in front of him and he wrapped his fiddler's hands around it.

"I guess you don't make grits round here."

"Not that I know of."

"I'll have to make you some."

"No man ever cooked for me before."

"Then it's about time."

"I notice you aren't actually moving."

"I didn't mean today."

"Of course not." She poured herself a cup from the percolator and sat across from him. "Last night sure was..." She didn't finish her sentence.

"Yes," he said. "Wasn't it, though."

"I guess you're used to it."

"They aren't all the same. That one was particularly gratifying."

"And that man, Endicott, didn't raise any fuss."

"No. I've got to admit I was surprised. I want to think that the music convinced him otherwise. That there was no point in harming such angelically talented musicianers as us."

"If you say so. I've got to feed the animals before they start bellowing. Seems a shame that real life has to come back."

"I guess that's what we've been trying to avoid all these years. But I'll help. Treyf gets anxious if I don't check in on him. You notice he's already grown a lot?"

"Course he has. Pa's already arranged to sell him to the butcher in town once he's big enough. We don't need another boar."

"Turn Treyf into chops and bacon? Talk about spoiling a mood. You're the one who asked me to take care of him. It's clear that he's some pig and destined for greater things."

"What sort of things might that be?"

"That's just it. How can we tell?"

The sound of footsteps came from overhead. Moses didn't want to waste this private moment with Desdemona. But taking advantage required him to have some vision of the future, a gift that had always eluded him. And now came the other sisters, followed by his brothers and the father himself.

"I can't believe it, Pa," Juliet said. "You are the last one down. Write that in your diary and put stars around it."

"I was not asleep," Johansson said. "I was working out our seed order for next spring."

"And here we thought you were writing poetry. Did I just say that out loud?"

"Let me pour you some coffee, Pa," said Desdemona. She was halfway to the pot when the sound of furious hooves made her stop. They were all listening now.

"A fast horse never brings good news," Johansson said.

Moses moved toward the window and pushed aside the curtain. He saw a man in a Stetson on a tall horse silhouetted against the sun. The dust was still settling around them. "Looks like Jack Endicott has come to pay a social call."

"We could hide in the attic," Douglas said.

"And give him cause to burn down my house?" Johansson said. "You have no choice but to meet him."

"If you put it that way," Moses said. "Let's go, boys. Don't slump, now. Remember there's three of us."

"I'm going with you," said Desdemona.

"I'm coming, too," said Cordelia.

"And I'm not being left out," said Juliet.

"Now we're bound to strike fear in the man's heart," Moses

said. "Where's that shotgun of yours, Mr. Johansson?"

The old man licked his dry lips. "I left it in the barn."

"Very sensible. Wouldn't want it to go off by accident. Come on, then."

Moses went to the door, the others behind him. They stepped out into the light. Jack Endicott was still on his horse.

"If you are here to apologize, we accept," Moses said.

Endicott got down, his long coat opening to reveal the Colt .45 in his belt. "Stay where you are," he said. "You three should have let me play."

"But then we wouldn't have won the contest," Douglas said. "You sound like a dying raccoon on that thing."

"Perhaps it's not the time to offer criticism, brother," Moses said.

"You know what you are?" Endicott said. "You're snobs. People think a man like me couldn't have any artistry in his soul. I've got plenty. I am brimming over with artistry. It needs to come out."

"Maybe you could take up house painting," Desdemona said.

Everyone turned to look at her. Jimmy said, "You sound just like Moses."

"The object of attention ought to be the man with the gun," Endicott said. "On top of debasing my ability, you killed my dog. Using my own gun."

"I didn't mean to," Jimmy said. "I thought that was you under the covers. I don't mean it as a joke. It is just bad luck that I have been responsible for the death of certain animals."

Endicott spit into the dirt. "I am tired of listening to you talk. I've come all this way to kill the three of you and I won't let this be a wasted trip. If you don't want your lady friends to get hurt, I suggest you step away from them.

"It isn't even a fair fight you're suggesting," Cordelia said. "They're musicianers, not fighters."

"I don't intend this to be a fight. More of an execution. Come on now, move over."

He pulled out the Colt and motioned with it. A whistle sounded in the prairie air and they all saw Johansson with two fingers in his mouth. "Keep out of it, you Swedish corncob," Endicott said. "This is between them and me." A low rumbling sound had them turning their heads again, this time to see Brutus moving on surprisingly nimble hooves. The beast stopped some twenty yards away and shook its massive head.

"Jesus Christ," said Endicott. "Isn't that a buffalo?"

"It is," said Johansson.

"I thought they were all hunted out."

"Not all, as you can see."

"And he's tame?"

"As a kitten," Moses said. "If you want, you can have a ride."

"You're not shitting me?"

Johansson whistled again, two sharp notes, and the beast snorted and lowered itself onto its front knees. Endicott looked at Johansson and then back at the buffalo. "Nobody better try anything," he said. He walked toward it, slowing as he got closer. They could all hear the buffalo breathing. It kept a passive eye on Endicott. "Okay, boy, take it easy now," he said. He came up to put a hand on the animal's side. "Warm as a steam engine."

"Don't keep him waiting too long," Johansson called out. "He doesn't like being on his knees."

"All right. Here we go, nice buffalo. I'll just get on your back for a minute or two."

Endicott had to hop on one leg to get the other up over the buffalo. He grasped onto the curls between its horns and pulled himself the rest of the way. Johansson whistled and Brutus rose up from one knee and then the other, lurching a little so that Endicott swayed back and forth.

"Yee-haw!" shouted Endicott, pulling out his gun and waving it around. "I sure wish that photographer fella I run into before was here. Go on now, walk in a circle."

Brutus began to move.

"He's like a cowboy in a dime novel," Douglas said.

"He better not shoot that pistol," Johansson said. "Brutus doesn't like the sound of gunfire."

"That so?" Moses asked.

"Brings back bad memories."

"I guess we've all got those." He put his hands together and called out, "Hey, Jack, we took a vote. It was unanimous except for Jimmy. We're making you a part of our band."

"Now, Mose—" started Douglas, but his brothers each put a hand on him.

"You are? You're letting me join?" cried Endicott. "You hear that, everybody? I'm in! I'm in! This is cause for celebrating!" He pointed the gun in the air.

"Don't fire that gun," Moses said in a whisper. Endicott pulled the trigger and as the barrel flashed the sound echoed off the house. Brutus stopped. "We'll need a name. How about Jack Endicott and the Pot Lickers? That's got a good ring to it. I can't wait for us to play together. Woo-wee!"

Endicott shot again, three times. Brutus pawed the ground. Raised its head and bellowed. And began to run.

"Bad memories," Johansson said.

They had to pull Jack Endicott from the creek. For one thing, it was the civilized thing to do. For another, he would have poisoned their water source. They put his broken body in the barn overnight and then dug a grave in Johansson's back field. Jimmy was given the task of gouging the man's name into a wooden board; it was his own idea to carve an image of a concertina, which Moses pronounced a nice touch. His instrument being found tied to his saddle, they placed it by the corpse's feet. Then they filled in the grave, the sisters and Johansson taking turns with the shovel.

"Pa," said Desdemona. "Maybe you've got some words from Shakespeare."

The old man cleared his throat. "'If I must die,'" he intoned,

"'I will encounter darkness as a bride, and hug it in mine arms.'"

"The immortal bard has come through nicely," Moses said. "Let me add a few words of my own."

"Just don't get long-winded," Douglas said.

Moses stepped forward, bowler in his hands. "Down in that hole is Jack Endicott, formerly of Asheville, North Carolina, but born in Arkansas, I believe. Someone might ask, what did he die of? The answer is, crushed by a buffalo. And also drowned in a creek. But it might be best summed up this way: he died from a lack of natural talent."

"That's a little harsh," said Jimmy.

"So was his playing."

"You always have to have the last word." Douglas shook his head.

"And that," Moses said, stepping back, "brings this part of our particular story just about to an end."

The sisters prepared a roast chicken and potatoes and beans and they sat down at the table.

Desdemona said, "I'm sorry, Pa, but me and Moses are going to get married. And then we're going on the road. He's giving me lessons on the mandolin. I can strum rhythm for him and even play some tunes if they aren't too fast."

"This is news to me but awfully welcome," Moses said, looking at her. "And you can sing like a bluebird. I never heard a more beautiful rendering of 'Barbara Allen.'"

"So I am to lose my eldest," Johansson said, chewing grimly. "'Here I and sorrows sit.'"

"That's right, Pa. You find solace in your Shakespeare."

"Desdemona isn't the only one who's got an announcement," said Cordelia. "Me and Douglas are going to see the world. We raised enough money at the dance to get us started, take a train east, and get on a ship to London or Paris or Budapest or Constantinople."

Johansson slapped his hand down on the table, making their dishes jump. "And I suppose my youngest is deserting me, too?

"No, Pa," said Juliet. "No, I'm not. This is my home. I want Jimmy to stay with me. We can run the farm with you, can't we, Jimmy? He's not like his brothers. He doesn't mind working hard."

"I won't object to that last statement if you both promise to take care of my pig," Moses said. "You can't slaughter him, Jimmy, either by accident or on purpose."

Everyone was silent a moment. Then Douglas said, "I guess our little string band is no more. But we had a good run. We even won us a prize."

"True enough," Moses said. "Although prizes aren't everything. They're mostly good for waving in the face of someone else."

"At least we'll have that photograph, if it ever arrives," Jimmy said. "I'll send you both a copy."

"I am resigned," Johansson said. "Now let's go outside."

"Outside, Pa?" asked Cordelia. "It's night."

"I want to see the night sky with my daughters one last time. And with no smart remarks from these musicianers here."

"Moses is going to find that a challenge," Douglas said. "I told you he's got to have the last word. Even when it comes to the firmament."

"That just isn't true," Moses said as they all started to rise.

Desdemona opened the door and they filed out. The women stood by the men but did not take their hands. Brutus trotted over to rub his giant head against Johansson's shoulder.

Johansson led them some distance from the lighted windows of the house. All seven of them tilted their heads back and looked up. They saw the great wash of stars against the darkness. A shooting star passed over them, and then another. Even Moses fell silent for several minutes.

Acknowledgements

My thanks to Jay and Hazel Millar and all the talented folk at Book*hug, Peter Norman for his sharp-eyed editing and helpful suggestions, Stuart Ross for the clean copyedit, proofreader Susan Sanford Blades, and Philippa Dowding for telling me about a scene in Cormac McCarthy's *Blood Meridian* that I immediately adapted for my own use, although I have yet to read the book.

About the Author

CARY FAGAN is the author of eight novels and six short story collections. He has won many awards, including the Foreword INDIES Award for Humor, the Canadian Jewish Literary Award for Fiction, and the Toronto Book Award. He has also been shortlisted for various prizes, including the Governor General's Literary Award for Fiction, the Atwood Gibson Writers' Trust Fiction Prize, and the Giller Prize. Fagan's work has been translated into French, Italian, German, Dutch, Spanish, Catalan, Turkish, Russian, Polish, Chinese, Korean, and Persian, and he is also a "beloved" (*Quill & Quire*) author of books for children. He lives in Toronto.

PHOTO: JOSH LEVINE

Colophon

Manufactured as the first edition of
A Fast Horse Never Brings Good News
in the fall of 2025 by Book*hug Press

Edited for the press by Peter Norman
Copy-edited by Stuart Ross
Proofread by Susan Sanford Blades
Type + design by Malcolm Sutton
Cover images: birch tree/public domain; euphonium/public domain;
Giovanni Rivalta, 'Still life with a cat and a mackerel on a table top'/
public domain; Sophie Lemire, 'Portrait of a gentleman holding a red
book'/public domain; Albert Bierstadt, 'The wild west'/public domain

Printed in Canada

bookhugpress.ca